Without A Word

A Ghostwriter Mystery
(Book 7)

C. A. LARMER

Published by Larmer Media
NSW Australia
www.calarmer.com

ISBN: 978-0-6488009-0-3
Cover design: Stuart Eadie
Cover image: piskunov (iStock by Getty Images)
Edited by The Editing Pen
& Elaine Rivers (with heartfelt thanks)

This one's for Michelle,
for asking

ALSO BY C.A. LARMER

The Ghostwriter Mystery series:
Killer Twist (Book 1)
A Plot to Die For (Book 2)
Last Writes (Book 3)
Dying Words (Book 4)
Words Can Kill (Book 5)
A Note Before Dying (Book 6)

The Murder Mystery Book Club series:
The Murder Mystery Book Club (Book 1)
Danger On the SS Orient (Book 2)
Death Under the Stars (Book 3)
When There Were 9 (Book 4)
The Widow on the Honeymoon Cruise (Book 5)
Gone Guest (Book 6)

The Posthumous Mystery series:
Do Not Go Gentle
Do Not Go Alone

The Sleuths of Last Resort:
Blind Men Don't Dial Zero
Smart Girls Don't Trust Strangers
Good Girls Don't Drink Vodka

PLUS
*After the Ferry: A Gripping
Psychological Novel*

An Island Lost

CONTENTS

PROLOGUE

It was the silence that made Phoebe want to scream. As she creaked open her bedroom door and glanced out, she thought, *That's odd.*

Where was the thud-thud-thud of her little brother's feet, louder than his tiny frame belied, racing from one end of the house to the next like a freckle-faced wind-up toy? And the theatrical lilt of her mother's voice as she made her way through last night's dishes and the entire *Grease* soundtrack, the odd Bee Gees song thrown in for good measure? And why wasn't her father yelling at her to "Get up, lazy bones, the bus waits for no one"?

She stared at her Swatch watch and gulped.

Yikes! School! It started ten minutes ago!

Phoebe bolted back to her bedroom to get changed, then stopped and returned to the hallway, crumpled uniform in hand, her eyes darting about.

Hang on a minute…

She checked Danny's room first, then her folks', then blinked as she realised that Bouncer was also missing. The family Labrador was usually sprawled out in the hallway, his fat tail thumping the carpet.

"Hell-oooo? Where is everybody?" she called out,

her voice calm at this point, curiosity edging out the panic. A tiny smile flickered at her lips. Waiting for the punch line.

The kitchen was empty too, and there were no crusty breakfast bowls. No note—although she didn't think to look for that yet, that would come later when a grown-up stepped in—and when she opened the front door, she noticed the garage was open and the family's station wagon was gone.

Had something happened? Had she forgotten something?

Phoebe swivelled and returned inside, making her way back to her parents' bedroom, where she finally noticed what had been obvious from the start. The master bed was bare. No duvet, no pillows, no sheets. There was nothing on the bedside cabinets, her dad's usual stack of music bios all missing. She raced to the cupboard. Apart from a few bent coat hangers, it, too, was empty.

"Hello?" she said again, her voice breaking now as she ran for Daniel's room and pulled his drawers open. Nothing. His bed was bare, his toy box missing, his posters ripped from the walls, just a few specks of Blu-Tack to prove they ever existed.

She blinked. Needed to wake up. Blinked again.

What the hell… what the hell… what the hell!

Phoebe staggered back along the hallway and out the front door, racing down the path to stare out at Baker Street, frantically looking this way and that, hoping to see the wagon's tail lights, a removal van—anything! She swung around and around, as though trying to reset the clock as the realisation hit her like a smack of cement: she was completely and utterly alone.

It was the eve of Phoebe Fisher's tenth birthday and her entire family had vanished.

The young girl stopped twirling, fell to her knees on the patchy lawn, and began to scream.

CHAPTER 1

Lorraine Jones stared with narrowing eyes at the panting dog. She pursed her frosted lips and exhaled through flared nostrils. She was glad to have her daughter back, really she was, but her so-called travelling companion was a whole other kettle of fish.

"He won't bite, Mum, I can assure you," Roxy Parker said as she placed one of her mother's best Tupperware containers full of water in front of the black-and-white dog.

Lorraine watched as it slurped away, splashing water in all directions, and decided to let that one go—for now—but she couldn't warm to the idea of having a canine move in with them. It would be hard enough having Roxy for the fortnight. And what if it barked all night? *Whatever would the neighbours say?*

"I'm just here to do the book and then we'll both be out of your hair," Roxy told her mother as she arrived late that afternoon in an unfamiliar white Jeep with the mutt in the passenger seat (not in the back where he belonged!).

"I just don't understand why you had to bring the dog," she replied, twiddling with the pearls around her neck. "You live on a hundred acres up there in

Byron Bay, don't you?"

"Eleven, actually, but as I told you, Sam's away and Lunar can't be on his own."

"Why not? It's an animal, Roxanne, have we forgotten that?"

Roxy reached down to pat the border collie-Alsatian-cross.

"Don't listen to her, Lunar, she's not great with dogs." *Or kids*, she might have added, but she'd already decided it was time to forgive her mother's bad parenting.

Roxy was in her midthirties, after all. Time, perhaps, to grow up, which was another reason she was there… But she didn't want to get into that just yet. She had some big news, news that would change absolutely everything, but one glance at her mother's cocked eyebrow and she decided to hold off on that.

She would need to pick her time carefully.

"Will he be okay out here while we get ourselves some tea?" Lorraine asked.

Roxy smiled. "It's an *animal*, remember, Mum? Not a toddler. He'll be fine."

"And what about his… business?"

"Business?"

The second eyebrow nudged up. "Yes, has he… you know, done a doo-doo?"

"A *doo-doo*? Really? Are we still calling it that?" Roxy laughed. "We stopped along the way. He'll be fine. Come on, where's that lovely tea set of yours. Let's live large."

Roxy marched back inside the house, through her mother's cluttered living area to the refurbished kitchen at one side. She had never been a big fan of the overstuffed bungalow her mother shared with second husband Charlie, with its bulky antique furniture and clashing floral vibe, but she was grateful for the offer and for the decent-sized backyard. Most of all she was grateful for the cosy guest bedroom in which she could hide away—or she would be down the track, that much was certain.

When Roxy's agent, Oliver Horowitz, first called about the autobiography he wanted her to ghostwrite, she had leapt at it, and not just because she was intrigued by the client, Phoebe Fisher, a young woman with an extraordinary story to tell. From what Roxy knew, Phoebe's entire family had simply vanished overnight when she was just a child… and were never seen again. It was the kind of mystery Roxy lived for, but the truth was this was more about earning a living. She would have taken the work even if the client was a hundred and spent her entire life in a convent.

Roxy was in dire need of paid work. She had officially moved to the countryside with her new partner Sam Forrest—the electrician she'd met on her last adventure, the one with the three-day growth, the matching penchant for mystery and the handsome mutt—and while her new home was certainly lush (think rolling green hills and koala-littered gum trees), the work was sparse. Not so much as a sentence of paid writing to be found. Not even the local rag would hire her. She wasn't local enough for them apparently. Give it twenty more years, they told her, and she could drop her CV in.

So when Oliver called a few weeks ago to invite her to Sydney to meet the book's client, she had just one reservation—where, oh where, would she stay?

Roxy had officially moved into Sam's cosy timber cottage in Northern NSW, subletting her even cosier inner-Sydney apartment for the year, so she couldn't exactly oust her tenants for a fortnight, and there was no room for Lunar there anyway. She had to bring the dog along; Sam was working for a regional power company and was currently in Far North Queensland, patching up after a recent cyclone.

Lunar's presence also precluded the people Roxy really wanted to spend time with—her best friend, detective Gilda Maltin, her agent Oliver, and even crazy Caroline Farrell, sister of a certain bloke she once dated who was still ensconced in Berlin. *Thank God.* All three friends lived in inner-city haunts smaller than shoeboxes and *sans* backyards.

No place for Lunar then.

Roxy's only option was Lorraine and Charlie's lower North Shore pad. So she had swallowed her pride—and her better judgement—and asked her mother for a bed.

"I only need to be in town while I'm interviewing the client. Then once I've done all that, I can transcribe the recordings and start writing the book back at home. So, two weeks, three tops."

Lorraine had jumped at the chance to spend some quality time with her prodigal daughter, but she suspected Charlie was less than keen—he knew what these two were like; they'd be at each other's throats by the end of the first day. Now Roxy wondered whether they'd last the hour.

"Where do you keep your tea bags again?" she called out.

"Oh, let me do it, dear. Tea bags are so common. I'll make us a fresh pot."

As Lorraine got busy scooping tea leaves into a Royal Doulton pot, Roxy sent a quick text to Sam, letting him know they'd arrived safely, then stretched her body out after the 800-kilometre drive. She had left well before the crack of dawn and, despite a few pit stops, mostly for Lunar's benefit, had made very good time. It was just late afternoon.

"Charlie's making his special salmon dish this evening," Lorraine purred as she worked and Roxy frowned.

"Mum, I already told you I'd be out tonight. I'm meeting my agent to discuss the book."

"But you've only just arrived! I've barely seen you! Charlie hasn't even said hello yet."

She sighed. "Mum, this isn't a social visit. I'm here on business."

"Still, Charlie's at the farmers' market now, sourcing all the ingredients. He'll be most disappointed."

She hid her own disappointment. "I can stay for dinner, I guess"—although she had been so looking forward to meeting Oliver at her favourite inner-city Thai restaurant—"but we'll need to eat early so I can head out after that."

Lorraine flashed her a victory smile, then continued making the tea while Roxy reached for her mobile and began texting the news to Oliver.

It was going to be a very long fortnight indeed.

CHAPTER 2

This *better not take long*, Detective Inspector Gilda Maltin thought as she steered her new vintage Mercedes through the car park turnstile at Sydney's domestic airport.

She was overdressed for the occasion in a clingy black dress and heels that would make a handy ice pick, but that was Roxy Parker's fault. They were supposed to be catching up tonight, cracking open a bottle of merlot at this very moment, but then Gilda's boss had called and here she was, winding her way through the bowels of the car park and up towards the rooftop.

Towards a body in a car. Circumstances suspicious.

As she nodded at the waving police officer, Gilda wondered why there wasn't a larger police presence. There was just one uniformed officer waiting at the entrance and another at the top of the fourth level to point her towards one of the empty undercover parks.

"Inspector Wiles has asked you to leave your car here, ma'am, and walk the rest of the way up," he called out over the sound of her engine, and she smiled, wondering if her boyfriend was trying to encourage some much-needed exercise. Then she glanced down at her heels, groaned, and got out.

"Gilda!" Detective Chief Inspector Brent Wiles yelled when she'd finally clickity-clacked her way to the open-air top level and glanced about.

The roof was packed with cars, many dusty, some covered over, and there wasn't a soul in sight, apart from a sharply dressed man with a chiselled goatee and a woman with a low ponytail and a cheap polyester suit.

The younger woman's eyes flickered down Gilda's dress to her shoes as she approached, a tiny frown appearing on her forehead, and Gilda said, "Manolo Blahniks, darling. You can borrow them if you like."

Detective Doreen Oliver blushed and looked away while Gilda turned her eyes to Wiles and said, "I gave up a hot date for this. Better be good."

"Roxy can wait," he replied, deliberately glancing behind her. "I'm surprised she didn't tag along, knowing her track record."

"Oh, she's got her own mystery to worry about. So, what've we got?"

Wiles waved her closer to an old model white Toyota Corolla where a body sat, slouched in the driver's seat. It was a middle-aged woman, grey roots obvious at the tips of her dyed brown hair, dark sunglasses on. She was carrying a bit of weight, her hands resting on her bulging belly, her chin tilted awkwardly to one side, her eyes just visible through the lenses. She appeared to be staring at the car door handle, like she was contemplating whether to use it.

"Been here since daylight, I assume," Gilda said, indicating the sunglasses, and he nodded.

"Security have her hatchback logging through the entrance turnstile just on midday. She took a ticket but didn't have a long-term booking, so we can only assume she was supposed to be here briefly, but something happened. It's the *something* we need to investigate."

Gilda glanced at her watch. It was just after 7:00 p.m.

"You think she's been sitting here since *midday?*"

He shrugged. "No cameras in the immediate vicinity but there is a walk bridge from this level across to the domestic departure terminal, and there's CCTV there, so we'll get ahold of that and see if she went through at any stage. We're also looking into next of kin. Doreen must be Googling your shoes because I'm still waiting to hear about that."

Doreen frowned again and tapped at her iPhone. "It's odd. I'm just not finding anything."

"Vonnie's sending someone over now," Wiles added, speaking of Evonne Cressida, head of the State's Forensic Services Group. "I'm sure it'll all make sense in the end. I'm just keen to get your take on it."

Gilda took that as a compliment and leaned into the vehicle and then recoiled backwards as Wiles's blue eyes twinkled.

"Sorry, forgot to warn you."

She glared at him and leaned back in again, careful this time not to inhale the overwhelming stench of body fluids and decomposing flesh as she inspected the scene.

It was certainly a strange one. The woman was dressed in dark trousers and a red-and-white-striped business shirt with a small *Australia Post* insignia on the breast pocket, her seat belt off, a sensible black handbag on the passenger seat. Her cheeks looked sunburnt.

"No obvious signs of a struggle, no suspicious circumstances. Her wallet and mobile are in the bag next to her," Wiles said. "All her ID. Name's Paisley

Smith, aged fifty-three, obviously works for *Aus Post*, not sure which outlet yet. According to her licence, she resides in Gerroa, small place down the south coast."

"I know it," Gilda said. "That's a two-hour drive from Sydney. Heading away do you think?"

"No luggage in the boot."

"Who phoned it in?"

"Security guard doing the rounds about an hour ago. About *two* hours earlier, someone had mentioned a woman 'sleeping' in her car, some suit rushing past. He told the guard, and the guard said he meant to come up sooner, got waylaid."

Wiles's jutted jaw told her what he thought of that, and she had to agree. Could the woman have been saved?

"Too busy to help a dying woman?"

"The guard's devastated, if that helps."

"So how come no one else spotted her? Airport car parks are busy places."

"Not this level. The roof's used exclusively for long-term parking—most people who are collecting loved ones from flights choose the shadier parking below, but they're welcome to park up here if they can find a spot and aren't too fussed about the heat. And it's midsummer; it would've been hot."

"You think she died of heat exposure or dehydration or something?"

"Wouldn't be a first."

And he was right. Australia was a hot country. Vehicles were even hotter, but you couldn't tell that to the idiots who left their dogs and kids locked up inside them. And it would have been beyond hot up there on the cement rooftop today. It would have been sizzling. Gilda had plenty of experience with humans overheating. Was still haunted by an early case she had attended, a toddler who was found expired in the back seat just an hour after her harried father had rushed to work, forgetting she was strapped in. No doubt the father never got over that one either.

"No obvious signs of drug or alcohol consumption," Gilda said, thinking aloud, stretching her mind, knowing this was why Wiles wanted her on the case. "Doesn't mean much at this stage though." She leaned in closer again. "So, a middle-aged woman leaves work—by the looks of the getup—and drives all the way from a small village on the south coast and comes and parks at the hottest possible place on a very hot summer's day. We'll worry about the *why* in a moment, but first I want to know *how*. Unless she died of an unexpected medical episode—a heart attack, a brain aneurysm, maybe?—you could be right; it could be heat exposure. Could she have somehow locked herself in?"

She didn't wait for an answer, glancing down at the woman's door. It was unlocked and had been when the guard first reached the scene, Wiles told her.

"All four doors were unlocked. The two front windows"—he pointed to where they were half down—"were exactly like that. Her car horn works; we've already tested it. She could have beeped for help at any point or used her mobile. As I said, it's in her bag, still half-charged. I've had a quick look, but it's password protected. Once forensics are done with it, we'll get that to our techies, see if they can crack into it. In the meantime, Doreen's going to obtain her phone records and see if she used it during this ordeal."

"You think she phoned for help?"

"Well, she wouldn't be phoning for pizza."

Doreen sniggered at that.

Gilda offered her a smirk, then said to Wiles, "Could she simply have fallen asleep? Maybe waiting for someone to get off a flight? Do we have any idea if anyone's missing their lift?"

"Not yet. I've got young Mattheson in the terminal now, checking the CCTV and asking about stray passengers. But surely they'd call her on her mobile, wake her up. I doubt you could sleep in the heat anyway."

"She did have the windows down a bit."

"Still would've been boiling without cover. Cars are all metal and glass. Surely it'd get so uncomfortable you'd exit the vehicle at some stage."

"You'd think so. Unless…" She caught his eye. "Maybe she didn't *want* to get out?"

He frowned. "What are you saying? Suicide by sunbaking?"

"I'm just thinking aloud."

"Let's wait and see what Vonnie's lot says. There will probably be a very obvious explanation."

Gilda nodded. She hoped he was right because the alternative was that the woman simply sat in her car and baked herself to death.

And who would do such a thing? And, more importantly, *why?*

CHAPTER 3

"Well, stone the crows! Our country girl is back in the Big Smoke," said Oliver, using his broadest Aussie accent, as Roxy rushed into WonTon Thai Restaurant in her old stomping ground, Elizabeth Bay.

She dropped her oversized handbag, leaned in and kissed him on both chubby cheeks.

"Sorry I'm late, Olie, and cut it out. I'm hardly a country girl."

"You're wearing a checked shirt."

She glanced down at the silky red-and-black-checked shirt she'd styled with dangly necklaces, blue skinny jeans and black heeled boots, and winced. "Better than Hawaiian print." She nodded at his usual garb. "Besides, this look is in at the moment."

"In small-town Bumpkinville, perhaps."

Roxy rolled her eyes and then darted them towards a bottle on the table. "Merlot?"

"What else? Although it might be a bit sophisticated for you now. What do they drink in the country? Home brew? Whisky and rye?"

"Just pour us a glass, Olie. This joke is wearing thin."

"Bit like you!" he said, reaching for an empty glass.

"You lost some weight."

"I'm outdoors a lot now. Nothing like a dog to get you walking daily."

"How is Sam going?"

Roxy smirked at him as she took the glass and then a good gulp.

"Just kiddin', Rox. I like your boyfriend, you know that. It's just that he took you away from all of us, so I'm still having trouble forgiving him."

"You and Gilda alike." She thought of her friend and how unfriendly she had once been towards Sam. "Where is she? I thought she'd be here by now. Caroline too."

"Gilda got called to a case, and Caroline, well, truth is I didn't invite her." He looked sheepish. "I love Caro, you know that, but she's like a bloody vacuum cleaner that woman. Sucks the life out of everything around her. I wanted you to myself and so did Gilda."

"And now you've got me all alone."

He smiled wickedly. "I know. How lucky am I that a corpse showed up? Maybe we should get straight to it in case she finds a pulse and suddenly appears."

Roxy nodded and Oliver reached for a file from a bag at his feet, pushing his half-empty bowls aside and spreading the file open before her.

"So, you'd heard of Forgotten Phoebe before I called you, yes?" He handed her what looked like a contract, the name Phoebe Fisher typed at the top.

"Heard of her? I've been fascinated by her for twenty years!"

Roxy pushed the bowls even farther away, reached into her bag, and produced her own file, really an oversized scrapbook with newspaper clippings poking out from within.

Oliver's eyes widened. "The infamous Book of Death!"

"The very first one, in fact," she said, adding, "and it's a Crime Catalogue, thank you very much."

Roxy had always loathed her agent's nickname for these scrapbooks, even though she had to admit he wasn't far off the mark. The vast majority of the articles she had cut out of newspapers over the years and pasted in did involve pretty horrendous deaths, but not all. Not this particular case for instance. This was a missing-person's story, or more correctly a missing *family*, and one that lingered in her memory.

"This case is so haunting," she told Olie as she handed it over. "I was still at school when it happened, and we were all fascinated and horrified in equal measure. I collected every article I could find. It was decades ago, but I still recall cutting every single story out and pasting it in. I remember the smell of the Clag glue, the way I had to hide it from Mum. She would not have been happy with my new occupation."

Roxy laughed at that, but Olie wasn't laughing. "Her and me alike."

He turned to the front cover and raised his scruffy eyebrows. Roxy had certainly hidden the scrapbook's content well. It gave nothing away, with crazy doodles all over the front, mostly of loopy flowers and silly faces, as well as a variety of stickers for bands like Nirvana and Pearl Jam.

"I was into grunge rock," Roxy explained.

"You don't say?"

"I actually did mean to collect snippets on my favourite bands but… Well, I got a bit distracted."

Oliver opened it and started leafing through. "So where's the stuff on Phoebe?"

"Around page five. Hers wasn't the news story that set it all off—that takes up the first few pages and is a really gruesome murder of a little boy that was never solved. He was kidnapped from a shopping centre and found days later, chopped into little pieces." Roxy shuddered. "The hours I spent wondering about that poor kid, about who could do such a thing, how his family were coping. Suddenly pasting in stories of rock bands seemed too trivial. I think…" She chewed on her glass for a few moments. "I think I started pasting it all in to try to make sense of the horror somehow."

"And did you?"

"Of course not. How can you make sense of that? But it did help with one thing." She offered him a slim, sad smile. "It helped me get over my dad's death."

"I'm sorry, Roxy, but how does more death help you get over death?"

"My therapist would tell you—if I could afford one—that it was a coping mechanism. I started scrapbooking a few years after he passed. I was still moping a lot, feeling sorry for myself, and it really helped. I think, in a strange way, it reminded me that so many others had it so much worse." She flashed Olie another apologetic smile. "Does that make sense?"

"Less a 'Crime Catalogue' than a macabre 'There but for the Grace of God Go I'?"

"Something like that." She shook herself out, reached for her wine. "Anyway, Phoebe's story has always stayed with me."

"Literally. It's in your files."

"But then, who *wasn't* fascinated by it?"

Indeed the story had the entire nation engrossed for weeks, with every newspaper and current-affairs program speculating on exactly what had happened and falling over themselves to try to get access to Forgotten Phoebe, as she was promptly dubbed—the sad little suburban girl who was left home alone. For life.

Roxy couldn't imagine what the poor child had gone through, and that didn't even include the media intrusion. It must have been such a shock, the utter feeling of loneliness and rejection—all feelings Roxy had endured when her father had died too young from cancer. Even in her selfish teen angst, she understood that Phoebe was in a much, much darker place. Roxy's dad had not *chosen* to leave. Because, yes, when it came to it, the only conclusion the police had ever reached was that Phoebe's family had deliberately taken off from their Baker Street, Coogee, home, and left her behind. There was no other way to explain it. No signs of violence or a struggle, no blood or bodies or kidnapping note or letter to justify why. They had secretly packed their belongings in the dead of night, including Phoebe's five-year-old brother and pet Labrador, and just vanished.

Poor Forgotten Phoebe.

How does someone survive that? And why, pray tell, would they want to rehash it two decades later?

"You can ask her that yourself," Oliver replied, pointing a pudgy finger at the contract. "The publisher's deets are at the top. Company called Swanson Smight. Nonfiction publisher's name is Persephone Daley. She's arranged a preliminary meet and greet between you and Phoebe. Tomorrow morning. At eleven. I suggested Lockie's." He winked. "Thought you might appreciate it."

Roxy smiled. She did. Her Scottish friend Loghlen ran a Surry Hills café, and she had missed him, his delicious fare, and the eatery's bohemian vibe. There was a café just near Sam's property, but it was more hippy than boho and hard to get a decent latte. The problem was, the last time she met a client at Lockie's, things turned very nasty very fast, triggering a series of murders that almost ended Roxy's life. She thought she was simply interviewing a boring Sydney socialite, but the socialite's secrets turned out to be anything but, and she was soon hunting for a killer in the dusty outback. Oliver appeared to read her mind.

"Don't worry, Rox. The crime here has already happened—if you can call it a crime."

"Oh I think we can call it a crime," Roxy countered, snatching the scrapbook back. "You wake up on the eve of your tenth birthday to find your entire family has vanished; that's not exactly a benign event. What happened to them? Were they all kidnapped and killed? Did they desert her? Either way, it's a crime and a pretty horrendous one."

"Well, whatever it is, you're not there to solve the mystery, right? That's not what they're looking for. They just need a ghostwriter to pen her story for her, and it's not in the bag yet; you need to win her over. So maybe don't mention your Book of Death—it's just creepy. And let's leave out the fact that clients tend to drop dead around you."

She scowled at him, but he was right on all fronts. "Why *is* Phoebe doing this?" she asked, picking away at his leftover pad thai. "Why now?"

"Maybe she needs some closure? I don't know. Persephone tells me it took a lot of convincing. They've been at her since she turned twenty-one. She's now thirty. Just between you and me, I think they finally offered enough money to change her mind."

Roxy nodded. She wasn't going to judge the woman.

She had bills like everyone else and no family to help her out. "So, if she does give me the green light, how long have I got to write this thing?"

"You have one week to interview her and then two weeks to write it. Just the first draft, then they'll take it from there."

"Cripes, that's fast. Why the sudden urgency?"

"She's a busy woman, wants it off the to-do list, I guess. At least you've already done your homework." He nudged towards the scrapbook. "And there's a lot of stuff on Google. Lots of trash magazines have revisited it over the years. That'll give you some background. Phoebe can fill in the rest. But the key is to win her over. Meet with her tomorrow and be on your best behaviour."

"I'm always on my best behaviour with clients!"

He stared at her. "You know what I mean. Don't start interrogating her about the mystery of what happened to her folks. Just play it cool. Pretend that's not the entire reason you want this job."

"It's not!" Roxy said, but they both knew that was a lie.

CHAPTER 4

Paisley Smith's husband had no idea why his wife had been sitting in the boiling sun at Sydney airport for hours, but then again he refused to concede she was even there, accusing them all of fabricating the entire event.

Bordering on hysterical when he arrived at Sydney's forensic mortuary very early the next morning to identify his wife's body, the balding man in the budget-store jeans and grey T-shirt adamantly refused to accept that Paisley Smith was anywhere near the airport that day.

"She would never go to Sydney, not without me. It's all *bullshit*!" Presley bellowed as the police officer who had driven him up from Gerroa shepherded him into the mortuary. "You bastards are lying to me! Why are you lying?"

The officer, a skinny twenty-something constable called Oscar Flannery, gave Wiles a strained look—it had been a long drive—and he stepped forward and offered his hand.

"Mr Smith, I'm Detective Chief Inspector Brent Wiles. I'm the one in charge of this case, and I'm very sorry for your loss."

"Bullshit!" Presley yelled again, his red eyes bulging. "This is not happening, this can't be! Please, God, not this. Not now!"

Gilda watched from the side, her heart breaking for the man. She had seen grief so many times, and disbelief was just one of its many tragic stages. Death was so final, so hard to accept, that lashing out was an easier, more consoling option. Life had just run out of control, and many tried to wrestle it back, often by wrestling with the truth or with the people around them. Gilda had been slapped once by a woman who'd just learned her daughter had been killed in a car crash and demanded she take the words back. Was spat on by a grieving widower, screamed at by many, many more. Anything could happen when emotions were wrought.

"I want to see my wife!" he said suddenly, and Wiles waved the pathologist's assistant across.

Her name was Kay Chong, and Gilda knew her personally. A tiny woman with a giggly personality, she was a good friend of Oliver Horowitz. But she wasn't giggling now. Kay stepped solemnly from behind the front counter and gently guided Presley through the main door and down a brightly lit corridor towards a large, angled window. There was another assistant waiting behind the glass and beside a trolley bearing a body bag.

It contained Paisley Smith, of course, and no sooner had she unzipped the top to reveal the victim's face, the husband began to buckle. His legs gave way and Kay could barely hold him as Wiles rushed up to take the weight.

"No, no, no, no, no… My beautiful, beautiful wife!" he spluttered, then looked around, pushing himself back up. "I want to get in there! Why can't I get in there?"

"I'm very sorry, Mr Smith," Kay said, her voice surprisingly firm. "We must preserve your wife's body for now."

Preserve the evidence, Gilda thought while he continued to shake his head.

"You will be able to take her home in a few days," Kay continued. "Until then, we need you to formally identify your wife."

He looked at her through smudged eyes, confused and distraught.

"We do need you to say your wife's full name aloud, please, for the record."

"What?" He looked at her furiously, as though he wanted to clobber her, and for a moment there Gilda thought he was going to dispute it all again, but then he stood a little taller and said, "Yes…" Sniff. "That…" Sniff. "That is my wife. *Paisley Smith*."

The words were spat out, like he was spitting out poison, then he turned to look at the body and began to gasp in heavy, heaving sobs. "I'm so sorry, honey. So, so sorry."

Gilda's ears pricked up. *What was he sorry about? Did he have something to do with this? Did he drive her to it?* She tried not to think the worst—he was clearly devastated, there was no way he was faking that—but she made a mental note of his words anyway. Then she continued to watch as Kay and Wiles both let go of the man and stepped back so he could have a moment to himself.

After just a few minutes, he brushed a hand across his face and looked around vaguely like he'd just woken from a deep sleep, a nightmare no doubt. His face was pinched, his eyes drooping, his anger assuaged.

"What happens now?" he croaked, wiping his face again.

"Now we try to work out exactly what happened."

Wiles drew Presley away from the window and back to the foyer and into a stiff vinyl sofa set that smelled of industrial-strength disinfectant.

"Do you have any idea why your wife might have been at Sydney airport?"

He stared at Wiles like he was going to dispute the fact again, then shook his head.

"She didn't leave you a note or—"

"Last time I saw Paisley she was going to work."

"That was yesterday morning?"

He nodded vaguely.

"Can you say roughly what time?"

"What? Um…" He shook himself a little as if trying to focus. "About sevenish, I guess. We had breakfast together; she seemed fine. She was just… she was just heading to work. Same as always."

"She works at a post office, Mr Smith?" Gilda asked.

He looked at Gilda like he'd only just noticed her and said, "Yep, the main one in central Wollongong."

Nowhere near Sydney then, she thought.

"One more question if you don't mind, and then we'll get you out of here," Wiles said. "Was your wife taking any medication? Did she suffer from alcoholism or any chronic diseases?"

He looked in a clobbering mood again. "No, she did not! Paisley never touched a drop, and don't let anybody tell you any different! She was fit as a bloody fiddle, my wife!"

Wiles nodded quickly and waved Flannery over. "I'll get Constable Flannery here to drive you home, Mr Smith, unless there's somewhere else you'd like—"

"Where else would you like me to go? Hey?"

Wiles waved Flannery closer. "Let's get you home."

"Shouldn't we interview him properly?" Gilda asked, watching as the officer escorted Presley Smith through the foyer and out onto the footpath towards his patrol car. "See if he can shed more light on all this? He could hold the key."

Wiles shook his head. "I don't think he's in any state to be interviewed, do you? Let's give him some time to digest it all, and we'll talk to him later."

Party pooper, she thought. If Roxy was here, she'd be throwing out more questions than a quizmaster. Gilda had a few of her own, like why would Paisley Smith drive all the way to Sydney airport and then just sit in her car for six hours?

Did the couple have a fight?

Was she leaving him?

Was there something he was hiding?

Gilda sighed and followed Wiles outside. "Why did you ask about medication and alcohol?"

He stopped and pointed his car keys at a sparkly silver sedan. "Vonnie says there's a greater chance of an adult dying from heatstroke in a vehicle if they have some kind of chronic condition, even alcoholism." His vehicle made a squeaking sound and lit up as the doors unlocked. "Of course, Mr Smith may not know or may be lying. The autopsy will tell us more. We should have it back early next week. Tuesday at the latest."

"That's quick for an autopsy."

"They want to tick it off before the full moon hits." He flashed her a grin.

She smiled back as she waved her own key towards her car parked a few doors down. "You returning to headquarters? Shall I follow you in?"

"Don't you have a hot date?"

"It's ten in the morning, Wiles. I think we can assume Roxy's left the restaurant by now."

"Either way, you just pulled an all-nighter, so take the day off. Go home to bed."

She nudged her eyebrows upwards. "Is that an offer?"

He frowned and glanced around furtively as if worried they'd been overheard.

"I don't think the corpses care, Wiles," she told him as she watched him get into his vehicle.

He strapped his seat belt on and smirked back at her. "Yeah, but the Department might. Listen, I've got a fair bit of paperwork to catch up on, but I'll see if I can get away." His blue eyes twinkled now, but not that brightly. "Can't make any promises."

Then he slammed the door, started the engine and drove away while she stood staring in his wake, wondering if she should be offended or worried or both.

CHAPTER 5

Forgotten Phoebe had changed dramatically since she'd first hit the press and not just because she was now a grown woman. The difference was startling. From the grainy photos in Roxy's scrapbook and images she had found online, Phoebe Fisher had been a scrawny ten-year-old with pale features, knobbly knees and mousy plaits.

Mousy was no longer a word that applied.

Adult Phoebe was stunning. Her skin was now bronzed brown, her body strong and muscular beneath a figure-hugging designer suit, and her hair was the most vivid shade of blue—like the heroine in the Disney film *Frozen*. Roxy tried not to stare as she watched Phoebe chat briefly with Lockie, placing a hand on his arm and laughing, before turning to look in Roxy's direction where he was pointing. She turned back to Lockie and gave him a shimmering smile, then made her way across the floor, towards the ghostwriter, every eye in the room—and quite a few outside— upon her.

Roxy had shown up a good half hour early, and not just to get her thoughts in order. She was keen to catch up with the café owner who was a longtime friend.

"The place is never the same without you," Lockie told her in his thick Scottish lilt. "I've reserved the quiet corner table for you, just as you like it, and I have Sophie whipping up your favourite smoothie. But I'm guessing you're gonna want a latte and a focaccia later?"

"That all depends how well it goes with this client."

Roxy didn't have long to fill him in before Phoebe arrived, also early, and Roxy wondered about that. Did Phoebe show up everywhere early now? Was she constantly worried people would not hang around?

Stop psychoanalysing her! she told herself as she pushed her chair out to shake the approaching woman's hand.

"Thank you so much for meeting me, Roxy," Phoebe said as she offered her one of her sparkling smiles, and Roxy wondered about that too. It must have taken a lot of hard work to rebuild any sort of confidence in herself and in life.

"Actually we can thank my mother for my confidence—my fairy godmother, that is," she told Roxy after they had settled in and Roxy had repeated the sentiment. "Margie Means is my hero and my saviour."

This was not an official interview, just a chance for the two women to sniff each other out and decide if they could work together. So far it was going well.

"To be honest, Margie was originally just the grumpy lady who lived next door," Phoebe was saying, playing with a small macchiato. "I never really thought much of her, until… well, until it happened. Margie adopted me, and I guess she saved my life."

"That was incredibly generous of her. Did she have her own kids?"

Phoebe shook her head sadly. "She lost a baby very

early, in childbirth, I believe. I think that's what broke her marriage up, long before I came along—but you didn't hear that from me." She smiled grimly. "I guess her loss was my gain. I was like her surrogate child. It was a win-win for both of us."

"And you remained living there, in Coogee, right next door to your parents' house?"

She stared at Roxy as though reading the subtext. "It does seem a little cruel, doesn't it? But what choice did I have? It was where Margie lived and I was a day shy of my tenth birthday. Didn't have a lot of say in the matter. Did what I was told." A tiny crinkle appeared above her left eye. "Perhaps it would have been kinder if they had moved me elsewhere, but then..." She was now staring into the distance. "I think we all thought they would return. They would show up again and all would be right with the world." Meeting Roxy's eyes again, she added, "But of course they didn't and here we are."

Roxy smiled warmly back at her. "Well, you look amazing and you sound incredibly resilient, and I don't mean to patronise you by saying that. I have to ask you this, though, if you don't mind. Why *are* you telling your story? Why now?"

Phoebe dusted something from her blouse and shook her glossy blue locks. "Because I'm sick to death of being asked about it. Constantly. Now I can say 'Read the book!' Plus I also get the royalties, so it's another win-win!"

Phoebe laughed, but that answer felt like the first disingenuous thing she had said since she'd arrived, and Roxy wasn't buying it. She had a hunch there was an ulterior motive, and it had nothing to do with people-pleasing or profit. She wondered whether Phoebe was attempting to find out what had happened to her family. Perhaps it was wishful thinking on Roxy's part, or perhaps it really was a chance for Phoebe to reach out to them, to try to bring them out from hiding?

She put the suggestion to Phoebe, who seemed genuinely surprised by the notion.

"Absolutely not! Those bastards can rot in hell as far as I'm concerned. I have no interest in ever seeing them again. Ever."

"But what if your book draws them out? What if they make contact?"

Phoebe held a manicured finger up. "First of all, you're assuming they're still alive, and we have no evidence of that. And secondly, even if they were, I'd tell them to go to hell. Or better yet, I'd have them arrested for child abandonment."

She was half smiling, but there was a definite steeliness to her tone. "I doubt very much that they'll reach out anyway. I mean, why would they? They're cowards. Lowlife. Scum. No, you have to believe me when I tell you: I have zero interest in those animals who walked out on me and never looked back."

Roxy took a long, slow sip of her drink and contemplated that. "Fair enough, Phoebe. I get that, really I do, but aren't you even a little bit curious? What if they had a very reasonable explanation for everything? Wouldn't you *want* to know?"

Roxy knew she was pushing things now and had probably just ruined her chances of scoring the job, but she simply couldn't understand Phoebe's lack of curiosity.

Surely any answer was better than none?

Phoebe looked annoyed for a few moments, and Roxy feared she was about to get up and walk away, then something else crossed her face. It was sadness, simple as that.

"Do you seriously think anything could justify what happened to me?" she said. "That any words from those people would make it all okay? Would erase the past twenty years of my life?"

"You're right. I'm sorry." She gave a sheepish smile. "I have a terrible tendency to want answers. It's the journalist in me."

"Oh I get that, I really do, but sometimes the answers aren't worth it."

Phoebe drained her coffee and then dabbed at her lips with a serviette. "Please understand this, Roxy. I am not interested in those people who once called themselves my…" She swallowed hard. "My *parents*. Nor am I interested in whatever excuses they might want to offer all these years later. Honestly, I'm not doing this for them, I'm doing this for me."

Roxy did believe her now. Her bitterness towards her folks was obvious not just in the words she used— *bastards*, *lowlife*, *scum*—but in the words she left out. At no point in the half hour they'd been chatting did Phoebe utter their names, Shane and Karen Fisher, let alone call them Mum and Dad.

The younger woman smiled suddenly, her eyes as bright as her teeth. "I know you love investigating mysteries, Roxy." She laughed at Roxy's surprise. "You're not the only one who does her research! But that's not why I am considering you for the book, please understand that. I've read everything you've written. I like your style. I like your smart but conversational tone, the way you cut to the chase. It's very much my style, and it's how I want my autobiography to sound." She leaned in closer. "I want to get my story out, then I want it all to be over and I want to get back to my boring, mundane life."

She stood up and reached across the table to shake Roxy's hand. "That's all this is, I'm afraid, Ms Amateur Sleuth. Just good old-fashioned closure."

"Spoilsport!" Roxy said, pretending to be disappointed and making the woman laugh again as they said their goodbyes.

As she returned to her seat and watched Phoebe zigzag her way back through the busy café and outside again, every eye back upon her, Roxy realised there was nothing boring or mundane about Phoebe Fisher. She was as dazzling as she was delightful, and it went beyond the blue locks and toothpaste-commercial smile.

Roxy wasn't sure if it had happened organically or was as deliberate as the dye, but no one who ever met this woman was likely to forget her in a hurry.

There was no doubt about it. Forgotten Phoebe had been left behind.

CHAPTER 6

"I don't remember her at all," said Caroline, batting her oversized eyelashes at Roxy.

"How can you not remember Phoebe Fisher?" She gasped. "Forgotten Phoebe? She was famous! The story was everywhere when it happened."

The two friends were chatting at Pico's, a small, dimly lit wine bar, and Roxy was describing her latest ghostwriting gig. And it *was* now officially her gig. Phoebe's agent had rung Oliver just ten minutes after Phoebe left Lockie's café to say Roxy had the job.

"I can't believe it," Roxy told Oliver. "I was sure I'd botched it up."

"Quite the contrary. She told the publisher you were perfect. I don't know what you did, Rox, but good work, girl."

Roxy didn't know either but was grateful, and not just for the income. After meeting Phoebe in the flesh, she was even more intrigued by her story than she'd been before.

"We have no time to waste," Oliver was saying. "She wants you at her apartment first thing in the morning."

"On a Saturday? Wow, she doesn't muck around."

"Well, you're not here to twiddle your thumbs, and you're getting Sunday off. The publisher's texting over Phoebe's home address now, so I'll forward it on, and you'll need to come into my office at some point to sign the contract, but I'll look it over, make sure it's all in order."

She thanked Oliver and then got busy phoning her friends. She had planned to spend all tomorrow with them, but she would have to bring it forward, and so they hastily agreed to meet for happy hour cocktails at the moody, inner-city bar, once a place she used to haunt with her ex-boyfriend Max.

Caroline was uncharacteristically early but soon confessed, "I wanted to get you all to myself before that bloody detective arrives and dominates!"

Roxy smiled, remembering what Oliver had said. "No one ever dominates when you're in the room, Caro, you know that. So, how have you been? You look great."

"Of course I do, darling, but I want to hear your news first. How's that guy you're seeing?"

"More than *seeing*, Caroline. Sam and I are shacked up, although we can't seem to connect at the moment." Roxy peered at the mobile beside her wineglass. "We've been playing phone tag since I arrived."

"And why are you in town? Again?"

And so Roxy had described the job and Caroline had said, "Sounds like a sad story but, nah, I don't remember Forgotten Phoebe."

Of course Caroline had been a lot younger when it happened and was not one to look beyond her own world anyway. She probably wouldn't have remembered it if it had happened last month.

"Anyhoo, that's all very interesting, darling," she

said, sweeping her blond locks from her face, "but I have some even more gripping news."

Roxy smiled and reached for the glass. "Yes?"

"Max is back."

She almost spilled the merlot across her lap. "Again? Really? From Berlin?"

Caroline smiled cheekily. "Yes indeed! Big brother flies in on Sunday, back for good this time. The German job's done and dusted, and he's moving into his old place."

"Lucky him," Roxy said, remembering how beautiful Max's large warehouse was and missing her own minuscule apartment. She probably could have stayed with him after all. There was plenty of space for a dog, but was there enough room to contain their enormous history?

"No, lucky *you*!" Caroline was saying. "What good timing is this? A bit spooky don't you think? A bit fatalistic!"

Max's sister had long harboured a dream that the ex-couple would reunite. Maybe trip down the aisle while they were at it.

Roxy tried to ignore that as Caroline said, "So you two will have to get together!"

Now Roxy wasn't sure if she meant for a catch-up or for life and decided not to pursue it. Caroline knew she was living with Sam in the Byron hinterland. She knew what was what and so did Max.

"It'd be great to see him, to spend time with all of you," she said. "But I *am* here to do a book, so my days will be busy with that."

"Then you'll have to hook up with him at night!" Caroline's eyes were twinkling. "He's still single, you know. Never did find himself a gorgeous Fräulein."

"I think the term's offensive, Caro, and I find that hard to believe."

"Well, he never stayed with one for long then."

"Tell him I'd love to see him, of course I would. Now, enough about him, what have you been up to?"

And so the subject lightened to stories of Caroline's own dating disasters. She was never able to keep a man for long—too high expectations and not enough give and take (on her part that is). But she was a striking-looking woman—luscious hair, long legs, an ever-growing ensemble of flowery tattoos—she was rarely without offers and by the end of the evening had batted off several men who assumed, as Aussie men often did, that two women chatting at a bar must be in want of a man to interrupt them.

"Roxy bloody Parker!" came a cry from the front of the bar, and they swung around to find Gilda Maltin tottering towards them on heels again. "He let you out of his sight, did he?"

She groaned. Gilda had never been Sam's biggest fan, and time hadn't changed that. It was more to do with distance than personality, but she had to let that drop too, she was just so happy to see her.

As they embraced, Roxy said, "I could say the same about you. Can't believe Wiles let you out of his grasp!"

"I'm barely in it these days," she replied, then shook her head at Roxy's enquiring gaze and said, "I've been napping all day, so I'm due back on duty tonight. I've got about two hours, tops."

"Then let's get this party started!" Caroline said, clicking her fingers at the ogling barmen.

And it certainly felt like a party as the three friends laughed and gossiped and caught up on their lives. They were soon joined by Oliver—"Just a quick one"—and

Lockie—"Can't believe we're seeing each other twice in one day!"—but Roxy noticed that Gilda was sticking to the soda and sneaking surreptitious peeks at her phone.

"You can go if you need to, Gilda. I'm here for another week, so it's not like we won't see each other again."

Gilda almost jumped from her chair. "Thank you, Roxy. I just feel so bad, after my no-show last night."

"Last night?" said Caroline. "What happened last night?"

"Oh, um…," Roxy began and Gilda swooped in for a hug.

"Sorry for landing you in it," Gilda whispered, laughing as she dashed away.

Luckily Roxy didn't have a chance to explain. Gilda's departure caused an instant domino effect, and Lockie was now bidding them farewell and then Oliver was making his apologies—something about a "bloody contract to read over"—and so Roxy found herself leaning at the bar, alone again with Caroline.

"I think I'd better be off too, honey," Roxy said.

"Nooooo! I was just about to order shots!"

"Sorry, I have a big day tomorrow. My first official interview with Phoebe. I need to be alert. Besides, I owe Sam a phone call and Lunar a bit of one-on-one time."

Caroline scowled. "Seriously? You're choosing a mutt over *moi*?"

Roxy hugged her close and apologised again, but the truth was she didn't want to get stuck talking about Max again, and she had a hunch that's where the conversation would end up.

And she was scared of what she might end up saying.

CHAPTER 7

Phoebe's home was almost as eye-catching as she was. Set in the heart of the city, in a towering York Street skyscraper, the luxury split-level penthouse apartment with its own doorman and private elevator, would easily have blended in on New York's Upper East side. The place screamed of cutting-edge style—duck egg blue walls, rich velvet furnishings and pierced metal chandeliers dangling from high ceilings. It had clearly been expertly decorated, and only recently by the looks of things, and Roxy couldn't imagine her affording it from her victim's compensation payout.

"Goodness, no!" Phoebe tsked when asked. "Lucky to buy a toaster with that paltry sum. I started a public relations business a few years ago, and it's doing quite well," she explained as she led Roxy across the geometric-patterned carpet, past several oversized artworks, and out sliding glass doors to the wide, covered balcony.

Her PR business, MakeAMark, was doing better than well by the looks of the interior, and the exterior was just as swanky. There was a six-piece modular lounge setting atop Verona cement tiles, a stone water feature at one end and ceramic pots with neat topiary ficus throughout.

Phoebe led Roxy to the lounge where a matching coffee table contained a jug of kombucha, two tall glasses, and a bowl of fresh tulips, Roxy's favourite flower.

"I hope this will do," she said, waving Roxy into a seat. "I know it's a little steamy today, but I prefer the outdoors, don't you?"

Not really, Roxy wanted to tell her. She'd never been much of an outdoor girl until she moved to Byron, and was keen to return to that lovely, air-conditioned interior, but she wasn't here for her own comfort. She was here to get a great story out of her client, and if her client wanted to sit outdoors, then so be it.

Phoebe's husband, James Van Beurden, was older by the look of the photos Roxy had spotted on her way through—mostly of James in the arms of various children, probably nieces and nephews if her research was correct. He had been married before but had no kids, too busy running his own investment company— or at least that's what the gossip mags had said. Perhaps *that's* what really paid for this glamorous pad she thought, a little unkindly, as she placed her small digital recorder on the table, adjusted the volume and pressed Record.

The story, as it trickled out, was a gripping one. Some of it had not appeared in the media, so Roxy was as fascinated now as she had been back then. More so because here was the victim filling in the dots or, as Roxy soon discovered, hazy smudges. Phoebe's memory was not as reliable as she'd hoped.

"I don't remember that morning so well," she confessed. "I just remember waking to find them gone and then screaming and sobbing and finally having the wherewithal to knock on my neighbour's door."

"Is this the neighbour who ended up adopting you?"

She nodded. "Margaret Means." She spelled out the name for Roxy. "Margie called the police, they came swiftly and… well, I guess it was an absolute nightmare after that. The next few days are still a blur, but at some point I woke up to my reality. At some point the horror set in."

"You were probably drugged."

"Sorry?"

"No, I'm sorry!" Roxy flung a hand to her lips. "That was a bit brusque. I was just wondering whether some kindly doctor medicated you so you could get through it. Do you think that might be why it's difficult to remember?"

Phoebe frowned but in a thoughtful way, as though it had never occurred to her. Then she shrugged. "Who knows? I did have a lot of counselling afterwards—still see someone from time to time—and it was explained to me that I was in a lot of shock. That the mind does blank out the horrible bits to get through."

The tiny crinkle appeared above Phoebe's left eye, and she bat her eyelashes quickly, as though trying to beat some dark memory away.

"Are you okay?" Roxy asked. "Do you want to take a break?"

"No, no." She gave her shoulders a wriggle and plastered a smile to her lips, her eyelashes steady, both eyebrows raised, waiting for the next question.

Roxy softened her voice and said, "So how did you, in the end? How did you get up each day and get off to school and get on with living?"

"Just that. I got up each day and I went to school and I got on with living. But it was mostly because of Margie. She's the real hero here, not me. She's the real reason I'm writing this book—a tribute of sorts. She's the one who wouldn't let me wallow or use it to my advantage, although I did try." She gave a ghost of a smile. "I was a bit of a brat at first. You know: 'I can't possibly do my homework, I'm too traumatised!' and 'You all have to be nice to me after what I've been through.'"

"There's some validity in that," Roxy said, but she shook her head.

"I would have been unbearable! No, Margie just told me to suck it up and move on. It was tough love, but it worked."

Roxy was impressed. "I'd like to interview Margie, if that's okay. Is she still in the same house in Coogee? The one next door to your childhood home?"

"Yes, she is still there, but she's not a fan. Of the book, I mean." The crinkle above her eye returned. "She thinks I'm a fool to dredge it all up. Must you talk to her? I thought this was my story, in my words?"

Now she sounded petulant, and it surprised Roxy.

"It *is* your story, absolutely, but I should have explained all of this from the start. When I write a client's story—any client's—I always try to speak to the client's family, colleagues, friends, just to get an idea of what to ask about. Often clients forget entire incidents, experiences or, heaven forbid, *people* that they later wished they'd included. My job is to ensure there are no regrets, and one way of doing that is by independently chatting to the parties involved. Often someone will mention something that the client had completely— *innocently*—forgotten but, when prodded, produces a fantastic story or anecdote. It enriches, embellishes."

"You think this story needs any *more* embellishing?"

Roxy smiled politely. "It's just part of the process."

Phoebe looked at her for a few quiet moments, then her expression relaxed and she said, "No, I'm sorry, I don't mean to tell you how to do your job. It's… well, it's just painful, for both of us. To be honest, I'm not sure how much you'll get out of Margie. She's not a big fan of the book."

"Leave that to me. I often get pushback from family and friends. Most are just scared of what might come out. The truth can unsettle the horses."

Phoebe scoffed at that as she scooped her extraordinary blue hair into a loose knot at the top of her head. "I can't imagine Margie scared of anything! No, I think she just questions everyone's motives for doing the book, and I've been thinking it over since we chatted yesterday. Why *am* I doing this book?"

She offered an apologetic smile. "I wasn't being entirely honest with you, Roxy. I'm certainly not doing it for the money." Her eyes danced across the terraced deck and out to the million-dollar view. "And it's not so much that I want closure or to satisfy the curiosity of strangers. The truth is, I just want to set the record straight, and by that I don't mean what happened on that dreadful day. I don't care anymore about *that*. Honestly I don't. I only really care about what came *afterwards*."

Roxy must have looked concerned because she smiled her gleaming smile again.

"Don't worry! You will get all the details about that hideous morning. I am in public relations; I know *that's* why people will be picking up this book. But like I told Persephone, I have to get something out of it too, or what's the point? I want to show everyone just how far I've come. I want it to be a story of success, of overcoming tribulations. It's not about rehashing the past, it's about stepping into the future."

"Sounds like good motivation to me," Roxy said, smiling back at her as she continued the interview. "Let's make this a tribute to where you are now and how far you've come."

Phoebe looked relieved and sat back with a gleaming smile.

CHAPTER 8

"What a load of crock!" said Roxy's mother when she relayed the conversation to her in the backyard of Lane Cove that evening. "*Where you are now*, indeed! Roxanne Parker, you do not fool me."

"Sorry?"

Lorraine laughed. "You don't agree with that sentiment at all. You adore the past; you wallow in it sometimes! You desperately want to know what happened that day the family vanished, and you're just waiting for her to ask you to investigate!"

"No, I'm not."

"Yes, darling, you are."

Lorraine winked at her and returned inside while Roxy smarted at her mother's comments.

Urgh, she was so infuriating! Always telling her who she was and what she was thinking! Roxy did not wallow in the past! But… but even if she did, what was wrong with the past anyway? Where was the harm in wanting to set the record straight? To find out what really happened? It was an intriguing mystery after all! How could anyone not want to find answers? The fact that no one had ever worked out what had happened was almost as bad as the crime itself!

"And way too tantalising for an amateur sleuth to ignore," added Gilda as Roxy huffed and puffed along the leafy streets of Lane Cove half an hour later.

Gilda had been given an early pass at work and told not to come in on Sunday. Despite what Presley Smith had said of his wife's death—the fact that she had no health conditions and would never just take her own life—Wiles insisted any further investigation would be a waste of their time. Until the postmortem was finished, she was off the hook.

And Gilda was secretly glad, happy to catch up with the friend she missed so badly now that they were separated by a full day's drive. She wasn't glad about the timing, however, and no sooner had she shown up at Lane Cove, Roxy was shoving a pair of Lorraine's sneakers on her feet and insisting they walk Lunar.

Gilda loathed exercise. With her busy life she just could not see the point. Walking was something you did to get from A to B or, as she put it, "From HQ to corpse. But I'll make an exception for you, Roxy Parker. Not for that bloody dog!"

She scowled at Lunar who simply waved his tail back.

"Hey, don't take your mood out on my beautiful pooch."

"Yours or Sam's?"

Roxy ignored that and told her all about the day's interview. Gilda had immediately agreed with Lorraine—Roxy was fooling nobody.

"But if uncovering the mystery really is your motive for doing the book, then you're wasting Phoebe's time and your own."

"It absolutely isn't!" Roxy said before sneaking a sideways glance at Gilda as they walked. "Why would I be wasting my time?"

"Because if Phoebe's adoptive mother couldn't work out *whodunit*—or *whydunit* in this particular case—nobody can."

"Margie? Why should she work it out? She was just the kindly neighbour who took her in."

"The *kindly neighbour*?" Gilda erupted with laughter, her shaggy blond head dropping back, and she had to stop and catch her breath for a moment.

Roxy stopped too and scowled at her. "What?"

"I've heard her called some names in my time, but never that!" Gilda was wiping tears from under her eyes. "Margie wasn't just the *neighbour*, Roxy. She used to be the hottest detective in the nation." The look she shot Roxy said *How do you not know that?*

Roxy blinked rapidly and released Lunar so he could have a roam. "Hang on, are you talking about Margie Means?"

"Margie to some, darling! Detective Chief Superintendent Margaret Means to others. To me, she'll always be *SuperMeans*. A real-life superhero."

As Roxy stared at her, wide-eyed, Gilda explained.

"Before she took Phoebe in, Margaret Means was Australia's first female director of crime operations, a shining beacon. She broke new ground for the rest of us, crashed through that bulletproof glass ceiling, which was no mean feat."

"Wow, okay, I did not know that. I have some more homework to do, clearly."

"Clearly," Gilda echoed. "So I can't imagine that SuperMeans did not investigate the disappearance thoroughly, and as I say, if *she* couldn't find any trace of the missing family, I doubt anyone else could, even the great Roxy Parker."

Roxy ignored that comment, especially the sarcastic undertow and said, "And did she investigate? Do you know?"

"How could she not? She lived right next door; ended up with the kid. Which has got me wondering—how *did* such a successful career woman end up burdened with somebody else's child?"

"'Burdened' is a bit rich," Roxy said, frowning, "but this I do know."

She whistled for Lunar, who had taken the opportunity to bury his nose deep into a tipped-over rubbish bin. He looked around and came running back as they resumed the walk.

"Turns out, Margie had known the family for years and offered to take Phoebe in when they vanished. Department of Community Services refused at first and stuck the poor kid in foster care, but then she got lucky and they let Margie—*SuperMeans*—have her. Now I can see that some strings were obviously pulled..." She squished her lips to one side. "I'm surprised Phoebe didn't mention Margie's background though." She groaned. "I still have so many questions to ask and just a week to ask them!"

Gilda looked at Roxy. "Here's another one for you: Ask SuperMeans why she gave up a brilliant career to turn SuperMum. From what I hear, that's when she dropped out of the force entirely. She went from being married to her career to Phoebe's full-time caregiver. She wouldn't even do it for own kid, so it seems like a pretty big sacrifice to make for someone else's bloody child."

"Well, that bloody child is eternally grateful," Roxy snapped now, Gilda's comments making her testy. "Phoebe says Margie lost a baby very young and it destroyed her marriage, so maybe she was looking for a second chance…"

"Young? Really?" Gilda said but Roxy was smarting now.

"You know, you can't dedicate your entire life to the job. There could be more to life than work, work, work."

Gilda snuck a peek at Roxy as they walked. "Are we still talking about Margie here?"

"Of course! And Phoebe is grateful, that I know for sure. Margie gave that child a second chance."

"Still, I can't imagine giving up my career so flippantly."

Roxy stopped again and stared hard at Gilda. "You *really* think having a child is flippant?"

"Not flippant, perhaps, but…" She mock shuddered. "I'd rather be skinned alive than stuck with a snotty-nosed brat."

"I didn't know you hated kids so much."

"I don't *hate* them, sweetie, I just don't *want* them. There's a difference. Besides, I am getting a bit long in the tooth for all that. Come on, let's catch this green light."

They bolted across the main road and headed back to Lorraine's house on the other side of the street. Roxy was a little thrown by Gilda's remarks and a little irked too.

"I'm meeting Margie tomorrow, so I guess I can find out what possessed her to destroy her life and become a mother."

Roxy's sarcasm washed straight over Gilda who grabbed her arm and said, "You're meeting SuperMeans? Tomorrow?"

"Yes. Phoebe set it up. Why? Want me to get her

autograph for you?"

"God no! Then *you'd* be skinned alive. I hear she's a tough old bird. Still, I wish I could tag along. I could really use her thoughts on my current case."

"Oh?"

As they made the final leg home, the sun setting just below the motley mixture of sandstone and slate houses, 1920s bungalows and modern apartments, Gilda filled Roxy in on Paisley Presley's shocking death.

"The pathologist will hand down her report on Tuesday, but until then we've got a wager going. I'm thinking it has to be a sudden heart attack or stroke. Doreen has her money on drugs or alcohol, and Wiles is far too grown-up to hazard a guess. But I think he's leaning towards heat exposure."

A smile snaked onto Roxy's lips. "How is wily Wiles?"

"Oh he's fine," Gilda said, waving the subject off. "If she really did die from heat exposure, what a way to go, hey?"

"How long would it have taken?"

"Judging by the temperature that day, not that long, but long enough. Maybe an hour and a half, two hours tops. It would have been extremely unpleasant."

Roxy shivered suddenly and picked up the pace. The sun was almost gone, and the temperature was beginning to drop. Even Lunar was pulling at the leash as though eager to get back.

"I'm with Doreen," Roxy said. "She must have been bombed out of her brain on something."

"I hope so, for her sake. Otherwise, it would not have been a nice way to die."

Roxy shivered again.

"You'd think your survival instincts would kick in

subconsciously and you'd jump out."

"Mmm, that's what Wiles said. She must have strong willpower."

"Either that," said Roxy, "or a pretty strong desire to die."

CHAPTER 9

Just as Gilda was pulling Lorraine's walking shoes off, her mobile phone began to ring, and she broke into a smile.

"Couldn't live without me, hey Wiles?" she said as she answered it.

"What?" he replied, and then, "There's been a development in the Paisley Smith case."

"What kind of development?"

"The suicide note kind."

She didn't miss a beat. "I'll be right in."

Half an hour later Gilda was sitting across from Wiles in the homicide department of the state's crime command centre in Sydney's west, staring at his computer screen. It was a photograph of a text message that had been emailed from the police station in Gerringong, the neighbouring town to Gerroa.

She read it aloud for the second time.

"I'm sorry, my love. I have to do this. I hope in time you will understand. xo."

She looked up at Wiles. "Do what? Exactly? Sit in the car and expire?" He shrugged. "This was sent to Presley Smith? And he's only just telling us now?"

"Hubby rarely uses his mobile phone. Only just noticed it."

Gilda blew a stream of air from her lips. "You really think this is a suicide note?"

He scratched his goatee. "It suggests suicide, but it's not conclusive. We need the postmortem to determine exactly how Mrs Smith died, but you saw her yourself. No obvious signs of a struggle. Doors were unlocked. And if the husband is to be believed, no medical conditions that might have caused her death."

"When did she send this text, do we know?"

"Smack on ten, Friday morning, from central Wollongong. We assume from the post office where she works. Flannery spoke to them on Friday, and they have her leaving the premises around that time, so it all adds up."

"But if she was going to kill herself, why not do it closer to home? There must be a steamy, hot car park in Wollongong she could have availed herself of." She read the message again. "'*I have to do this.*' Maybe she just meant, I have to leave you. She was at the airport, after all. It's pretty ambiguous."

"Don't forget, she didn't have any luggage."

"Yeah, but she was clearly emotional, mightn't have thought to pack anything. Might have been leaving in a hurry. What do we know about the husband? Their relationship? Maybe he was unfaithful or abusive? Maybe he's lying and he did get the message and followed her there. Somehow restrained her in the car or suffocated her or something."

"I thought you suspected a heart attack," Wiles said, smiling. "One night with Roxy and you're pointing fingers at the husband." Before she could respond, he said, "It's an interesting theory, but we've checked his alibi. Presley Smith also works for *Australia Post*—"

"That's cosy."

"He's at their Nowra branch—opposite direction to Wollongong. Anyway, Presley was at work from nine to five, according to his boss, and had his usual hour lunch break. No way he could have got to Sydney and back in that time. Pathologist has the death clocked at between 1:00 p.m. and 4:00 p.m. at the latest, but that's a guestimate at this stage."

He leaned back in his chair and put his feet up on his desk. "I don't know what this tells us, to be honest. As I say, let's wait for the full report and then take it from there. I didn't mean to drag you away from your friend. I could have read this over the phone."

"I wanted to come in." She offered him a provocative smile. "Good excuse to see you."

He returned her smile, but it didn't quite reach his eyes. "I am still working, Gilda."

Doesn't mean you can't spend time with me, she thought grumpily, *or heaven forbid, give me a half-convincing smile.*

~~~

Roxy hadn't had a decent conversation with her boyfriend since she'd arrived two days earlier and was relieved when he finally answered his mobile. She was in her mother's backyard again, sipping a glass of wine and pretending to keep Lunar company, but really she was hiding out.

"Hey Roxy, how's it all going?" Sam said over a crystal-clear line that almost had her convinced he was about to step through the back gate.

In fact, she knew he was still on the job in the middle of *Nowhereville, Queensland.*
~~~

"Great, can you talk? Or are you busy?"

He laughed. "Kind of. I'm hanging from a pole, checking wires as we speak."

"This late? Seriously?"

"Big backlog to get through, the locals are getting angsty. We're working round the clock at the moment."

"I'd better leave you to it then."

"Don't you dare! I've been trying to reach you for days. I want to hear your beautiful voice. Just let me secure this…" There was a scratchy sound, a few heavy pants, and then he was back. "Okay, that should do it. If I suddenly drop out, dial triple zero."

"Now you're really freaking me out."

He laughed again and assured her he was exaggerating, then demanded to hear how she was doing and then asked about Lunar.

"I miss my old mate. How's he coping in the Big Smoke?"

"He's fine. In fact, it's an exciting holiday for him. The smells! The sounds! So many things to sniff out. I'm not sure he's bonded with Mum, though, and not through any fault of his own. He wags his tail madly every time she comes near, and she doesn't seem to notice."

"Not everybody's a dog person, Rox."

"That's her excuse and she's sticking to it."

"So…" He hesitated. "Have you, you know, mentioned anything?"

Roxy hesitated too. She knew what he was talking about, and she knew he wouldn't like the answer. "Not yet, but only because I've barely been home. If I'm not interviewing Phoebe, I'm catching up with all my mates and—"

"What about *them*?" he said. "What about Gilda?

You tell her?"

She scrunched her eyes shut. "Just hasn't felt right."

"Okay. Interesting." He paused again. "Are you having second thoughts, babe?"

Her eyes flew open. "No! Absolutely not!"

"Then what's the problem?"

"I… I don't know. It's big news. I'm…" She heard the interior sliding doors squeak and could see Lorraine making her way out. "I better go. I was just checking in. Everything good there?"

"Yep, all good."

His tone was polite, but she knew she had hurt him.

"I *will* tell them, Sam," she said, whispering now as her mother closed in. "I just need to find—"

"The right time, yeah, yeah. Well, you're only there for another week, right? So you better find it fast." The line went dead, and she had a horrible feeling he'd hung up on her. Either that or he'd plummeted to the ground, and she wasn't sure which was worse. Then he said, "I gotta go too. I love you, Rox. Give that dog a squeeze from me."

And then he was gone and she was the one left dangling.

CHAPTER 10

Margaret Means was naturally greyer and more wrinkled than the tabloid shots in Roxy's scrapbooks, but they were her only concessions to aging. The seventy-year-old's voice was still deep and commanding, and her handshake, when she offered it to Roxy, was verging on the painful.

Her attitude also packed a punch.

"I'd like to say I'm pleased to meet you, but that would be a lie," she announced as she released Roxy's hand. "Nothing personal, mind. I'm just not a fan of this ridiculous book. You're only here because Phee has begged me to see you, and I would do anything for that girl. And she knows it."

Whoah, thought Roxy. *Tell me how you really feel!* "Well, I appreciate your making the time," she said instead. No use getting off to a bad start.

They were standing on the stoop of 55 Baker Street, the one next door to where Phoebe first lived, and Roxy couldn't help ogling number 53 as she arrived.

From the outside, the old Fisher house looked relatively benign, just a nondescript brick structure with a sandy garden out the front. It was just a few streets back from Coogee Beach, a family-friendly spot on the city's east coast, not too far from world-famous Bondi. If you hadn't done your research, you would never have known the history that had unfolded there twenty years earlier.

Roxy *had* done her due diligence and knew that it had been bought and sold many times over the years, as though no family had ever really settled in, so perhaps its unsettling past permeated from inside. She was itching to knock on the door and take a look around. Get a sense of the place herself.

"I've only got twenty minutes to spare, so let's get on with it," Margie said, waving her through and securing the door behind them.

She then marched Roxy down a short hallway to a small kitchen. Her home was what you might call minimalist, although "no fuss" was probably how Margie would describe it—lots of clean lines and neutral colours and barely a decorative item in sight. The appliances all sparkled within an inch of their lives, and she headed straight for one of them, the kettle, and began to fill it up from the tap.

"Phee is a very determined young lass," Margie said as she set about making some tea, "and there's nothing I can do or say to change her mind. But I do fear she's being manipulated by her publishers and"—she paused and gave Roxy the once-over— "*others*, and I do hope you treat her story with kid gloves and kindness."

"Of course," Roxy said. "I'm just the ghostwriter, Mrs Means—"

"Margie."

She nodded, but the moniker didn't suit her. It was homely, motherly, soft around the edges, everything this woman was not. "This is Phoebe's firsthand account, so everything I write comes straight from her lips, not mine. It really is in her hands."

The woman ran her eyes across Roxy's face, and she felt as though a spotlight had just been switched on.

"So why are you here then?" Margie said. "Why are you wasting my time?"

Cripes! Roxy tried hard to hold back a frown, and when she answered, her voice wobbled slightly.

"I'm not here to waste your time, Margie. I'm sorry if that's how you feel. I'm here to get some background on Phoebe, a bit of context. It's all just part of the process, and I do this with every book I write—and I have written a few." *You're not the only expert in her field*, she wanted to add. "As I explained to Phoebe, it's important to establish a client's complete background so I know exactly what to ask about. And as she was a child when her parents vanished, she may remember things differently."

"Incorrectly, you mean?"

Roxy smiled stiffly. "I just want to get the facts straight. It's as simple as that."

The woman's eyes narrowed, and she was clearly weighing Roxy up, deciding whether she could trust her. Eventually she said, "I will need to see your version before it goes to print."

"That's not up to me, I'm afraid. You'll need to talk to the publisher. And Phoebe of course."

"Are you denying me this?"

The spotlight was back on Roxy, and she couldn't help frowning now. She was growing impatient with Mrs Grumpybum.

"I'm telling you who's in charge of this book. And it certainly isn't me."

That seemed to satisfy Margie, who stared at her for a moment longer before returning to the tea, which she was scooping out of a large tin and into a simple white teapot. As she did this, Roxy took a few settling breaths. She had been expecting some pushback, but that was quite a tussle.

She understood why the woman was being defensive. *Offensive*, in fact. As she'd explained to Phoebe, it was not unusual for at least one family member—often many more—to pull her aside and read her the riot act. People simply didn't like the idea of the family laundry being aired, even when it was their own loved one doing the airing and the laundry was Omo-clean. Even the most benign stories were met with anxiety and trepidation. But there was nothing benign about this one, and Margie was right at the heart of it. She was the one who took a young, distraught Phoebe home, the person who protected and nurtured and turned the child's life around. She'd probably fended off countless tabloid journalists and paparazzi over the years. Add to that a long career in the police force, and it was little wonder she didn't trust anyone.

Roxy decided to harden up and cut her some slack, and by the time tea had been served and they settled on sturdy wooden chairs at Margie's kitchen table, the mood lightened, but only just. Roxy felt like the woman was going through the motions, answering the questions but offering little else. No colour. No anecdotes. Nothing beyond what Phoebe had already offered.

She noticed the clock. It was time to tighten the rope.

"I'd like to get some more details about that morning, if you don't mind," Roxy said. "At what point did *you* know the family had vanished?"

Margie's lips drooped downwards. It was a habit,

Roxy soon discovered, something she did after almost every single question, and it only emphasised her grumpiness. Roxy wondered if it was deliberate.

"I had no idea what was going on until I heard the screaming," Margie said. "Wailing really. Coming from next door. I thought the dog had been hit by a car, it was that raw." Her jaw tightened, and Roxy could see it still had an effect all these years later. "But, if I'm being honest, I didn't think too much of it at the time. I always kept my distance from that lot."

"Really? Why?"

She paused, lips drooping again. "I wasn't *fond* of the parents, shall we say. Phoebe was fine… I mean, she could be a bit precocious back then, a bit *rambunctious* you could say, and the boy was far too boisterous for my liking, but he was still an innocent, still a child. The parents though… "

She picked at a stray thread on her sleeve, lost in thought, and Roxy made a note to ask more questions about Phoebe's brother, Daniel. He was five years old when the family vanished, yet Phoebe had barely mentioned him in the preliminary interview yesterday, and Roxy wondered whether they'd been close and how much she missed him.

Even if she didn't want to find her parents, surely Phoebe was curious about her only sibling? As Margie said, Danny was an innocent back then. Surely she couldn't bear him any grudge?

Eventually Margie said, "They just weren't the greatest human beings, let's leave it at that."

"So you weren't surprised when they took off?"

"I didn't say that." The woman gave Roxy a warning look: *don't put words in my mouth.* "My reservations with the Fishers were entirely separate to their departure.

They simply weren't of good character, but I won't elaborate, so stop asking me to. I'm not a gossip, and I don't think young Phoebe would appreciate me smearing her folks, even if they did desert her."

She offered her first smile, a sad, wistful one, and said, "Phee may say she doesn't care for them, but how can she not?"

Roxy nodded. "Fair enough. So, you heard Phoebe crying. Then what?"

"Then the poor child suddenly knocked at my door. I don't believe she'd ever come to my house before. She looked frantic. She told me her family had vanished, but she was barely coherent at that stage, and I had some trouble understanding what had happened. I'm ashamed to say I told her to snap out of it, then I told her to wait on my doorstep while I went across to investigate."

Margie folded her arms. Frowned. "It was strange. I've seen some sights in my lifetime, let me tell you that, but those empty rooms, the utter quiet..." She closed her eyes as she said, "I could not believe they'd taken off. And all they'd left behind was a scrappy old tea towel, hanging on the oven door."

"And a child," Roxy said, and Margie's eyes flew open.

"That goes without saying," she snapped.

Roxy took some soothing sips of her tea, then asked, "Did you have any idea where the family might have gone? Did they ever mention anything to you? Give you any indication?"

"Of course not. Otherwise I would have tracked them down and slapped them with a reckless abandonment charge! And why would they tell me anyway? Like I said, we were never close, didn't exactly chat over the garden fence."

"And you didn't see or hear them moving out? I mean, it must have taken them quite a few trips to the car with all their stuff."

Now Margie's glare was full throttle. "Are you suggesting I heard them leave and kept that information to myself?"

"No, of course not. I was just—"

"You were hypothesising, young lady, and I'm not a fan of hypotheticals. You said you were here to check the facts."

"I am, absolutely," Roxy stammered. "I guess I'm just curious, that's all. It is an extraordinary story, and I'm trying to wrap my head around it for the book. Forgive me. I know I'm being intrusive, too inquisitive. It's a flaw of mine."

Her attempt at humility thawed Margie again. "Yes, well, I can't really blame you. It is an extraordinary mystery. Had the world on edge for weeks, months really, and it's continued to baffle some of us for decades. How did it happen? How *could* it happen? And right next door to where I live!"

Margie stared into her cup as if contemplating her own question. "They did have a large garage, the Fishers. They must have done it all in there, under the cloak of darkness, I suppose. But if I'm being honest, I have to wonder what I missed."

She looked up at Roxy then, and there was a glimmer of remorse in her eyes and something else. Was it humility? Shame?

"I've wracked my brain for years, Miss Parker, wondering what I missed, how an entire family could vanish from the house next door and how I did not suspect a thing. Me? Of all people!" The humility had vanished, and she was now looking at Roxy shrewdly again. "As you will have already learned—or I hope you have; if not, Phoebe has chosen quite the wrong author—I was high up in the State Crime Command at the time." Roxy nodded. "I certainly pulled out all the stops once the family took off. We did everything we could. Searched high and low. But it was hopeless. They had vanished."

As she spoke, Roxy wondered if that's why she took young Phoebe in—because she could not get past the fact that she had lived so close and hadn't seen the warning signs. *Had somehow let it happen.*

Roxy kept those thoughts to herself. She knew the steely ex-copper would not appreciate her psychoanalysis, but she did feel a little braver now and asked, "Do you have any idea why Phoebe never heard anything?"

"I suspect she was drugged."

"Drugged? You mean before they left?"

"We didn't think to check it at the time. In all the madness, we… well, we didn't do our due diligence. But I have wondered over the years—did they put something in her food to knock her out while they packed everything up and left? How else would she have slept right through? I have no idea, of course, and you will not put that in the book. It's pure supposition."

Damn it. She said, "Of course. And I gather their car was never found; there was no evidence which way they even went?"

"You have to understand, Miss Parker, there weren't cameras on every corner and in front of every shop back then. It was a very different time."

"It was only twenty years ago."

"Doesn't change the facts."

"Do you mind me asking why you decided to adopt Phoebe? How that came about."

The older woman did her drooped lips thing and said in a matter-of-fact tone, "She needed stability. I was prepared to give her that."

No emotional platitudes then.

It all sounded a little too convenient for Roxy and far too clinical. Phoebe was a living, breathing human being, not discarded furniture or an abandoned puppy. There *had* to be more to it than that, but she doubted the ex-detective was going to share any more with her today. She would try to squeeze some emotion from her next time.

"Oh there won't be a next time," Margie remarked when Roxy tried to pencil in a second interview as they wrapped up. "You said it yourself, this is Phoebe's book. I have said more than enough."

Then, with no interest in negotiating, she marched Roxy back down the corridor to her front door and swept it open.

Roxy wasn't quite prepared to leave it at that, so she stopped on the doorstep and said, "Can I ask just one more question then?"

The woman smudged her lips downwards.

"Do you have your own theory about *why* Phoebe's family took off?" Then, noticing Margie's blossoming frown, she quickly added, "Again, please forgive my nosiness, but with your extraordinary background, I'm just keen to hear your take on it. Off the record of course."

Roxy half expected Margie to tell her she was immune to flattery and slam the door in her face.

Instead, Margie simply leaned on it and said, "Of course I've given it a great deal of thought. Even done a little *sleuthing* of my own, if you must know. I have a few theories, but theories aren't evidence of anything."

Then, sensing Roxy's disappointment, she added, "I will tell you this for good measure: I've met all kinds of human beings in my time, the good, the bad and the ugly, and people *always* hurt the people they love. It's as though they can't help themselves. We might want to explain it in neat plotlines and pop them away in tidy little boxes, but who knows why anybody does anything. Twenty-five years in the force taught me that. There is no explanation for you, Miss Parker, none for Phee either, I'm afraid. We're all just animals trying to survive, and some of us are doing it better than others. Quite frankly, nothing surprises me anymore."

Then she dropped her lips downwards and swung the door shut, leaving Roxy standing on the doorstep, feeling completely and utterly surprised.

CHAPTER 11

"What did I tell you? Margaret Means is a legend," Gilda said when Roxy relayed the conversation to her an hour later at Peepers café, the one down from Roxy's old pad in Elizabeth Bay.

The ghostwriter was doing a tour of sorts, trying to revisit all her favourite haunts, and simply had to fit this place into the mix, although she hadn't factored in how wistful she would feel as she strolled through her old neighbourhood and past her shabby brick apartment block on her way to the street-side eatery. She wished she could buzz her way into apartment 8A and spend just a few moments in the small but sundrenched space that she had loved. *Still* loved and was not sure she could ever part with, no matter what happened with Sam.

Sam owned a place in Sydney too, a "shitbox" he called it, in nearby Newtown, which he also rented out, but he didn't yearn for it, as she did, and she wondered about that. He didn't have anywhere near the attachment she had for the Big Smoke.

Would that become a problem?

It was lunchtime on Sunday, and Roxy wasn't due back at Phoebe's apartment until Monday morning, so she had scheduled another catch-up with Gilda. Or, to be more precise, Gilda had scheduled it with Roxy to hear all about the former Detective Chief Superintendent Means.

"She was very intimidating," Roxy told her. "She clearly didn't trust me at the start, was highly suspicious of my motives, but I feel like she chilled out in the end. You're right, she's a tough old bird."

"And who can blame her?" Gilda said. "You know how hard it is for *me* today, imagine Margaret's days. The sexism and misogyny; it would have been dinosauric!"

"Dino-whatie?"

"You know what I mean. You had to be tough to make it back then. I guess she never softened."

"I would have thought taking a child in might have helped," Roxy said, ordering another coffee from the waiter as he passed.

Roxy didn't normally drink caffeine post-midday, but she needed a second hit for what lay ahead. Caroline had just messaged to say she'd collected Max from the airport and they'd swing by the café to say g'day.

Gilda could see that Roxy's heart was aflutter and tried to keep the conversation light, first getting details of SuperMeans, then drawing her into a discussion on her latest case, now dubbed Death by Sunbaking.

Roxy took a few moments to switch her thoughts from Forgotten Phoebe to the body at Sydney airport.

"So," she said, dropping several teaspoons of sugar into her cup, "the poor woman sent a suicide text, then drove all the way to Sydney, parked on a hot roof and just, what? Sat in the car and waited to die?"

"I know, it's ludicrous, right?" Gilda frowned.

"I'm not prepared to call it suicide. Not yet. That text might just have been a Dear John letter for the hubby. She was at the airport, which suggests she was heading somewhere, we can't forget that. I'm waiting to see the autopsy results, but I suspect we'll find she died of a medical episode that incapacitated her, which then led to prolonged heat exposure. Mostly, I'm baffled by the timeline. If she was leaving her husband, why drive to work, then run off again, *sans* suitcase, so quickly? Why not pack a bag like a normal person?"

"*That's* what's got you baffled?"

"True, the whole case is strange."

"Could it be murder?"

Gilda swept an eyebrow high. "Trust you to mention the *M* word. We have considered it. It is our shtick, after all, but I'm not sure about that either. I did wonder if the hubby chased her down, but he has a watertight alibi."

"Strangers like to murder too, you know? Could some creep have come across her in the car park? Was she sexually assaulted?"

"No obvious signs but we'll know more in a few days. I suppose someone could have suffocated her afterwards, but again, there are no obvious injuries or bruises, no sign of violence or physical restraints. She had a mobile phone within reaching distance, a horn at her disposal. It was a public space for goodness' sake."

"He could have held a knife to her throat or pointed a gun at her or something?" She bit her lower lip; it did sound improbable. "Any other family members in the frame?"

"There's an adult son I spoke to briefly on the phone. He could barely speak he was so upset, poor love. He also lives down south, nowhere near Sydney airport."

"Doesn't mean he couldn't have driven up, done the deed and driven home again."

"And there she goes again, swinging it back to murder," Gilda said.

"Sounds like nothing's changed."

This was a new voice, a deep voice, and both women swung around to find Max Farrell leaning in with his trademark sloppy smile.

Roxy's breath caught in the back of her throat. Her ex-boyfriend was paler than usual but otherwise looked fighting fit and nowhere near as rumpled as he normally looked, *should* have looked after a long-haul flight. Max was wearing a smart black jacket over a white T-shirt and blue jeans, and his once floppy fringe had been recently trimmed.

"Goodness, you look fresh as a daisy!" Gilda agreed as she jumped up to smother him with a hug.

Roxy followed suit, glad of the opportunity to let her heartbeat relax a little before he crushed her to his chest.

"Where's Caroline?" Gilda asked.

"Struggling to find a park. Wow, you both look good too. Really good."

Gilda tossed a shoulder back and ruffled her shaggy blond hair. "We're like fine wine, darling."

"You get better with age?"

"No! We're fabulous *all* the time."

He laughed while Roxy just rolled her eyes.

"Grab a seat and we'll get you a coffee, something to eat," Gilda said, but he was tapping his stomach.

"No need, they fed me on the flight." He yawned suddenly. "Sorry, jetlag is starting to hit, but Caro said you were here, and I was so keen to see you."

"Thank you, honey!" Gilda winked, knowing only too well he was referring to Roxy. She also knew Roxy was struggling to find her voice, so she added, "Tell us why you left Berlin. It all seems so sudden."

"Straight to the tough questions I see, Detective Maltin!" He laughed as he took the seat next to Roxy so their arms just touched.

Roxy felt a shot run through her and instantly shifted away.

"Truth is, I loved Berlin, loved the job even, just couldn't stop missing home."

Missing Roxy he would have added if he wasn't feeling quite so washed out. Travel hadn't made him any braver either, and he already knew the story. He knew she'd moved up north and in with some handsome bugger. He hated the very idea of Sam Forrest, spurred on by Caroline who hadn't even met him but decided she hated him too, but he was determined not to let on. At least not now.

He might be jetlagged, but he was no fool. He'd noticed how quickly she'd moved her arm away. Like she couldn't bear to touch him.

"Oh my God!" came a squeal from the front door. "The band's back together!"

Caroline swooped in, scraping a seat from another table on the way.

"How good does he look, ladies? You'd never know he'd been flying for twenty-nine hours straight!"

"I was in business class all the way," Max said. "Company's final gift to me before I scuttle back with the masses."

"Got a job lined up?" Roxy asked, finally snapping out of it, and Caroline answered for him.

"He'll have every company in Sydney lining up, don't you worry about that!"

Max turned his eyes to Roxy. "I don't want to work for a corporation again. I want to go back to freelance. Like you."

"Hard life these days," she replied, and now they all eyed her. "I'm just saying. Everybody's got a blog now; everybody's got an iPhone camera. Less call for the likes of us, Max."

"Is that why you've stayed up north?" He remembered how career focused she once was, then blushed as he realised—as they all did—that the answer had more to do with a new love interest.

Caroline leapt to her feet. "Time to break up the band again! I'm in a loading zone, and this one needs his beauty sleep."

Max looked relieved and jumped up almost as quickly, then waved awkwardly to them both and fled the café while Gilda gave her friend a worried glance.

Roxy was staring after him, chewing her lower lip, a quizzical look on her face.

"You okay?" Gilda asked.

"Yes, of course." She offered a quick, relieved smile. "To be honest, I'm just glad that's over with."

She laughed and Gilda nodded reassuringly, but she knew these two well, and she had a feeling it was just the beginning.

Again.

CHAPTER 12

When Phoebe was very young, her entire neighbourhood went from a happy-go-lucky environment to a sad, bleak place, and it had nothing to do with the Fisher family, she told Roxy as they began the second day of interviews.

Long before Phoebe's *Home Alone* horror, a neighbouring family had experienced a horror of their own, losing their only child to a backyard drowning. Phoebe was very young at the time and only learned later—and only in hushed, sketchy detail from dear Mrs Dorey next door—how the poor child had been playing in a neighbour's backyard, unsupervised, when she slipped through their faulty pool fence and fell into the deep end. The supervising mother found her just minutes later, but she could not be revived.

Rumour has it the woman had been drinking, but Delvine Dorey wouldn't elaborate further. Only saying that the neighbour got off lightly while the entire neighbourhood got a death sentence of sorts.

"We were such a close-knit group before that, regular barbecues with each other on weekends, all minding each other's littlies," she told eight-year-old Phoebe as she dished out a bowl of ice cream from her cosy kitchen one steamy summer's day.

She had quietly ushered the child in for a sneaky treat, something she did from time to time when no one was watching, like she was breaking some silent bond between the parents.

"After that… Well, that's when we all sort of closed our doors and shut each other out. Which is a great pity, really. It's like none of us were ever the same again."

Mrs Dorey died quite suddenly of a heart attack, not long after Phoebe's family vanished, which seemed almost as cruel a blow. She had adored that old lady, would have preferred to be taken in by her, if truth be told, but of course the woman was gone and the only one putting her hand up to help was the cranky copper who lived on the other side.

Margie never talked about the drowning either, but it had clearly reverberated because she insisted Phoebe get swimming lessons even though she was ten by then and a competent swimmer, thanks very much!

"We never had a pool when I was growing up," Phoebe told Roxy now, "but I don't remember ever not knowing how to swim. I guess those *people* must have got me lessons at an early age. I guess the neighbourhood drowning must have shocked everyone, even *them*."

She was referring, of course, to her biological parents but was still unwilling to use their names, as though simply uttering the words was far too painful. Or was more than they deserved.

"But that didn't stop Margie," Phoebe continued. "She booked me in for weekly stroke lessons and forced me to join squad—which I absolutely loathed." She smiled vaguely. "Funnily enough it ended up being quite therapeutic. There's nothing quite like swimming laps over and over and over again to wash away your anger. I eventually warmed to it."

She eventually warmed to Margie, too, and then grew to love her as her own mother, but she always thought fondly of Mrs Dorey and told Roxy how she would sneak in to visit her like she was some sort of double agent and would always find an enormous bowl of something sweet and enticing.

"She would have made a terrific surrogate mother. Of course she would've been far too old to take in a deeply distressed ten-year-old, but then what did I know?"

"Did you ever hear any more about the child who drowned?"

"No. It was a taboo topic in our street." She sighed. "It's funny how people don't like to talk about sad things. Like they're scared it'll rub off on them or something."

She sighed again and Roxy sighed along, even though she disagreed. In her experience, most people had a touch of schadenfreude and loved mulling over others' misfortune. Most slowed down when driving past crash sites and watched news bulletins with just a glint of anticipation.

What did they teach you at journalism school about prioritising disaster stories? *If it bleeds, it leads.* She was guilty of that herself. More than most, in fact. Had a collection of grisly scrapbooks to prove it.

As Phoebe went inside to prepare some lunch, Roxy thought about the drowning and realised there had been more than one lost child on Baker Street in Coogee. Unlike Phoebe, however, that child had not been rescued by a competent cop, nor was she around to tell her sad story or show how far she'd come.

By midafternoon, Roxy had a much clearer idea of how Phoebe had grown up and what had happened to her. But there were still plenty of gaps.

"Margie says she feared you were drugged that night your family vanished," Roxy said, and the younger woman looked at her, startled.

"Really? She said that?"

"Off the record, yes. She never mentioned it to you?"

Phoebe shook her head. "Goodness, they were loose with the pills back then! I guess it could explain why I didn't wake up."

"It's a pity they didn't think to check your blood at the time."

"They did everything wrong," she replied. "Margie told me much later that she was very disappointed in the two guys who investigated. Says they were useless, a waste of space."

"Still, I'd like to interview them if possible. Are they still around, do you know?"

"No idea. But why waste time on them? I don't want those losers anywhere near my book."

"I understand that, Phoebe, but they were a pivotal part of the story, so we can't ignore them either. At the very least I need to get their recollection of events."

Phoebe's meticulously drawn eyebrows nudged together and her lips pursed a little. The petulant look was back. "You don't trust my recollection?"

"This isn't a trust exercise, Phoebe, it's a nonfiction book. I need to get the story straight. How much did you see? How much did the adults *let* you see? Believe me, if we get so much as one fact wrong—

something as tiny as the police officer's rank—we'll have some pedant calling it a whitewash and discrediting the whole book."

Phoebe thought that over and relaxed her features. "Talk to Margie," she said eventually. "She'll know all of that."

Margie echoed Phoebe's words when Roxy called her later that night, her tone huffy as she recalled just how inept the two investigating officers had been. Roxy was back at Lane Cove and had set up camp in Charlie's study. Her scrapbook was open beside her, and she had the names of the two men but little else. They were Detective Senior Constable Gary Pollard and his junior Michael DeSanto, although the latter had been spelled in various ways in various articles, which was yet more reason to track them down.

"That's right," Margie said, "Pollard and DeSanto. Couldn't find their way out of a paper bag those two, although they had so much potential at the start."

"I thought you said there wasn't much to find."

"There *might* have been something if those bozos hadn't messed with the evidence! They let the cleaning lady in just a day after the parents vanished. Can you imagine it?"

"Why would they do that?"

"You'll have to ask them!"

"Hence my call. Any idea where they're based now? Are they still in Sydney? I can't find anything on them, and Phoebe doesn't seem to know."

"She wouldn't. They were just two suits who badgered her silly with inane questions and botched everything up." She humphed on the other end. "I have no idea where either officer is now, and frankly, I don't want to know. Honestly, they're not worth your time."

"Still, I would like to chase them up."

Another humph! "I'll see what I can find."

Roxy thanked her and hung up, but she had a feeling she would not hear from Margie on that subject again.

CHAPTER 13

Gilda had to read the report through twice before it sunk in. It was early Tuesday morning and the chief pathologist had just emailed Mrs Presley's preliminary postmortem results. It was now up on her computer screen, and Wiles was hovering just behind her, reading along.

"Cause of death: hyperthermia following severe heat exhaustion and heatstroke." She stared at the report. "No sign of a heart attack or stroke? Seriously?"

He held his palm out. "Want to pay up now or later?"

She frowned. "I really wish I'd been right about the heart attack and not because I'm losing ten bucks. I mean, who would put themselves through that?" She glanced back at the email. "I know Paisley wanted to leave her husband, but I still can't believe her survival instincts didn't kick in at some point, that she didn't jump out or turn on the air-conditioning."

"Keep reading," he said, tapping at her screen. "Says here there was severe damage to the body cells, which would have first led to shock and/or unconsciousness followed fairly quickly by organ failure and then death. She might have passed out before she got a chance to save herself."

He took control of her mouse and scrolled down farther, and she could smell his spicy aftershave as he leaned across. She inhaled deeply, smiling to herself as he continued.

"Vonnie hasn't ruled out suicide, but you'll see she's leaning towards misadventure. There was no sign of alcohol or any drugs in her system, but she does say, if you read the second part, that the temperature in the vehicle would have been at an extreme level at the time she died, and she can't rule out Mrs Smith fainting from the heat involuntarily."

Wiles noticed her sneaky smile and stepped back. "If she'd sat in the car long enough, that might have been the cause."

Then he walked around the desk and stood in front of Gilda, who kept reading.

"Time of death between 1:00 p.m. and 3:00 p.m. So we think she sat there the whole time? Never left her vehicle?"

"There's no vision of her anywhere other than driving through the turnstile at midday," Wiles said. "The only cameras on the top level are right near the terminal entrance, and Mattheson says there's no footage of her entering or leaving at any point. So, yeah, it looks like she just sat there. Intentionally or not, Mrs Smith baked herself to death."

"But why would she do that?"

"You saw the text, Gilda. She wasn't a happy camper. As strange as this is, we can only assume that was a suicide note. It is not our job to wonder why."

She frowned. "That's *all* our job is!"

"Not when it comes to suicide, or misadventure for that matter. Last time I looked, we worked homicide."

He noticed her firming frown and said, "Look, for all we know, Mrs Smith was intending to fly somewhere but couldn't bring herself to do it. Maybe she passed out while she was working up the courage. Or maybe she'd lost all will to live. Either way, the case is officially out of our hands."

"But it's so *strange*. Don't you have any curiosity about it? At all?"

"Of course I'm curious, Gilda, but it's not my job to make sense of other people's madness." He smiled lightly. "Listen, we've got to fill Mr Smith in on all this. Can you find out when Vonnie is officially releasing the body and let him know? He'll have to alert his funeral director, arrange for the body to be collected."

"Nicely delegated," she said, not returning the smile. "Mr Smith won't take this lightly. He'll probably turn into a madman like last time."

"He *had* just identified his wife's body. Give him a break."

"All I'm saying is, if I'm having trouble grasping the findings, I can't imagine how he'll take it."

"You might be surprised." He perched on the edge of the desk. "Nobody ever likes to admit that someone they love didn't love them enough to hang around, but in my experience, most people come to terms with suicide pretty quickly. Before you're out the door, they're explaining how their loved one had been down in the dumps lately or tried to take their own life before—stuff they'll never tell you in the preliminary interview."

He stood up and walked towards the door, then turned around to catch the frown that was still clinging to her forehead.

"You've got to let this one go, Gilda. Even if it

doesn't make sense, it's not ours to question."

She disagreed heartily but tried to hide that from her eyes as she returned to the screen and began tapping back to the top of the report, looking for the chief pathologist's number.

~~~

Elsewhere, a man was tapping at his computer too, speed-reading the latest gossip on various news sites, when a headline caught his eye.

Forgotten Phoebe Finally Speaks!

His brow furrowed and he stopped and reread the clickbait, then tapped again, hooked, as the full story appeared before him.

In what's being hailed the memoir of the century, publisher Persephone Daley has confirmed the rumours that have been circulating for weeks, that PR doyenne Phoebe Van Beurden (nee Fisher) has just signed a multimillion-dollar publishing deal for a tell-all book.

'Forgotten Phoebe,' as she was dubbed by the tabloid press, was living in the beachside suburb of Coogee in 1999 when she woke up one morning to find her entire family, including parents Shane and Karen, and five-year-old brother Daniel, had vanished. The then-ten-year-old was taken in by a kindly neighbour and has never spoken publicly about the ordeal since.

Now married to financial mogul James Van Beurden and residing in his luxurious Wynard apartment, Ms Van Beurden, now thirty, was not available for comment, but her publisher did confirm
~~~

that the autobiography would be out by Christmas.

The man dropped his iPad to his lap, looking as though he'd just been slapped. Then he glanced around, pulled it back up and read it all again, his hands shaking violently this time.

CHAPTER 14

The early-morning air was crisp and dry, and Lunar wagged his tail as Roxy walked him through the Lane Cove backstreets that were becoming a little too familiar for her liking. The poor dog was not used to being strapped to a leash, let alone locked up in a backyard all day, even one as pretty as her mother's, so he champed at the bit as he bounded from tree to car tyre, or—in his world—one delicious odour to the next.

As she lingered, letting Lunar have a good sniff, Roxy decided to phone Sam. Then hesitated. He was usually an early riser, but what if he'd done another late shift? She groaned, feeling suddenly out of sorts. So *disconnected*.

Lunar returned to her side, his eyes wide, his ears low, and she bent down to give him a good pat. "I know you miss Sam, matey," she said. "I miss him too."

And the Byron hinterland, although not as much as she expected.

She and Sam had been living in each other's pockets since the day they first hooked up. They hadn't bothered with formal dates like most new relationships; she had simply moved straight in. It was partly because they felt so comfortable with each other and partly because she was from out of town. If she was being completely honest, she had to admit she had nowhere else to go. No one else to hang with.

Now back in Sydney and surrounded by friends and family—all clamouring for her time—Roxy had to remind herself to think of Sam more, to call him more often, to remember that she was going back.

What was that about?

"Just face it, Roxy, you're not a country girl," Oliver told her as she sat across from him in his office an hour later. "You're a natural born city slicker, like the rest of us,"

"Not true," she retorted. "I love it out there."

"Not enough to miss it."

She scowled, wishing she hadn't just 'fessed up, then produced a thumb drive and tossed it towards him. "Here are the first lot of interviews."

Oliver had agreed to get them transcribed, and she was dropping them in on her way to Phoebe's apartment for the next appointment. Normally transcriptions were part of her job description—and not an especially enjoyable part. An hour of chatter could take three hours to type out and could be boring at best (she'd already heard it all, right?), but it was also deemed a necessary evil. Hearing it again not only consolidated the narrative in her head, it allowed her to catch things she might have missed, including subtle sighs, surprising bursts of laughter, all the little things that actually spoke volumes and made the story richer. But Roxy didn't have time for subtleties with this one, and so Oliver had arranged for a contractor to do the transcription and free her up to keep writing.

"How's the first draft coming along? Got any idea where you'll start?"

She stared at him. Hard. "The only place it can start. That shocking morning when the poor child woke up and found her entire family had vanished."

"Oh, yeah, right." He chuckled, his stubbled chin wobbling along with him. "That's why you write the books and I write the contracts. Want a coffee?" He didn't wait for a reply as he yelled out, "Shazza! You there, love?"

"I'm not your lover, Oliver H. Not that desperate yet!" came a croaky voice from deep within the office.

A moment later, Sharon appeared, offering Roxy a sly wink. She was Oliver's long-suffering assistant, a scrawny woman with spiky red hair and a smoker's pucker.

"Coffees all round?"

Roxy nodded and said, "Lookin' good, Sharon!"

She turned back. "Been doing boxercise, if you must know."

"Goodness, that sounds energetic."

"Well, one of us has got to make an effort."

She nudged her pencilled eyebrows at Oliver's flabby stomach that was protruding through the buttons on his vintage bowling shirt, and he mocked outrage as she shuffled out. Then he reached for a sheaf of papers on his desk and flung them towards Roxy.

"Here's the full contract. I've read it over and everything's in order. This is your copy. There's just one caveat that was phoned through last night. Margaret Means wants a full check of the manuscript before publication—that's for the publishers to worry about—but she also asked that her real name not be used. Nor does she want Phoebe's current residential address mentioned. Not even the suburb.”

“My lips are sealed, but it's a little late for that, I'm afraid. I saw a story on it only this morning.”

“As long as they can't blame you for the spill, you won't void your contract. You know how this works, Rox. This book is going to be huge. The press are going to be all over it like… like…”

“…like you on the dance floor?” Roxy offered. “Like your hands on a first date?”

He smirked back. “Persephone tells me they're already fielding calls from the *Today Show*, *7.30 Report*, *60 Minutes*.”

“Impressive.”

“But not surprising, right? It's a great yarn. Or at least I hope it will be. You haven't written for a while.”

She scowled at him as Shazza returned with their coffees, plonked them on the desk and left again. As she brought her cup to her lips and tested the heat, Roxy had to agree it had all the hallmarks of a gripping memoir. This was the first time Forgotten Phoebe had spoken since that *fateful day*. She just hoped she was up to the task. Staring gloomily into her cup, she felt an immense pressure to get it right.

“I was kidding, Rox. You'll do a great job. And don't worry too much about the press. I'm told Phoebe doesn't intend to do any interviews, which is a bit bloody odd considering the woman is in public relations. You'd think she'd be working it like… like…”

She groaned. “Don't start that again.”

He snickered. “Of course Persephone didn't sound too happy about her PR blackout. I mean, who's going to knock back *60 Minutes*? Sales would go through the roof.”

“Sales will go through the roof anyway. And Phoebe

did tell me she's not doing it for sales. She's doing it to set the record straight. Or something."

"You don't believe her?"

Roxy took another gulp of her coffee while she considered this. "It's not that I don't believe her. I think there's an ulterior motive. I just haven't worked out what it is."

"*Yet*," Oliver added, knowing his client well, and she smiled mischievously.

Then she noticed the time on the clock behind him and dropped the cup back with a start. "I better get my skates on."

She scooped up the contract, thrust it into her bag, and got to her feet.

"Another full day with Phoebe?" Oliver asked, and she was about to contradict him when something stopped her.

"Yeah, that's right."

It wasn't a lie exactly. She had blocked off most of the day for the interview, but there was a small gap in the middle—a thirty-minute lunch break Phoebe had scheduled in for her own purposes—and so Roxy had organised a catch-up with a certain ex-boyfriend who always got her heart pumping and her friends' tongues wagging.

She wasn't about to give Oliver the satisfaction, so she blew him a kiss from the door and left him none the wiser.

~~~

Gilda knocked gently on Evonne Cressida's open office door, and the chief pathologist looked up from her desktop computer and smiled.
~~~

"Got a moment?" Gilda asked.

Vonnie tapped the keyboard, then waved Gilda into a seat. "You're here about the Death by Hyperthermia."

That was how Vonnie tended to describe her cases—by cause of death, not name or status—and Gilda didn't blame her. Slicing into cadavers was gruesome enough without placing them in too human a context. Better to call a body Death by Manual Strangulation or Fatal Stab Wound to the Torso than Timmy Jones, son of pushy parents or Nerida Keen, wrong place, wrong time.

Or in this case: Paisley Smith, desperately unhappy wife.

Gilda said, "Her next of kin, Presley Smith, will be here soon to collect the body, but I wanted to have a word with you first."

"He's not sending the funeral director?" She looked alarmed at this.

"I did try to persuade him, but he wants to do it himself."

Most grieving families left the collection process to the person performing the final rites. They had the appropriate transportation and an objective attitude, but not Mr Smith. Gilda had a feeling there would be nothing objective about the distressed husband today, and she wanted to be prepared.

"I know he's going to have a lot of questions, and to be frank, I have a few of my own."

Vonnie leaned back in her seat, crossed her hands over her lap and said, "Shoot."

"Have you ever come across this kind of death before? An adult dying of heat exposure in an unlocked vehicle?"

"An *adult* in a vehicle? No. I have come across fatal

heat exposure in young children many times, but they don't have the ability or wherewithal to get themselves out of a hot car. An adult usually does. I did hear of a middle-aged man in Japan who expired in his car one winter though."

"*Winter?*"

She smiled grimly. "It seems he had the car heater on full blast and was parked for a period of time. But he also suffered from alcoholism, which exacerbated things. I found nothing similar with your case. No signs of liver damage or the like. Of course I do see many cases of adults dying in their *homes* during heat waves. They're mostly elderly people living in poky apartments without proper ventilation or air-conditioning. Those victims are usually isolated, disabled or incapacitated, otherwise we'd expect them to seek out a cooler environment."

"So they just sit in their hot house and waste away?"

"Not everybody has a good support network, Detective. And many of the elderly and disabled don't want to be a bother, so they suffer in silence. What's sad is, the effects can be reversed quite quickly if they do seek to reduce their body temperature—loosening clothing, taking a cold shower, moving to a cooler environment, rehydrating. It's usually when they can't find relief that they die, which is why it tends to happen to the elderly or the mentally ill."

"But this is an otherwise healthy, middle-aged woman with a job, a husband and an adult son. She was right outside an air-conditioned airport terminal. How about this: Can a person—a healthy adult—really just sit in a hot car and wait to die? You haven't ruled out suicide. Could she really have done it deliberately, do you think?"

Vonnie tipped her chair farther back and gave that some thought. "A person can do almost anything if they set their mind to it, I suppose. Sure, it would have been uncomfortable, especially if she was sweating profusely, although we don't always sweat when under extreme heart stress. Sometimes our body retains water. Mrs Smith did release her bowels, but we have no way of knowing if she was conscious for that. If she was lucky, she would have passed out before the real damage was done."

"And you found no signs that she'd attempted to get out?"

"You inspected the vehicle, Detective Maltin, not me. But she would have become delirious at some stage and might not have been in any position to help herself. That's not unusual either, of course. We often hear of plane crash victims who might have survived had they worked out how to unbuckle their seat belts. Humans can forget how to perform even the simplest of tasks when under extreme distress."

"And she had no medical conditions that might help to explain it?"

She tipped forward again and glanced at her computer screen, tapping it a few times to bring up her report. "We did find evidence of microhemorrages, which are like tiny strokes..." She glanced back at Gilda. "Don't get excited, that's fairly typical following heat stroke." She looked at the screen again. "From what I could tell, your victim was in good shape. Fighting fit as they say."

"And yet she didn't fight for her life," Gilda said, feeling none the wiser.

CHAPTER 15

It had been four days since a distraught Presley Smith had first identified his wife's body, and when he walked into the mortuary that day, he seemed as shell-shocked as before and just as delusional, insisting again that there was no way his wife would deliberately sit in a hot car and perish.

So much for Wiles's theory that the husband would be moving into the acceptance stage, thought Gilda as she sat with him in the foyer, waiting for Paisley's body to be brought out. Gilda had handed Presley a copy of Vonnie's preliminary postmortem and reminded him that he needn't have come. His funeral director could have taken care of it.

"I had to get out of that bloody house," he mumbled, flicking through the report. "Everywhere I look, all I see is Paisley. The life she built there for us. The home she tried to make happy. It's… it's hard."

"I understand—"

"Really? You just lost someone, did you?"

Gilda didn't answer. She'd had that question thrown in her face plenty of times before and knew there was no correct answer, no words for angry mourners.

He closed the file and slammed it on the small table

in front of them, catching the eye of a young man with long black hair who was working behind the desk today. He shot Gilda a curious look.

"This is a setup," Presley said. "There's something seriously fishy going on. Paisley wasn't leaving me, and she wasn't bloody suicidal—she's the strongest woman I know. She was fine. Nothing wrong with her!"

Gilda took a deep breath. "Had anything happened that might have changed that?"

"No! Nothing."

"So until this incident she was perfectly happy?"

"Easy there. I never said that. Happy wasn't a word you'd use for Paisley. She just, got on with it, you know? It wasn't her nature to be happy, but she was fine. Fine!" He looked at her, then away, then back again. "I mean, life hadn't dished us out a bowl of roses or anything."

"What had life dished out?"

"Not a lot. We're both still working full time, not a lot of cash in the bank, but we do all right. Of course it would help if our son got a bloody job, but don't get me started on that subject." He grimaced. "Hell, can't blame him, not really. There's not a lot of work around our parts…" He ran a hand across his patchy head. "Look, we were okay, Detective. Paisley was okay. She was not suicidal. It's bloody nonsense. She wouldn't do it, and she certainly wouldn't do it to me. She would never just leave me!"

She left your son too, Gilda thought, but his selfishness didn't surprise her either. It was hard to think beyond yourself when you were in so much pain. She wondered about the son now. Why wasn't he here helping his dad? Why weren't they supporting each other through it?

Gilda gave Presley a moment and then said, "It is a *preliminary* report, Mr Smith, and if you read it, you will see that cause of death is still open-ended."

"It's rubbish is what it is."

She dipped her head to one side. "I know this is hard, but you are forgetting the text message your wife sent you. It does suggest a certain frame of mind."

"Frame of mind, my arse! The text's a phony too. It's all a setup. She was murdered. That's all there is to it!"

Gilda straightened her head and stared at him, gobsmacked. The assistant was also staring, intrigued now while Presley just glared at the report like he wanted to rip it to shreds.

"Murdered?" she repeated.

Was he being fair dinkum? Did he really believe that his wife had met with foul play?

Gilda knew she should be dousing his concerns, handing over the body and closing the case down, but her curiosity was growing.

"Why are you saying all this, Mr Smith? Who would want to kill your wife?"

He said nothing, his eyes still on the report.

"Was your wife ever threatened in any way? Have you any proof of these allegations?"

Still, his eyes would not meet Gilda's, and she could feel her instincts tingle. He was hiding something; that much was obvious. There was more to this story than he was letting on, a secret he wasn't prepared to share. She pulled out her notebook and flicked through it.

"Your wife worked at a post office in Wollongong, is that correct?"

Finally he looked up. He nodded and cleared his throat. "The one right in the CBD. Forty-five-minute commute but she made the slog."

"Full-time, you said?"

"Monday to Friday. It was decent work. Been there forever, managing deliveries and despatch, working the front desk when they needed. Shitty work sometimes but we got bills like everyone else."

Gilda turned to a blank page in her notebook. "Can you remind me again when you last saw your wife?"

He was frowning now as he watched her produce a pen. "That morning. Like I said, she was perfectly fine. Normal. We had some breaky. I went to work. I thought she was heading to work too."

"So you had no idea she was driving to Sydney until her body was found?"

He shook his head.

"Can you think of any reason she would be at the airport?"

He shook his head again.

"Did she receive any phone calls? Any messages or give you any indication…"

"No! I'm telling you, she was going to work, that's all that she was doing. It was a normal day. Just another bloody day. Nothing wrong with her."

"And yet she's dead, Mr Smith. So something was wrong. Very wrong."

"That's what I'm telling you! It stinks!"

Gilda chewed on her pen for a moment and had a feeling she was going to regret her next words. "If you like I can make some enquiries."

"What?"

"I could look into it a bit further. Chat to some of her colleagues, maybe have a word to your son?"

Now the man looked confused, even a little wary.

"Why would you do that?"

"Well, I thought…"

"What would be the point?"

She blinked and swapped a frown with the guy on reception. "Mr Smith, you just said your wife was murdered, that the text was a fake, that she was perfectly fine and there was no reason for her to be at Sydney airport. Do you want me to investigate further or not?"

Presley's features turned stony, and she thought for a moment that he was about to yell again when he said, almost coldly, "Will it bring Paisley back?"

"Well, no, but—"

"Then what difference does it make?"

"It's about the truth, Mr Smith. Don't you want me to find the truth?"

He laughed then, like he'd never heard anything so preposterous, his face contorting to reveal a set of messy, overlapping teeth in his lower gum. Then he stopped just as suddenly and stared at her with a look of pity and disgust.

"You will never find the truth, young lady. Don't waste your time trying." He stood up and looked around impatiently. "What's taking so bloody long? I need to get my wife away from this putrid place."

Gilda wasn't sure if he meant the mortuary or Sydney itself, but she knew one thing for sure. Despite his bitterness and bluster, Presley Smith had just thrown down the gauntlet, and she was up for the challenge.

Detective Chief Inspector Brent Wiles had other ideas.

No sooner was Gilda back in the office, her boss

was warning her off. "I told you before, Gilda, the man's just hurting. Paisley Smith wasn't murdered, he just wishes she was, then he's off the hook and doesn't have to feel like he let her down."

"He seemed pretty convincing to me. Says his wife was perfectly fine. Says she had no cause to be in Sydney."

"And yet she sent him a text saying she was leaving him." He let out a heavy breath, an impatient one. "We have Vonnie's report to back us up; there are no suspicious circumstances, no signs of any kind of interference or violence. No bruising, no sexual assault. There's nothing to investigate, Gilda."

"But—"

He held a palm up to quieten her, and she frowned. *She wasn't a child. She didn't like being silenced.*

"The official report will be released soon. Until then, I have something else I need you to do." Wiles turned to a folder on his desk and handed it across. "Mattheson's been working on this one for months. Giles Haymarket. Low-grade thug. That is, until he shot his business partner three months ago. He's currently in custody, awaiting trial. It's pretty open and shut, but I want you to check it over, make sure Mattie's crossed all his *T*s, that kind of thing."

This felt even more patronising, and Gilda's frown intensified as she opened the file and began scanning through it. She stopped at one page. "They found the shotgun in Haymarket's underwear drawer?" She looked up at Wiles. "The smoking gun in his jocks, seriously?"

He smiled. "Just do me a favour—and Mattie—and give it the once-over. Won't take you long."

Plastering a smile to her own face, she said, "Fine"

and left his office, but it didn't feel fine, and she wasn't just talking about the Smith case now.

Gilda had the distinct impression Wiles wasn't just being patronising, he was trying to distract her. Was he worried she was bored, or was there something else behind it?

CHAPTER 16

As he watched Roxy walk into the York Street café in her skinny jeans and oversized man's dress shirt, her eyes wide, her lips squished to one side as she glanced about, worriedly, Max knew he had made the right call.

Despite the frown, she had never looked more beautiful. She was thinner than normal, but that wasn't it; he couldn't care less what size she was. Roxy's trademark black bob had now grown out, so too her chunky fringe, but there was something else, something different that he couldn't quite put his finger on.

Was she glowing? Was that it?

"There you are!" Roxy announced when he finally caught her eye through the crowded restaurant.

"Shall we get a takeaway and take a hike?" Max said, indicating the boisterous lunch crowd.

"Brilliant plan. But I've only got half an hour and only because Phoebe has a million texts to answer. Then I'll have to get back. But thanks for coming into the city to meet me."

"No worries," he said, masking his disappointment.

As they waited in the coffee queue and then for the barista to work his magic, the two friends shared plenty of small talk, but it wasn't until they were settled side by side on a wooden park bench that Max finally said what he'd come to say.

"I miss you, Parker."

Her eyes flittered from him to a group of elderly people doing what looked like Tai Chi, their legs cemented to the grass, their arms flowing freely. She was grateful she wasn't seated across from Max at a table, was grateful he didn't see the small smile she now tried to swallow back.

"I missed you too," she managed, but he turned to face her now.

"No, I mean I still miss you."

Roxy's smile slipped and she felt her stomach flutter, then drop. *Oh no, not again.*

As if reading her mind, he quickly said, "Look, we could do what we always do and dance around each other for months, but I'm older and uglier now and I just don't have the time or energy. And you clearly don't."

She swept her eyes to him. "Are you saying I'm older and uglier now?"

He laughed. "I'm saying we haven't much time. You're heading back in a few days, right?"

"Yes I am. Back to my boyfriend. Sam."

He nodded. He got it. Mentioning Sam was her way of applying the hand brake.

"What's he like? This *Sam*?"

Roxy's expression lightened. "You'd like him; he's a good bloke. Salt of the earth. Huge heart. Really beautiful—"

"Okay," he said. "I get it. He's a gem."

She smiled at his deadpan tone. "You really would like him, if you met him. Maybe you should come visit us up north one day. Then you'd understand."

I'll never understand, he wanted to tell her. Instead, he said, "Maybe" as a lump formed in his throat. "How's that coffee coming along?"

She stared at the untouched cup in her hand and took a small sip. "It's good. Better than the almond milk nonsense they serve at my local café."

Roxy launched into a funny anecdote about the Goddess Café just down from Sam's property, and Max relayed stories of his own from his time in Berlin, and very soon they were laughing like they'd always done, and Max was forgetting why he had come and what he needed to say. But, after twenty minutes, as he watched her check her phone clock and drain her cup, he knew it was now or never. He also knew he was being selfish and that no matter how great this Sam fellow was, the guy would never forgive him for what he was about to say.

Max placed his cup on the bench, then turned to face her again.

"Parker, I'm really sorry, but I need to say something and you need to let me."

She held her breath and silently begged him to stop.

"I want us to try again."

She closed her eyes. "Oh, Max."

"Look, I know Sam's more than a good bloke. I know he's fantastic."

"*Fantastic?*" Her eyes were wide open now. "I'm not sure I'd go that far. Who told you he was fantastic?"

He smiled. "Well, that's not quite the word everyone uses. They all hate him, which makes me realise he must be fantastic, because I can smell their fear. They're terrified they've lost you." He grabbed her hand like he was grabbing a buoy. "I'm terrified too." He waited until she glanced back at him and added, "I want another chance."

Roxy snatched her hand back, grabbed her handbag, and jumped up. She took a step away then turned, frowning. "Max, honestly, again?"

He offered her his sweet, lopsided smile.

"I'm happy now," she said. "I'm settled."

"Settled? Is that what you want in life? To be settled?"

"Yes! Unapologetically so! You and me, we were never settled, always falling in and out of love—"

"Never out!" He held up a hand. "Never."

She sighed and shook her head.

"It's the only reason I came back, Roxy. I've tried a different city. I've tried different..." He didn't finish that. "None of it works. *I* don't work without you. I want a life with you. I'll move to Byron Bay if that's what you want."

"It's not about Byron."

"Then what's it about? Do you love this guy, like you love me?"

She shook her head. "I can't do this." She turned around again. "I've got a book to write."

And she did what she always did when Max declared his love. She ran for cover.

CHAPTER 17

"He declared his love?"

This was Gilda over the mobile phone as Roxy strode back to Phoebe's apartment block for the second half of the day.

She groaned. "He always declares his love, Gilda. Let's not act like it's a revelation."

Now Gilda was groaning. "And let's not act like it's nothing special either, Missy! I've been waiting a year for Wiles to even say he *likes* me! I don't think you get it. What Max feels for you is real and always has been, and it's clearly not going away."

Now Roxy was sighing. "I know. I know. I don't want to hurt him…"

"Then don't!"

"So what do I do? And don't tell me to break up with Sam just because you want me home. What should I do?"

"If you even have to ask the question, then you are more screwed up than I thought."

She stopped walking. "That's true. I am! I'm totally screwed. I need your help!"

"You can start by giving Max a break."

"Sorry?"

"Stop meeting him for cosy coffee dates and give the poor guy a chance to get over you."

"Hey! Now you're victim blaming."

"*Victim* blaming?"

"You're acting like it's all my fault. Max and I were friends first. I'm allowed to meet a mate for a coffee, aren't I?"

"Not when that mate's madly in love with you and you can't return the favour, no. I think that's mean. It's not fair to Max, and it's certainly not fair to Sam."

Roxy groaned, rolled her eyes, and kept walking. "You're right. Of course you're right. I'm pathetic."

"No, honey, you're just very confused. Oh, hang on a minute…" There was a muffled sound at Gilda's end, then she said, "Duty calls."

"Wait! I rang to get some help, and not about Max. Do you know how I can contact the two detectives who first investigated Phoebe's case?"

"Why don't you ask SuperMeans?"

"I have but she hasn't got back to me."

"Ask her again."

"That's like me saying, 'Why don't you ask Wiles why he hasn't said he loves you yet?' It's difficult." She paused. "Why hasn't Wiles said it yet, by the way?"

"No, no, I have no time for this conversation. All right, just quickly, what are their names?"

As Roxy recited the two names over the phone, Gilda scribbled away, not recognising either of them. "Give me a few hours. Shall we catch up at Pico's tonight? Might have something for you then."

Roxy agreed. "But gee my mother's going to kill me. I've barely spent an evening with them since I arrived."

Lorraine was more maudlin than murderous when

Roxy broke the news to her soon after arriving home that evening that she was heading back out, and Roxy decided she preferred murderous as she tried to cheer her depressed mother up.

"I'm sorry, but you do get to have breakfast with me every day."

"A bowl of muesli and some orange juice. Is that all I'm entitled to? Is that all your father deserves?"

"Charlie's not my father, Mum, you know that, and I'm sure he's fine with it. Sorry but this is work related. Gilda's helping me with my latest book, she has some info for me."

"Can't she give it to you over the phone like a normal person?"

"Not as much fun though, is it?" She wrinkled her nose cheekily. "I don't get out much up north. We're miles from restaurants and bars, so it's exciting for me to dress up and go out. But look, I've got a spare hour. Why don't we put on our sneakers and take Lunar for another walk. He really needs it."

And so do we, she thought.

Lorraine looked at her sulkily.

"I'll make sure I'm home for dessert, how about that? I'll even grab something on the way back. Be home by nine, I promise."

That seemed to do the trick, and Lorraine said, "Fine."

As she went to swap her stiff linen frock for a tracksuit and joggers, Roxy stepped outside to where Lunar had been pacing, excited by her return and what that might mean for him.

"Yes, you lucky dog," she said, laughing. "Two walkies in one day!"

Lunar's eyes lit up at the *W* word, and he raced

towards an outside hook where his leash was hanging, pulling it off with his mouth. Roxy laughed again as she clipped it to his collar, then reached for her own walking shoes, which were just outside the door where she'd dumped them that morning. As she tugged them on, she wondered about Phoebe's childhood pet and how much she must have missed her pooch when her family vanished. If they did leave of their own free will, why couldn't they have left her the dog for company?

Would that have been too much to ask?

~~~

Ninety minutes later, Roxy was breathing more easily at Pico's. It was strange, she thought as she surveyed the room, waiting for Gilda to arrive, how she could feel more comfortable in a dark, half-empty wine bar than she did at her mother's bright, overly furnished bungalow. How she preferred the company of strangers to her own flesh and blood. Of course her mother would see it as a fault, but the truth was the two women had never really got on. They tolerated each other at best. There was love there, that was genetic, but they were so very different and could never quite accept the differences in each other. Roxy liked to think it would all smooth over one day, but she was beginning to realise that it might not. Just as she was beginning to realise that Max would always love her and she had to live with that.

But did she love him back? In the way he needed her to? And was Gilda right? Was she being utterly selfish? Was it time to finally cut him loose? She thought about Sam then and knew what she needed to do. The one thing he had been asking her for.
~~~

The one thing that would send a very strong message to Max…

"Cheer up, darlin', can't be that bad," came a low drawl breaking through her thoughts, and Roxy looked around to find a heavily muscled man staring at her with a snaky grin. "Want me to buy you a drink and fix that frown?"

"No, thank you," she said, trying to sound polite. "I'm waiting for a friend."

"Doesn't mean I can't get you a drink."

"I'm fine. Thanks."

"Lesbian are you?"

"Sorry, what?"

"I'm just offering to buy you a drink, lady. It won't kill you." His tone was now dark.

"Yeah, but I might kill *you*," came a woman's voice, and Roxy was relieved to see Gilda standing behind the man, hands on her hips.

He turned and stared at her, looking foolishly unruffled. "Piss off, lady, I'm chatting here."

Gilda smiled. She was unruffled too. She produced her badge and flashed it in his face. "Beat it or I'll haul you in for harassment."

He glanced at the badge, then at Roxy, then sneered at them both and slumped to the back of the room.

The barman appeared and said, "Sorry, ladies, that guy's a serial nuisance. I was just coming to rescue you."

"We don't need rescuing, thanks, Johnno," Gilda informed him, offering a warm smile to lighten the tone. "But we do need a coupla drinks, am I right?"

Roxy nodded. "That'd be a start."

As the bartender fetched some wine, the two women settled onto stools at the farthest end of the bar where there was less chance of being interrupted by obnoxious drunks, and Gilda produced a slip of paper.

"The investigating officers from the Fisher case," she said. "Both no longer in the force."

"That's odd."

"Not really. Policing has a high attrition rate. One guy's left the country, living in New Zealand now apparently, that's Gary Pollard, but I can't find a contact number for him, sorry. The other one—Michael DeSanto—is working security at a bank in Martin Place."

"Okay, that's not too far from Phoebe's apartment. I might stop by on my way there tomorrow."

"Just tread carefully, okay? He's damaged goods."

"How do you mean?"

Gilda sipped the icy rosé Johnno had just handed over, then reached for a bar menu. "Micky D, as they called him, was very young when he first joined the force and not that much older when he was assigned to the Missing Persons Unit. Didn't last long after that. First went out on stress leave, then came back for all of eighteen months before dropping out entirely."

"Do you think Phoebe's case broke him?"

"Not sure exactly. I spoke to Wiles who spoke to someone further along the chain. He thinks it was more of a personality thing. Just wasn't suited to the work. He was certainly the wrong person to put on the Fisher case. Still had his training wheels on, and the guy supervising, this Gary Pollard chap, he was only a few years ahead of him. Wiles hasn't got a good word to say about the Missing Persons Unit back then. It's since been disbanded and replaced with a stand-alone investigative unit."

Her eyes flickered down the plastic menu and back

up. "It's a pity that wasn't in place when Phoebe's family went AWOL. Shall we get some calamari? Potato wedges too?"

Roxy nodded blankly, stunned by her earlier comment. "Are you saying Phoebe might very well have found her family if it wasn't for some incompetent detectives?"

"Who knows? People don't just vanish." She went to call Johnno over, then stopped and said, "Actually, they do—about 2,600 each year, would you believe?—but the vast majority turn up pretty fast and the rest leave some kind of trail. This is a family of four, three of them disappear overnight—"

"And their dog, Bouncer."

"Right. So how did they not find some bread crumbs? The parents must have hired a delivery van of some sort to move so much stuff so quickly. They must have stayed in a hotel somewhere with all their gear or been spotted on a highway. Someone must have said something to someone! It's very strange."

Gilda paused to place the order, then turned back to Roxy with a sly smile. "But of course you're not here to solve the mystery, you're just here to write about it, right?"

Roxy pressed her lips to her wineglass so she didn't have to fib to her best friend.

When she returned home later that night with a box of baked cheesecake as a peace offering, Roxy couldn't help thinking about Phoebe's case and how sad it was that a young girl's fate was put into the hands of two novices. What a different book she might be writing had someone like Gilda or Wiles been on the job.

Or SuperMeans for that matter.

She sighed wistfully and tried to put it out of her mind as she sliced the cake in the kitchen and let Charlie prepare beverages.

"You know, Roxanne, your mother really does miss you," he was saying as he dangled a bag of peppermint tea into one cup and two chamomiles into the others.

"I know. I'll be home for dinner tomorrow night. I promise."

He beamed. "Good. I'm cooking my famous lamb roast."

She stepped across the kitchen and gave the man a hug. "Thanks, Charlie. I know I'm a pain, but I do love you both, you know that, right?"

He pulled free to stare her in the eyes. "I do, but your mother needs more actual bodily proof."

CHAPTER 18

It was the lack of any kind of evidence at the Fisher's Baker Street residence that had ex-Detective Constable Michael DeSanto stumped, and he told this to Roxy as they sat sipping burnt coffee and discussing the Fisher family mystery early the next day.

He could blame Roxy for the coffee. She'd snagged it from a greasy bakery down from the bank where he worked and brought it as a bribe, but he seemed happy enough to chat with her as he waited out the front for the bank manager to unlock the door. Now overweight and missing most of his hair, he seemed like a friendly fellow to Roxy and older than she expected.

"I'm forty-three," he said when she asked. "So that made me, what? Twenty-three at the time? Not long out of the Academy. Very little experience and certainly none involving missing persons. I was assisting the Organised Crime Unit when they moved me across."

"So why were you assigned the case? Why not Margaret Means?"

"*Chief Superintendent Means?*" He looked at her like she was stupid. "She didn't work Missing Persons. Way too high up the chain of command for that. She was overseeing the OCU back then anyway, that and the Criminal Groups Squad; had her hands full with all the gangland murders that were happening around that time." His jaw tightened as he stared into his cup. "You probably don't remember, but there was a lot of blood on the streets back then, lots of drive-by shootings, drug dealers protecting their turf. Everyone was working overtime. Means more than anyone. She would've had the politicians on her back, not to mention the press. When this one landed, the Fisher case, they thought..." He hesitated. "Well, I don't think they gave it much thought at all. Everyone figured it'd be sorted in a day or two and I'd be returned to Organised Crime."

"Why would they think that?"

"We all figured it was *Home Alone* come to life. You've seen the movie, right? We figured the folks had packed the car, taken off and were halfway across the country before they realised they'd left a kid behind."

"But then day turned to night...?"

"And night turned to day, and days turned to weeks, and by then the scene had been compromised. If there had been a crime, we had no proof."

"Compromised?" she said, or *botched up* as Margie had claimed?

"Yeah. Some neighbour dropped by on the second day and scrubbed the place out before I got a chance to stop 'em."

She nodded. She had already heard. "Could it have been deliberate?"

He looked at her sharply. "Why would you say that?"

"I'm just wondering, that's all. It just feels a bit, like..."

"Sabotage?" he offered. "I did wonder that myself

but… well, I don't think so. It was just some old lady who did a bit of cleaning for the neighbourhood apparently. I think she was just trying to help. Didn't know any better."

"Was it Delvine Dorey?"

"Can't really remember. Sounds about right. Pollard questioned her, not me."

"And this lady, she just ducked under the police tape and went on in with her mop and bucket?"

"Well, no, I mean, there was no police tape." Micky blushed crimson then and Roxy was surprised by his reaction, even after all this time. He quickly added, "Remember, at that stage we were still expecting the parents to show up. We didn't think we had a crime on our hands, other than child neglect. Within three days we suspected abandonment, or worse."

Roxy blew a puff of air from her lips. "Do you have any theories why Phoebe's parents would abandon her?"

He shook his head but not convincingly. "We spoke to her teachers, the neighbours, friends' parents, trying to ascertain whether she was a nightmare child, you know? Someone you *would* leave behind. I've got one of them at home myself—a fifteen-year-old with a bad attitude." He smiled apologetically. "But according to all reports, Phoebe wasn't that bad. 'Little bit of mischief' I heard, but not deserving of that."

"What kind of mischief?"

He shrugged. "A few of the neighbours said something about raised voices coming from the house a few times. A few scraps and squabbles with the younger brother I believe. He was, like, five or six at the time. But that's just siblings, right?"

She nodded, not really knowing and wondering

about that. Did all brothers and sisters fight?

"Anyway," he was saying, "I don't care how naughty your kid is, you don't just dump and run. Didn't make sense at the time. Still doesn't." He sighed wistfully. "Still haunts me, to be honest."

"I can see that. Is that why you left the force?"

He looked at her sharply again. "Who told you that?"

"Nobody. I just wondered. You left soon after, so…"

"Had nothing to do with Phoebe Fisher. And I'd rather not go into it, not for your book."

"Okay, that's fine. So, tell me if you would, what do you think happened?"

He looked wary again. "Are you investigating?"

"Not at all. I'm just filling in the blanks for Phoebe. It will form the first part of the book, but that's it."

He thought about that, then said, "Well, since you're asking, I will tell you what I think. I think the parents were murdered."

"Really?" She wasn't expecting that.

"Yep. You know those gangland murders I told you about?"

"You think it's related?"

"Wouldn't surprise me. Those bastards were out of control back then, a real menace." His voice dropped. "This is off the record, right?" She nodded, reluctantly. "They're the reason I left the force. I came up against them just a few times, and it was a few times too many. The threats they made, the intel they had on me and my missus. She was pregnant with our first back then, scared the crap out of me." He shook his head. "Force wasn't paying me enough for that. So I left. Simple as that. But that's off the record, right?

Makes me sound like a wimp."

"It makes you sound like a protective husband actually."

"Ex-husband now," he said, a dark shadow crossing his face. "For all the good it did me."

"In any case, I won't mention it in the book. No need; it's Phoebe's story, not yours. But I will mention your theory to her and see if she wants to discuss it. Are you okay with that?"

He looked unfazed.

"You really think gangland criminals killed the parents? Did you find any evidence of that?"

"Like I said, we had very little to go on, but the parents were pretty dodgy by all accounts. I'm sure Phoebe hasn't told you that. Maybe she doesn't even know. Do any of us see our parents clearly at that age? If you ask my daughter, I'm a complete psychopath." He grinned. "From all reports, there were problems in the Fisher house, mother was a lush, father liked to gamble, had very little money in their bank accounts. Makes you wonder, that's all. Did he have loan sharks on his back?"

"And they never touched their bank accounts afterwards?"

"Wasn't much to touch."

"And what about the son and the dog? You think loan sharks killed them too?"

"Wouldn't put it past them."

"So why spare Phoebe?"

"Maybe they wanted someone alive to tell the tale, but she was so traumatised she doesn't remember it. Or maybe they only intended to hurt Mr Fisher but then had to take out the other witnesses, and Phoebe was fast asleep and survived."

"But why? How did she not hear it all? And what about all their stuff? Everything they owned was gone, all their clothes and personal effects. The dog."

"Yeah, that was the strange bit, the reason we never took my theory any further, but they could've done that to deflect the truth I guess. Make it look like abandonment. Or…"

He was warming to the topic, and she could see he'd given it considerable thought over the past two decades.

"Maybe the family were packing up, ready to flee, but someone found them first. Maybe they did a runner with what they'd packed—hadn't got to Phoebe yet. Maybe they were tracked down somewhere, murdered, and their bodies disposed of. Probably all lying with their gear under a cement overpass somewhere."

Roxy shuddered. "That's quite a theory."

"The truth is I haven't got a clue, but that theory feels nicer to me than imagining they simply upped sticks and left their little girl all alone, without a second glance."

And there it was again, the haunted look in Micky's eyes. This might not have been the case that drove him from his career, but it certainly stayed with him long after.

"So, what about your partner Gary?" Roxy asked. "What did he think?"

The dark look crossed Micky's face again. "Pollard had some crazy theories of his own."

"Such as?"

He shook his head. "You'd have to ask him."

"I wish I could. You don't happen to have a contact number? An address where I can find him?"

The head continued to shake. "He took off a long time ago, for New Zealand I heard. I don't think he wants to be found."

Before Roxy could enquire further, he was lobbing his cup into a nearby bin and stretching. "I better get on. I can hear them opening up in there."

She dropped her cup in behind his and said, "I appreciate you making time for me. Can I just double-check your name and spelling please?"

Roxy did that and then thanked Micky again, watching as he made his way down the side lane into the back of the bank where a worker was peering out, wondering where he was, offering him a welcoming smile. This job must have been a relief back then for the worried husband and father.

Roxy jotted some thoughts into her notepad, then turned to go, thinking what a pity it was that Michael DeSanto hadn't remained in the police force. He seemed like a genuine human being, someone who really cared, and someone who thought outside the box. She wasn't sure she agreed with his gangster theory, but she was pretty certain he would have matured into a very fine detective.

CHAPTER 19

Phoebe thought Micky D was the world's worst detective and dismissed his theory outright when Roxy relayed it to her an hour later at her apartment.

"He's covering his backside," she said, left eyebrow crinkling. "Even as a kid I could see the guy was in over his head. He kept asking me all sorts of questions about the criminal underworld; it just confused me and freaked me out, to be honest. Thanks to him, I started having nightmares that the Mafia would come for me in the dead of night. I still don't understand why you even spoke to him. Surely you could have checked the facts of the investigation with Margie? She'd know his name and rank." Then she shook her glossy locks. "Sorry, there I go again, telling you how to do your job."

She pulled her lips into a broad smile, like she was about to enter a PR event, and said, "What else do you need to know?"

"I just want to ask about your brother, Daniel, and then we'll move on."

Phoebe's smile tightened. "Danny? Really?"

"He was just five when it happened, yes?"

She nodded, her face suddenly drawn, her eyes tearing up, and Roxy reached a hand out to her, but she shook her off.

"Sorry, it's just… We were so close. I… I missed him so much at the start. It took me years to get over him, block him from my mind. We *adored* each other, really we did. He was like my little shadow. Followed me everywhere."

Roxy listened as Phoebe proceeded to share fond memories of her baby brother, but she couldn't quite compute that with what Micky had told her earlier—how the neighbours complained of screaming, how the siblings used to squabble.

She wondered if time had healed old wounds, as it often did, or if Phoebe was simply lying. In any case, it was her book, her story, so this was the version Roxy would write.

They moved on to Phoebe's high school years and then to university, and it was clear from her renewed enthusiasm that she really did want to leave the past behind. She brightened even further when the subject shifted to her PR business, and she wanted the world to know she was now doing okay.

"I'm better than okay," she told Roxy. "I'm great. I've got a successful business, a supportive husband."

Ah yes, thought Roxy, studying the notes she'd made about James Van Beurden, the founder of Van Beurden Enterprises, an ASX Top 200 company that was clearly very successful even though Roxy couldn't work out exactly what they did. Something to do with equities and investments?

"Let's move onto your husband then," Roxy said. "Tell me about him. How you met. First impressions. How he proposed. All that lovely stuff."

Phoebe's face lit up again at the mention of James, and she waxed lyrical for the next two hours, telling

Roxy every minute detail of their meeting and subsequent marriage.

"Even Margie likes him, and she doesn't like anyone!"

"So can I meet him? Have a chat?" Again, she held a hand up. "Just to check a few facts, get some colourful anecdotes."

"Of course," Phoebe replied as the small crinkle returned above her eye. "We're both sorry you haven't had a chance to meet before now. James has been away… on business. He runs his own finance company, and it's busy, busy, busy. But he's back now, so let me see if I can schedule something in." Her eyes lit up, and she offered Roxy one of her radiant smiles. "Shall I show you the wedding photos?"

As Phoebe got busy tapping away at her tablet, locating the best screen shots, Roxy checked her own phone and noticed two more missed calls from Sam. She quickly tapped him a message—*At work, will try you tonight*—then pressed Send, regretting it instantly.

Why didn't she think to add a few kisses or a love heart?

"Voilà!" Phoebe said, handing her iPad to Roxy, who took it and began to swipe.

The images were stunning. The wedding had taken place on a secluded Balinese beach, the sun impossibly bright, Phoebe's slinky ivory wedding dress vivid against the cerulean sky and the glistening aqua sea behind her.

As Roxy swept through them, she stopped at one shot that showed James with two kids in his arms, both girls who looked about eight or nine, a little too old to be held so high.

"Who are the kids?" she asked.

Phoebe glanced down. "Oh, they're James's nieces.

Charlotte and Samantha. He adores them! Lives for them in fact, or at least he did until I came along!"

She smiled and then her smile slipped a little and the crinkle reappeared above her eye.

"Will you have children, do you think?"

"Absolutely not." The answer was automatic. "James wants some, but I'd rather not. And he respects my wishes."

"Is that because of your past?"

Roxy instantly regretted the question. *Of course* it was because of her past, yet Phoebe was shaking her head emphatically.

"Not at all. Not one little bit! I'm just one of those women who don't want kids. I mean, I'm not an idiot, maybe if my childhood had been happier—and I'm not saying it wasn't since Margie took me in—but, well, who knows how I'd be feeling. But right now life is good. I have a great business, a lovely husband. I really can't see how a child would improve things."

Roxy's thoughts flickered to Sam, and she tried to shake him away.

"I don't want people thinking I'm bitter or feeling sorry for me, Roxy. Not anymore. I'm not having children because I *choose* not to have children and I don't need them to complete my life. I'm in charge now, okay? No one else. It's very important that the reader sees me as empowered, as happy, as having moved on. Do you understand?"

There was such vehemence in her tone, and Roxy chewed on her lower lip. Yet again this sounded more like a PR exercise than an autobiography, but then Phoebe was a public relations expert, and wasn't that half the reason people told their own stories anyway? Why she was hired in the first place? So the client was in control of the narrative?

As Roxy nodded and moved on again, she wondered if Phoebe had moved on herself or if her decision to marry an older man and forgo children was a sign that the past still haunted her more than she realised, was still impacting her present, whether she liked it or not.

And she wondered what Phoebe's child-doting husband felt about that.

~~~

Gilda ran a hand through her blond pixie cut and readjusted her stretchy cotton dress, which was clinging in all the right places, and then some. It was a tad sexier than her usual work garb, but it wouldn't hurt Wiles to remember she was more than a colleague, or at least she was last time she checked. As she knocked on his door and entered, she slipped her lips into a lovely, flirty smile but needn't have bothered.

He barely looked up.

Wiles was madly scribbling on a stack of papers in front of him, applying his signature at the bottom of each one. He glanced up at her, then back as he continued to scribble.

"How'd you go with the Haymarket case?" he said.

"Hello to you too!" she replied, but he just looked up now, waiting for her response. She did a mock salute and said, "Everything's in order, sir!"

He didn't laugh.

Gilda dropped her hand to her side. "It's all completely fine. Mattheson's done a good job." *He doesn't need babysitting* she might have added, but she was trying to play nice.

"Great. If that's cleared, maybe you could catch up
~~~

on your paperwork."

"Paperwork?"

"I still need to sign off on your last report, and Milo in accounts says he hasn't seen your expenses come through in a while."

"My expenses?"

He smiled, but only just. "I know maths isn't your strong suit, Gilda, and neither is sitting at a desk, but things are quiet at the moment, so it's a good time to tick those things off." He reached for the next page to sign.

"If things are so quiet…," she began as he continued to scribble. "Maybe I could poke around in the Smith case a bit more."

He looked up.

"It can't hurt," she added. "I still haven't interviewed the son—at least not in person."

"Flannery's already done that. There's no reason to harass the kid again."

Harass? Since when did he call police work *harassment?* "I also wouldn't mind checking in with Paisley Smith's colleagues. They were the last people to see her before she took off for the airport. She got some mysterious phone call—"

"Doreen's already onto that."

"But—"

"Gilda," he said, interrupting her again, his tone much firmer. "I'm telling you what I need you to do. Could you just do it, please? Get your bookwork in order, your expenses signed off, hell, wouldn't hurt to tidy your desk while you're at it. Use this downtime wisely. We all know it never lasts long."

"I just don't see how it will hurt to investigate—"

"Gilda, we already discussed this. There is nothing

to investigate."

"No, you discussed it, and I listened."

"And I'm your boss, right?"

"You're also my boyfriend."

He frowned. "What's that got to do with anything?"

Gilda felt like she'd been slapped. She also felt like a fool and wished more than anything that she wasn't standing before him in a sexy dress.

"Nothing. Sorry. My mistake." She stepped back towards the door. "I'll leave the Smith case alone then and get on with the all-important paperwork, shall I?"

Then she marched out of his office, stiff smile in place, several lies trailing behind her.

~~~

The Greek woman caught him sneaking another peek at her soft, spongy cleavage, and the man pulled his eyes away and up. With all that flesh on display, it was hard to focus on her craggy face, which was beaming back at him now, lips artificially plumped, foundation like wet cement. She wasn't beaming at the beginning, was openly hostile, determined he was wasting her time. But then he'd told her his sad little story and the tables had turned, as he knew they would.

Now the brassy magazine editor was clicking her fingers and demanding her young assistant fetch coffees, *pronto!*

"Or would you prefer something cold?" she asked, her voice raspy and just this side of desperate. He had her just where he wanted her.

"Black coffee'd be great," he said.

And so the pretty boy had marched off to do as he was told while the editor settled back in her seat like
~~~

she'd just won the lottery. But he was the one who was going to win big, and it was long overdue.

Twenty long years, in fact.

It had taken him a while to work out just how to go about it, without finding himself six feet under, and he hoped this plan would work. He didn't know a lot about Maria Constantinople, but he did know gossip magazines were always crying for a good story. But this was better than good, Maria told him, her claggy black eyes batting flirtatiously. This was "mind-blowing" and they could both make "a bloody motza."

"I just want what I'm owed," he'd told Maria, and she nodded like a lunatic, her breasts wobbling again.

"You'll get that and more, my sweet!"

"You understand this is dangerous, yeah? You can't just come right out with it. You need to get your ducks lined up."

She scoffed. "No need to tell me how to do my job, honey."

"I'm not telling you how to do your job, I'm telling you how not to get dead."

She snorted at that. She thought this was a lark. More fool her, he thought, his eyes dropping back to her décolletage as the coffee was placed before him.

"How're you going to do it?" he asked before taking a good long gulp.

"Don't you worry about a thing! I know just who to call."

Then she looked past him to the nervous lad hovering by the door and said, "Get me Roxy Parker's number. *Pronto!*"

CHAPTER 20

Roxy had been meaning to return to Phoebe's childhood home since the day she interviewed Margie, but she hadn't found the time.

It was now early Thursday morning, and hoping to grab the occupants before they left for work, she rang the buzzer at 53 Baker Street over and over and banged hard on the front door. There was no reply, and now it was her inner self she was kicking.

She should have come straight back!

It was as clear as a burglar's welcome mat that the occupants had gone away. The front blinds were down, rolled newspapers lay untouched on the lawn, and a light glowed beside the front door, despite the sunshine.

Damn it.

Looking around, Roxy noticed a small gate leading down one side of the house—the opposite side to Margie's place—and she strode across, checking over her shoulder before unlatching it and ducking down.

A narrow pathway led to the backyard, which was really just a large rectangular stretch of lawn with nothing but an empty clothesline in the middle and a few straggly palm trees. A real waste of space, Roxy thought. Clearly no green thumbs had ever lived here, or anyone needing a granny flat. She made her way across to the back door and knocked. Again, no answer. Peering through a back window, she could just make out what looked like a washing machine, a chest freezer beside it. She noticed another window, a larger one, and stepped closer.

Even if the current occupants did suddenly return, this might be her only chance for a sticky beak. There was no guarantee they would ever let her inside. The owners had no doubt dealt with streams of curious media and mystery buffs over the years and were probably as against the book as Margie was.

Through the smudged glass she could make out a small kitchen with pine cupboards and a black-and-white linoleum floor. She could just see a living area to one side and nothing much beyond that. As she balanced on tiptoe to see more, Roxy tripped over a rock by the back door, and that's when she spotted a flash of silver.

The key!

She stared at it, then glanced around, then stared at it some more, and was just about to pick it up when her mobile phone rang, catching her by surprise.

Her heart leapt into her throat.

Roxy took a steadying breath and answered it to find James Van Beurden on the other end—or his personal assistant, Lee Lin, to be more precise.

Lee Lin apologised to Roxy for the sudden notice but said Mr Van Beurden was available to see her now. "I realise it's very last minute, but if you can get straight in, he's all yours until eight thirty."

Roxy checked her watch. It was 7:45 a.m.

"I'm on my way," she said, then gave the key a final

glance as she turned away, silently cursing Phoebe's husband and thanking him, too, for saving her from committing breaking and entering.

James Van Beurden was a good fifteen years older than his wife and a lot less likely to turn heads as he walked, which he did now, through his already bustling office towards Roxy. He was shorter, too, and had enormous, protruding ears, a bulbous nose, and a neatly trimmed patch of light brown hair. He was verging on ugly, Roxy thought, immediately admonishing herself for the nasty sentiment. But it was true. He was not a good-looking man, yet the smile he offered his staff as he walked through, and then to Roxy as he closed in, one hand out to shake, was warm and welcoming, instantly disarming.

"Roxy Parker!" he said, recognising her face. "Apologies for dragging you in so early, but I wanted to meet you as soon as I possibly could. Phee has done nothing but gush since you started, and I'm so glad her story's in such capable hands."

"Thank you," she said.

"No, really. I'm just chuffed she's found such a competent author to help her tell her story. Both of us have pored over everything you've written. It's an impressive catalogue of work."

Roxy was beaming now. The man really knew how to gush! His compliment seemed sincere, and she could now see what Phoebe saw in him. His words were kind, his smile genuine. She felt immediately relaxed in his presence. *Perfect for someone who's survived so much.*

"I've arranged for us to talk in one of the conference rooms, so let me see…" He swivelled his head around and nodded at a petite, well-dressed woman who was waving from the other end of the foyer. She was standing by an open door with a water jug in one hand.

James led the way to the room where his assistant—the aforementioned Lee Lin—also brought glasses and offered Roxy coffee and tea. She accepted a coffee, then followed him in past a large oval desk and into two more comfortable armchairs by a window looking out over a lush, internal courtyard.

"You've got a lovely setup here," Roxy told him as she placed her recorder on the small glass table between them.

"My home away from home." He smiled. "Or at least it used to be before I met Phoebe. She gave me new life, a reason to leave the office." He smiled again.

Roxy thought of his nieces then and of what Phoebe had said. Hadn't they been his previous *raison d'être?* She was about to ask when he said, "We met at a PR function, two years ago last July. Best day of my life."

Roxy quickly reached down to the recorder and asked, "Do you mind if I switch this on?"

"Sure, let's get started. So, yes, we met at a function but we can give Lee Lin all the credit for that."

"Your personal assistant? Lee Lin…?"

"My *executive* assistant, yes. Lee Lin Zhao." He stopped to spell it for her. "Lee had hired MakeAMark—Phoebe's PR agency—and I'm embarrassed to admit it was love at first sight." Then he laughed again, leaning towards the recorder and adding, "Slight correction: it was love at first sight *for me*, not Phoebe. I can't imagine what she thought of the ugly little man who tried his luck."

Roxy laughed along. "But you hit it off straight away?"

"Yes," she said, "oddly enough we did. We were

married within the year."

He seemed proud of the fact, of the match itself, and she wondered about that. He might not have been handsome, but he was a mover and a shaker, a wealthy and powerful man, and she had already seen pictures of his first wife—an aging blond trophy—so he was clearly used to luring beautiful women, if only for his bank account. And Roxy wondered if that was also part of the allure for Phoebe and not because she thought Phoebe was a gold digger. There was safety and stability in a healthy bank balance. Not to mention an older man. The older he was, the less likely he was to leave her. Or to insist she have kids.

"And you've decided not to have children, I hear?"

"Have we?" he said, taking her by surprise.

"Oh, it's just, Phoebe mentioned…"

His smile had faltered slightly. "It's early days for us. Nothing's been decided."

She nodded, wondering what Phoebe would say about that but decided not to push it. This was personal. Not important to the book.

"And you're very close to your nieces, I hear. I saw a beautiful photo of them from your wedding."

The man's smile returned with full force as he launched into a story about their recent antics before stopping suddenly. "Sorry, this book is not about them. It's about my lovely Phee. What else do you need to know?"

"Oh, not a lot. It's Phoebe's story, of course, I just like to meet the important people and fill in some blanks—things like your family background, your business, that kind of thing."

"Then please, proceed."

And so Roxy did, and after twenty minutes she had

all the information she needed—his Dutch heritage, the full names and birth dates of his extended family, and how his company came into being. He was born working class, he told her, and had pulled himself up through hard work and determination. He made his first million by the age of twenty-one, floated the company by age thirty.

"We now have offices in New York, London and Mumbai, and are looking to start one in Tokyo later this year."

"Impressive," she said, and he laughed.

"But not that interesting, I'm sure. How about this—Phoebe and I now own five houses, including a lovely brick palace in Hunters Hill."

"A house in Sydney? Why don't you live there?" *Why stay cooped up in an apartment, even one as beautiful as theirs?*

"Phee prefers the York Street address. It's closer to everything, and I suppose it feels a little safer up there in the sky."

Safer? she thought, wondering what he meant by that, but he was staring pointedly at a large clock on the wall, so she knew she needed to get on with it, and she still had one set of questions to ask. They weren't strictly for the book.

"Do you ever wonder," she began as she gathered her things, "what happened to Phoebe's parents?"

"Margie's still alive and well."

Roxy smiled at him. He wasn't stupid. "You know what I mean."

His warm smile cooled considerably as his eyes dropped to the greenery below, and Roxy wasn't sure if it was her or the subject matter that had brought the change in temperature.

"What kind of parents would do that to a child?" he said eventually. "What kind of *vermin* would just scuttle off and leave a child so traumatised?" He looked back, pointedly. "And she is traumatised, Roxy, don't let her beautiful façade fool you like it does everyone else. Phoebe might seem confident and content—and in many ways she is—but the hurt runs deep, still haunts her daily. Did she tell you that?"

Roxy shook her head. *Quite the opposite, in fact.*

"She still wakes from time to time, screaming, sweating, clinging to me like I might suddenly…" He gave her a grim look. "Anyway, suffice it to say it's never been over for her, not really, and it never will be. At least not until those bastards get justice." His expression hardened. "Apologies, Roxy, I know I sound brusque, but you mess with my wife, you mess with me." Then he glanced at his watch and stood up, his voice bright and breezy again. "Now, if you'll excuse me, I really must get on with my day."

"Of course," she said, thanking him just as Lee Lin appeared as though by some silent cue to show her out.

As she watched James march back through the office, shaking hands with various subordinates, she wondered at his outburst and how infuriating it all must be. In many ways he was just like his wife. They had both pulled themselves up from nothing and created a life in which they called the shots. Yet this was one story over which neither of them had any control.

Phoebe's past clearly still nipped at the heels of their marriage and woke them both at night. It obviously impacted their decision to have children and even where they resided, "safely" in the sky, with a guard at the entrance and no chance of anyone sneaking off quietly in the dead of night.

As she made her way to interview her client, Roxy realised she had it all wrong at the start. Forgotten Phoebe hadn't been forgotten at all.

She was still a vivid memory.

CHAPTER 21

The highway to Gerroa was a picturesque one with stunning views of the Pacific Ocean and lush surrounding countryside, and as she steered her thirsty Merc carefully around the steep bends and past streams of Lycra-clad cyclists, Gilda couldn't help feeling a little guilty, but only a little.

How dare Wiles treat her like a lowly subordinate! Even *before* they had started dating, he treated her with more respect! Well, she would show him, she decided. Nobody put Gilda in a corner, not when there was a suspicious case to investigate!

"You okay?" came the voice beside her, and Gilda glanced across to Roxy, who had a thick pair of Gucci sunglasses on, her black hair flapping about in the breeze through the open passenger window.

"Yeah, just preoccupied," she said. Then, "I can't believe Phoebe gave you the day off. I thought you only had a few days left to interview her."

"I know. It's very frustrating, but she had some PR emergency. A client said something stupid on one of the morning shows. She has to mop up after him and will call me when that's done."

Roxy reached across the back seat to scratch Lunar's

neck. "I can't believe you let Lunar and me tag along for the ride!"

"I know how tiresome your mother can be, so I figured you could do with a break, him too." She glanced in the rearview mirror where Lunar sat, head out the window now, panting happily. "Just make sure he doesn't leave any hair on that back seat."

"Oh I think dog hair is the least of your worries."

Gilda shot her another glance and saw her smile. She hoped that meant she was joking.

"Why *are* we heading to Gerroa?" Roxy asked. "I thought you said the case was closed."

"Just chasing a few leads." Gilda didn't tell Roxy that Wiles had no idea where she was going. Thought she was spending the day at home, adding up her receipts. "The husband says his wife would never kill herself and had no reason to be in Sydney. I just want to hear what others think. Maybe the son will tell me differently. I hear he's unemployed and still living at home, so I'm hoping to get him on his own."

"How old is this kid?"

"About twenty-three, I think."

"Hasn't got a job? Still lives at home. That's a bit odd."

"Everything about this case is odd. Just add it to the list."

The Smith home was a simple, two-storey weatherboard structure set on a hill overlooking a small bay. In fact, the only interesting thing about it was the view of that bay, not that the house took advantage of it. There was no expansive deck or floor-to-ceiling windows like the other houses on the block, just a garage on the lower level and a rickety set of stairs leading up to the front door. It was as closed as the curtains that shrouded the windows that faced that extraordinary view.

There was no escaping the great location though, and Roxy gasped at the azure water below as Gilda pulled her car into an empty spot outside the Smith house. She hoped there was a path down that windswept cliff, because Lunar sensed the ocean, too, and was already bouncing about in the back seat.

As she put her Mercedes in park, Gilda spotted a young man with bobbing brown curls, walking around the side of the house towards the street. He glared at her and she turned to Roxy.

"This is official police business. You two better stay in the vehicle."

Roxy snorted. "In this heat? Have you learned nothing from this case?" She reached for her door handle. "I'll take Lunar down to that glorious beach I can see. Meet you back here in… how long do you need? Twenty? Thirty?"

Gilda studied the frowning man and said, "I'll be lucky to get ten."

Then they all got out and she locked the car, straightening her jacket and making her way towards him.

"My dad's at work!" he called out, his edgy tone not lost in the howling breeze.

"Good," she yelled back, producing her badge. "Because it's you I've come to see. Bob Smith, yes?"

The man's frown morphed from one of irritation to one of trepidation, and he nodded warily as she stepped closer. "I thought you were a real estate agent."

"My suit's not that bad is it?" Gilda offered him a smile and a handshake, introducing herself.

"Sorry. They're like vultures around here. Whole neighbourhood's been eyeing off this place. They all want to knock it down and build a McMansion."

"Not a bad idea," she replied, following his eyes to the view.

"It's never going to happen," he said, his voice edgy again.

"Can't say I blame you. I wouldn't want to give up the view either." She turned back. "Have you got a moment to chat?"

He nodded but stayed put, his chocolate-coloured curls flapping at the freckles across his face.

"I could do with a coffee after that drive. If you don't mind."

"Oh, yeah, right."

Bob led the way up the staircase at the front, then stopped at the screen door and noticed Roxy as she began walking Lunar in the opposite direction, down the steep cliff face.

"She taking the sniffer dog for a walk or something?"

"Something like that."

He led her inside to a pokey living and kitchen area that was notable for one thing and one thing alone—paisley.

"I'm guessing your mum did the decorating?" Gilda said, sweeping her eyes across the paisley-patterned curtains, cushions and throws.

Glancing around he said, "Yeah. I've never known anyone to take their name so literally."

"What about your dad? He an Elvis fan?"

Bob looked bemused for a moment. "Oh *Presely*, right. Nah, not particularly. How do you like your coffee?"

She told him milk and one, and he set about making it while Gilda surveyed the room again. The busy pattern was certainly cloying, and she felt an urge to sweep open those curtains and let the stunning view speak for itself. She would also knock out a few walls and open the space up while she was at it, but she wasn't there to renovate. She took another look around, this time with her detective hat on. She was interested in understanding the victim more, trying to see hints of what was to come, but apart from a penchant for paisley, there were few clues in the sparse furnishings.

The Smiths might have a million-dollar view, but it was clear the family was low-income—the sofa was just the right side of shabby, the ceiling ready for a fresh paint, flashes of a previous paint job, a faint apricot colour, poking through where parts were beginning to peel away.

"I kept offering to do it," Bob said, following her gaze as he prepared a mug of instant coffee. "But she wouldn't hear of it. Said it was a waste of my time. Wish I'd done it now."

His voice cracked as he said it, but there was bitterness along with regret.

"I'm very sorry for your loss," Gilda said quickly, belatedly, but he didn't reply, just handed her the cup and dropped onto the sofa, plonking his muddy boots up on the coffee table.

Helping herself to a chair from the nearby dining table, Gilda also sat down and placed her coffee aside. There was no way she was drinking instant coffee, thanks very much.

"I won't take too much of your time, Mr Smith—"

"It's Bob," he said, cutting in. "Although I've been thinking of changing it to Robert. Bob's a bit, you know, common."

"Isn't Bob short for Robert anyway?"

He smiled grimly. "You'd think so."

Gilda wasn't sure what he meant by that but pressed on. "So, *Robert*, I just have a few things to clear up and then I'll be out of your hair."

"Dad told me the autopsy was done, Mum's at the funeral parlour, so I'm a bit confused what this is about."

"Of course. Let me explain. The state's chief pathologist has brought in her preliminary postmortem report, and she has ruled it an 'open case, possible misadventure or suicide,' and the coroner still has to sign off on it, but there are still a few questions at this stage. We don't normally investigate suicide, but this is a very unusual case."

"Unusual? How?"

She stared at him. *Wasn't it obvious?* "The manner in which your mother died, it's… well let's just say we've never seen anything like it. Neither has the senior pathologist."

He shrugged at that, said nothing.

"We just have a few remaining questions." And by "we" she really just meant herself, but she wasn't about to tell Bob that.

"Like?"

Like why drive all the way to Sydney airport to kill yourself when there's a perfectly good cliff just metres from your doorstep? Of course she didn't say that either. He didn't look angry, like his dad, but he was clearly hurting.

"Do you know why your mother might have been at the airport that day? Your father has no idea, but I wondered whether you might?"

"If Dad doesn't know, I certainly wouldn't."

"If it really was suicide, do you have any idea why your mother might have wanted to take her own life? Did she ever give you any inkling of what was to come?"

The young man looked bruised then, and Gilda knew it was a difficult question—did suicide ever really make sense to the offspring?—but she stared back at him and waited. She really needed some answers.

Eventually he said, "I've been asking myself that over and over." He sniffed and wiped the back of his hand across his nose. "Why didn't she just get out of the car? Dad says the doors were unlocked. Why didn't she just step out?"

Gilda spotted a box of tissues, clad in a paisley cover (of course!), and jumped up to retrieve them, handing them over. He yanked a tissue out and blew into it.

She waited a few moments, then asked, "Did you ever see any sign that your mum was depressed or—"

"None. I mean, she was never one of those happy-go-lucky, smiley types anyway, you know? She kept to herself, went about her *thang*, did what she had to do." He sniffed again. "She was a good mum though, she was." His voice was louder and more determined. "She nearly died giving birth to me, you know." He nodded his head towards her. "I was born right there."

"Here?" She stared warily at the dining table.

"On the floor there, she said, blood everywhere. Mum used to be a hippy, thought a home birth would be cool."

"And it wasn't?"

"I'm an only child, aren't I? She can barely talk about the birth. Just says it was all worth it in the end. I don't feel so worthy now that she's…" His voice was cracking again. "I can't imagine how Dad feels."

Gilda pretended to sip her coffee before eventually breaking the silence.

"This question is a bit difficult, Bob, er, *Robert*, but I do need to ask. Did you ever see any friction between your parents, any fights?"

He looked up sharply, his curls bouncing. "You think *Dad* had something to do with this?"

"Was it a happy marriage?"

"Yes! Very!"

His answer was swift, almost aggressive and she wondered if he was lying, covering up, but then he added, "Truth is, they loved each other more than anything else, more than this house and its bloody view. More than me, that's for damn sure." He gave her a sad, pathetic grin. "Soz. I'm just feelin' blue. Look, I don't see what this has got to do with anything."

"If your parents did love each other so much, why would she leave him? And I'm referring to that text you found. It sounded like a goodbye message to your dad."

His eyes squinted. He said nothing.

"Could your dad be having an affair perhaps?" She waited for him to bristle at the suggestion—*who wants to admit that about a parent?*—but he didn't seem at all disturbed by the question. In fact, he almost laughed.

"You're joking, right? Dad? No way, man! He only had eyes for Mum. She only had eyes for him. Not in a million years. Never."

Gilda nodded, wondering if he was telling the truth or just had rose-tinted glasses on. She pushed her coffee aside—there was no point even pretending—and stood up.

"Would you mind if I took a very quick look in your mother's bedroom? I just want to try to understand her a bit better?"

"Help yourself." He waved her down the hallway. "But you won't find any answers in there."

And he was right. The bedroom, like much of the house, was sparsely furnished and decorated almost completely in—you guessed it—paisley, from the thin quilt to the fraying curtains. A double bed sat in the middle of the room, two mismatched bedside tables on either end. No pictures, no paintings, just an overwhelming sense of paisley. Gilda was a paisley fan herself but wasn't sure how they got to sleep under the frenetic pattern and thought it was a pity the woman's name wasn't Rose or Pearl instead.

Then she thanked Bob for his time and left him staring into his lap.

~~~

The small bay below the Smith house was windswept and littered with seaweed, but it was still pretty, and as Gilda trod along the wet sand, shoes in hand, towards the woman and the dog, she could see why you'd move here if you were married with kids. She could *not* see why you'd stay here if you were a single man in your twenties and on the cusp of life.

From what she knew of the place, there was little more than families, retirees and cashed-up weekenders, with just a general store and one restaurant to keep them entertained. She wondered why Bob—sorry, *Robert*—was still hanging around, especially if he was unemployed and his folks only had eyes for each other.

"Rox!" she called out, just catching her friend's attention before she started off in the opposite direction.
~~~

Lunar's ears pricked up, and then he started galloping back towards her, followed closely by Roxy.

"Sorry!" she said when she got to Gilda. "I lost track of the time. It's beautiful here."

"If you're old and boring. Come on, I have one more stop before we head back."

The stop was actually a good forty-five minutes down the road on the return leg to Sydney. The city of Wollongong is one of the largest in the state and home to the central post office where Paisley Smith once worked.

Along the way, Roxy's phone beeped several times and she ignored it, which caught Gilda's attention. "Are you avoiding Sam or Max? Or is it just your mother?"

Roxy frowned. "It's Maria Constantinople, actually."

"The editor?"

"Managing editor now of about a gazillion titles."

"So why don't you pick up? Maybe she's got more work for you."

"Frankly, I couldn't care less. I've been begging her all year for something, anything to keep my bills at bay, and she hasn't offered me so much as a morsel. Doesn't even bother calling me back these days so…"

"So you're giving her a dose of her own medicine?" Gilda laughed. "That'll help pay the mortgage. Ah here we are in the 'Gong at last."

She pulled the car into a public parking lot behind the post office, and Roxy said, "What are we supposed to do while you're in there?"

"I don't know. Find a dog-friendly café and be patient?"

As Roxy and Lunar headed off to do just that, Gilda

grabbed her bag and notebook and made her way down a busy laneway and into the post office. It was more like a gift shop, with a wide selection of books and toys and gadgets on offer, and she stopped to inspect a decently priced mobile phone before remembering her mission and making her way to the front desk.

"Yes, the days of just selling stamps are long over," the manager, Beverly Wendt, said after Gilda had introduced herself and was led out the back for a chat. "We make a lot of revenue from other sources now."

"It would have been a very different place when Paisley Smith started working here," Gilda said. "When was that, exactly?"

"Oh, I'd have to look that up to be certain," Beverly said, waving her into a chair in a cramped meeting room, "but she was here when I started fifteen years ago, and now I think about it, she's already had long service leave so, well, quite a while."

"And yet you were her boss, is that correct?"

Beverly looked a little awkward. "Paisley wasn't very ambitious. Just happy to do her job and head home to the hubby again."

How dull, Gilda thought. She'd go mad if she had worked in one place her whole life, let alone one that amounted to a gift shop.

"I know you're busy, so I'll try to be quick."

"That's fine, I'm happy to help in any way I can. We were all so shocked when it happened. It's just so sad! How is poor Presley? He'll be devastated. They were thick as thieves, those two. Did everything together."

"So I hear. He's holding up okay. Struggling with the idea of it, of course."

"We heard it was suicide, could that really be true?"

"It's still under investigation," she lied. "Can you tell me what happened that morning she died? Last Friday. She came into work at what time?"

"Um… about 8:55, same as always." She paused. "I did tell all this to that young man, the officer from Gerringong? He dropped in last week and ticked a few boxes."

Her tone suggested she thought he was just going through the motions.

"I'm here to double-check the boxes," Gilda said and she nodded.

"Rightio. Let me see… She was in before nine, had her usual takeaway coffee and muffin in hand, did a bit of despatch, checked some orders out the back here, and was just making her way to the front desk when she got the call."

"Call?"

"On her mobile. It must have been around 9:40, maybe 9:45. I remember because we hadn't been open long, and we were one man short that day. I just hoped the call wouldn't take long." She blushed, her eyes suddenly welling up. "I can't believe my insensitivity now."

"You weren't to know," Gilda said, trying to keep her on track. "Any idea who called her? Did she say?" Beverly shook her head. "How long did the call last?"

"Oh, just a few minutes. Then she began to serve customers, but I could tell she was distracted, and she started sending some texts, which she didn't often do. I mean, the younger ones live on their devices but not Paisley, not normally anyway. I was going to ask if everything was okay when she suddenly grabbed her bag and just left."

"Just left? No goodbye?"

"None! It was very out of character for Paisley. We were all quite shocked. That's when I knew something was wrong."

"What time was this, when she left?"

"Just on 10:00 a.m. At first I thought she had to move her car, to avoid a parking ticket perhaps? But then when she didn't return, I wondered whether Presley or Bob had been in some kind of accident…"

Beverly's eyes welled up again as her voice trailed off, and Gilda squeezed her hand, but her mind was racing, wondering about Paisley's mobile phone records.

Had Doreen followed them up?

"How close were you with the deceased?"

"Oh, not that close. I mean, we went out to lunch from time to time, but we never did much out of work hours. Our kids used to play together in the old depot during the school holidays, but that was about it. Paisley lived a fair way out as you probably know, and well, as I said, she spent a lot of time with her husband. And the boy of course. They were tight."

"She was close to her son?"

"Of course," she said, but Gilda sensed a shift in her tone. She wasn't quite as emphatic.

"Can you think of any reason Paisley suddenly upped and drove to Sydney last Friday? Any reason she might have gone to the airport?"

"None at all. We're all wondering the same thing." She hesitated. "How is young Bob?"

"He's holding up okay too."

The woman nodded, but Gilda sensed something again and asked, "How did they really get on, Paisley and her son?"

Beverly crossed her arms over her chest and said,

"Like I said, they were close."

Gilda waited a beat to let her start babbling, which she did, but not before glancing around surreptitiously like she didn't want to get caught gossiping.

"The truth is, they used to have a really close relationship, Paisley and Bob, but things started to fray recently."

"Do you know why?"

The woman looked around again, and Gilda gave her a reassuring smile. "It could be important, Beverly. I do need to get to the bottom of all this."

She nodded. "All I know is, she came into work one day very upset. She was ranting about Bob. She'd never done that before. I like to whinge about mine regularly, but she never had a bad word to say about the lad, even though he seems a bit… well… Anyway, this time was different. This time she had her blinkers off, said he was an *ungrateful shit*, if you'll excuse my French. They were her words. Not mine."

"Was she getting sick of him living at home, sponging off them?"

"Oh she can't blame *him* for that. She indulged the boy from the start. Spoiled him rotten. As far as I could tell, he did nothing around the house; she still did all his washing, even paid him pocket money I think. He certainly didn't have a job, and I'm not sure he's ever had one, which I think is strange now he's in his twenties. I mean, there's plenty of work if you want it. I even offered him a job here at one stage, but he refused, and she didn't seem to mind."

"She was a bit of a hippy I believe?"

Beverly frowned. "Don't know about that, but she was a good mother, just a bit, well, *tolerant* might be a better way of explaining it. She put up with a lot."

"How so?"

The woman looked deeply uncomfortable now; she clearly wasn't the gossipy type and was not enjoying how the conversation was unfolding. "He was just a bit of an odd bod, that's all. Never quite fitted in with the other kids, you know? Didn't have many friends, well, apart from an invisible friend he had until he was too old for that nonsense." She grimaced. "Maybe he has *issues*. Kids seem to have so many issues these days, don't they?"

Gilda nodded, wanting to get her back on track. "So she came in one day, whistling a different tune? When was this?"

"About a month or so ago. She was very upset. Said something about him wanting to sell the house from under them. I know the agents had been at them for years. It's the worst house in the best street—you know how they love that?" She glanced around again. "From what I could tell, Bob was super keen, even pressuring them to do it. Had gone to see a broker or something."

"Cheeky bugger."

"That's what I said! It all felt a little sneaky to me. Poor Paisley, she was so upset. So *disappointed*. But I think it was more than that. I think she felt betrayed. Like she'd always done the best by him and this is how he treats her."

Gilda thought about that. From what Bob had told her, the woman nearly died giving birth to him in the house, the very one he was trying to sell from underneath her. No wonder she felt let down. Gilda was about to enquire further when she noticed Beverly waving two fingers at a man through the window.

"I'm so sorry. I do have to get back."

As they walked out, the detective asked, "Do you think Bob might somehow be involved? In his mother's death?"

Beverly looked horrified at the suggestion but didn't exactly refute it either. She stopped and said, "Look, they were a loving family, I do believe that. But I always felt like the son…"

"Yes?"

"It wasn't just that she tolerated him. I always felt like she was scared of him or something. I know that sounds silly, but she seemed a little nervous around him, like she had to watch every word. Like she was scared he would suddenly explode."

CHAPTER 22

"Explode? What? Like a tantrum?" Roxy said as Gilda repeated the conversation on their drive back to Sydney.

"I guess, although a tantrum can turn violent if you're a grown son."

"You think he was abusive to his mum?"

"I don't know. Unfortunately, the manager had to get back to work, so I'll have to chase her up later. I also need to have another conversation with Presley. A frank discussion about his son."

"I only got a glimpse of Bob from the street, but did you sense he could lash out?"

"No, but then not every abusive man has fat hairy knuckles, of course," Gilda said as she changed lanes to pass a slow van in the left lane.

They had agreed to make a beeline straight for a trendy pub in Paddington, where Caroline was already ensconced with friends, enjoying happy hour, so Gilda carefully changed lanes again to take the requisite exit when her mobile phone rang.

"Should I get that?" Roxy asked, but Gilda shook her head and tapped something on her dashboard to activate the speaker.

"Hi, Wiles," she sang out. "I'm in the car with Roxy."

Roxy chirped in a quick, cheerful, "Hi Wiles!" before Gilda continued.

"We're just about to—"

"Where exactly are you?" He interrupted her, his deep voice booming across the car.

"On the way to the Paddington Inn. Want to join us?"

"No I do not. I need you back in the office. Now."

The voice was more than a boom. There was a bit of crash and opera in it too, and Gilda exchanged a quick frown with Roxy.

"Okay, I can do that. Is everything okay?"

"Just get in here, fast as you can."

Wiles sounded like he was about to sign off when his voice boomed again. "And leave Roxy at the pub where she belongs."

Then he hung up.

Roxy balked. "Is he saying I'm an alcoholic?" When Gilda didn't reply, she added, "I think he was saying I'm an alcoholic."

"Sorry, he must be very stressed. Maybe another case came in." At least she hoped it had, otherwise she could be in for some more fireworks. "I'd better get in."

"Of course, honey. Just drop me anywhere. I'll make my own way—"

"No! I'll drop you to Caroline first."

"But if it is a homicide…"

"Then the dead body isn't going anywhere, is it?"

The command centre was still bustling when Gilda finally arrived, and she felt a pang of guilt, which she swallowed down with a serious dose of pragmatism. Wiles was probably just wondering where she'd been all day. He wasn't a fan of working from home—which was where she told Doreen she'd be—and was even less a fan of lying.

He had also told her to leave the Smith case alone, and she'd done quite the opposite. But she had a hunch all would be forgiven when she revealed what she'd just learned. There were clearly issues in the Smith household, and the explosive son was a definite line of enquiry.

As she tapped lightly at his door and smiled meekly in, Wiles looked up from his computer screen and did not mirror her smile.

"Come in and shut the door behind you."

A few months ago she would have taken that as an invitation; today she wasn't about to pucker up.

"I'm sorry I was a no-show," she said quickly as she took the seat across from him. "But I did tell Doreen I wouldn't be in. The truth is, I was on police business."

"No, you were on a wild-goose chase." She stared at him. "I had Presley Smith on the phone earlier. He's irate."

Gilda's lips formed a perfect circle. "Oh."

"What were you thinking, Gilda? Going to his house uninvited? Rummaging through his dead wife's bedroom without permission?"

"I didn't rummage! And I was invited in by Bob."

"The distressed son?"

"He wasn't that distressed actually. Listen, I have some very interesting information about him that might be relevant to the case. I spoke to Paisley's manager at the Wollongong post office—"

"Hang on, what? Now you're interrogating her *boss*?"

"It wasn't exactly an interrogation. I'm just trying to get to the bottom of all this, trying to get a better idea of why Paisley did what she did. I heard something very interesting—"

"I don't want to hear it, Gilda. I want you to explain to me—*your* boss last time I checked—what the hell you think you were doing. And with a civilian in tow!"

"Civilian?" Gilda braced herself.

"According to Bob Smith, you turned up with"— he paused to read from a pad in front of him— "a 'pretty chick with black hair and a friendly German shepherd'." He stared at her deadpan. "Now why does that sound so familiar?"

"I can explain—"

"Jesus, Gilda! What were you doing, taking Roxy Parker and her bloody dog into a police investigation?"

"She didn't come in! She just came for the drive and stayed right out of it, I can assure you, but honestly Wiles, there's no need to be like this."

Gilda could feel her heart hammering, and it wasn't just Wiles's tone, it was the way he was staring at her— with such disappointment and disgust.

"I specifically told you to drop the case."

"And I ignored your advice."

He held up a palm. "That wasn't advice, Gilda, that was a command."

"Well, I disagreed with it."

He frowned. "You do get that I'm your boss, right? Or have you completely forgotten that?"

"No, you don't seem to let me."

"What does that mean?"

She just rolled her eyes and said nothing.

He threw the pad back down on his desk and began to scratch at his goatee. "I knew this would be a problem," he said, his voice a bit calmer.

She blinked back at him. "We're not talking about the case anymore, are we?"

"There is no case, and no we're bloody not." He took a few settling breaths. "I knew us going out would be a bad idea."

"Going out? Is that what we're doing? Really? Because it feels to me like we're always hiding in."

Now it was his turn to look confused. "What?"

"We've been 'going out'"—she did the quote marks with her fingers—"for a year now, Wiles. A full twelve months, but apart from police business, we haven't actually gone anywhere. We hide at your place or mine. You barely look at me when I'm at work; you certainly don't touch me. Why are we still pretending like it's not happening?"

"You know why that is, Gilda, and keep your voice down." He stared at the door. "I'm your superior officer."

"Oh come on, Wiles. You think they don't know?" She waved a hand outwards. "If they haven't worked it out by now, you should sack the lot of them. They're supposed to be detectives."

"It's unprofessional. It muddies the waters."

"So now our relationship is mud?"

"Don't be melodramatic. You know what I mean. You're taking advantage of my feelings for you—"

"I don't even know *what* your feelings for me are, so how can I possibly take advantage of them?"

He held his palms out again. "Look, we're getting way off the subject here. My point is you didn't follow orders; you went out on a limb. I told you to leave the Smiths alone."

"Ah, yes, but you also told me to question the

husband. You told me that would put my mind at ease, that he would soon admit she was suicidal and that would be that. He didn't, she wasn't. My mind was not put at ease, and so I investigated. It's my job. And I did try to tell you what I was doing today, but you didn't want to hear it, so I had to go 'out on a limb,' and I'm glad I did because I uncovered something that I think is consequential to the case."

"Like wha—"

"But I've always done that!" she rattled on, interrupting him this time. "Long before you and me started… well"—she looked him up and down—"whatever it is we started. I always ran my own leads. I never had to check it with you or anyone else for that matter. And I was always a rule breaker too. Just ask my other *superiors*. But I make no apologies for that. Thanks to my rule-breaking, I learned that Bob Smith might have been aggressive, maybe even explosive towards the victim in the past. He also has a motive to see her gone, a very good one. So I'm not prepared to just dump this case as another sad suicidal woman and leave it at that."

"Explosive? Motive? What are you talking about?"

She stood up. "Nope, I'm not on duty now, *boss*. I've got a hot date with a glass of champagne and some friends who don't talk down to me."

He almost smiled, his blue eyes twinkling suddenly. "You're being very churlish, you know."

"I'm being an employee, and according to my watch, it's knock-off time." She made her way to the door. "I'll see you on Monday."

"Oh come on, Gilda," he said as she kept walking. "Is that your way of saying don't bother calling over this weekend?"

She turned to glare at him. "Am I scheduled to work this weekend? Am I on the roster?" He looked at her, patiently, like he was looking at a petulant child. "Then unless we get another homicide, you won't be seeing me until Monday. *Boss*."

Then Gilda swivelled on her heels and stormed out of his office before she lost her nerve, while Wiles sat staring after her and wondering how that little chat went so belly up.

CHAPTER 23

The first thing Roxy thought as she peeled her eyes open late Saturday morning was thank goodness Phoebe still hadn't called. She was probably still over the limit, judging by how much they'd put away last night.

Roxy's head was pounding, and she sat up in bed and looked about.

Paracetamol! She needed headache tablets, and fast.

The evening had turned very wild very quickly. Mostly thanks to Gilda, who had returned from her "briefing" in a filthy mood, and the only thing for it was a bottle of wine, followed soon after by another. And then another.

By the end of the night, Gilda had declared her relationship dead and buried, and they all gleefully toasted the end of "Wicked Wiles" even though Roxy quite liked the smooth-dressing detective even if he did think she was an alcoholic.

She secretly hoped they'd kiss and make up, and she was secretly glad of the distraction too, because it left little time for Caroline to interrogate her over her relationship with Max and for her to interrogate herself over her relationship with Sam.

She checked her phone and winced. He'd left a bunch of messages yesterday, and she hadn't called him back.

Why wasn't she calling him back?

"Yoohoo, everything all right?" Lorraine sang from behind the closed door.

Roxy cleared her throat. "Come in, Mum!"

As the door swung open Lunar came flying in first, galloping across the room and straight onto the bed.

"Naughty boy!" Lorraine cried, hands holding a laden tray. "Off that bed! Now!"

The dog stared at Roxy, hoping she'd put up a fight for him, but she had no energy, and sensing this, he dropped off and slunk on the floor below her.

Lorraine's smile was victorious as she placed the tray on Roxy's lap. "This is your father's doing, not mine."

How many times do I have to say he's just my stepdad? Roxy thought, but she didn't have the energy to correct her either. Instead, she surveyed the offering and gave her own small smile.

"Bacon, eggs, juice and coffee. I love that man."

"He loves you too, don't you forget it." She reached across and brushed Roxy's messy hair from her face. "We thought you might need it. You were rather tipsy when you came in last night."

Roxy winced. "Sorry, Mum, how bad was it?"

"Oh darling, not bad so much as hilarious. Going on about men and how they could all take a flying leap."

She scowled again. "Did I say anything else?"

"Like what dear?"

"Oh I don't know…"

"Like how you're thinking of getting married?"

Roxy gulped. "*What?*"

"Last night, my dear, you said Sam wants more than

you're prepared to give and he could bugger off." She giggled. "I know you, Roxy. I know what that means. You've always found the idea of marriage terrifying, and your ranting last night only proves it. The poor man popped the question!"

Roxy must have been blushing, because Lorraine looked positively ebullient. "I knew it! I knew you had big news! You can't hide anything from your old mum."

Roxy smiled back, but in fact she was hiding something. It wasn't exactly marriage Sam had proposed. But she wasn't about to tell her mother that.

As Lorraine nibbled on a slice of Roxy's toast, she said, "Sam's a very brave man for even attempting to wrestle you into a white frock." Roxy went to say something but she held the toast up. "No, I don't want to hear it, Roxanne. I know you're terrified of commitment, but you do need to take this proposal seriously, and don't take long deciding. You're not getting any younger, and men like Sam don't drop from the sky, you know."

Except one just did, thought Roxy, her mind going to Max's recent arrival. She was so angry with herself. Had been so happy with Sam, but one look at Max, one moody conversation, and all her doubts were back.

"Do you think I might be able to meet this man before you actually walk down the aisle?" Lorraine was asking.

"Who said anything about an aisle, or a white frock for that matter? If I was going to get married—and I'm not saying I would, you've got that all wrong—it would be in a garden somewhere. Or on a beach."

"Oh don't be ridiculous, darling, you'd have to do it in a church. But I'd like to meet him first."

"You can meet him anyway. I'd like that too. I want

you to see what I see in him."

I want you to love him so you won't complain about him for the rest of your life, she might have added, but again, she had no energy.

Lorraine stood up. "Then I think Sam should get his backside to Sydney, and I think he should ask your father for your hand, like any decent suitor would."

"We're not Elizabeth and Darcy, Mum. It's not the 1800s."

"It's polite!" she retorted before glaring at the dog. "You don't forget your manners either, you hear? Stay off the bed!"

As she left the room, Roxy sat back on the cushion, picking at her breakfast—a kind gesture but her stomach was not cooperating—and thought of the lie she'd just let her mother believe. The truth was, it wasn't so much that Sam wanted to get married, although he did. What he really wanted was children, and *that* was why she was hesitating.

For the life of her she wasn't sure she wanted *either*.

"Children? Have you gone completely bonkers?"

This was Oliver, who'd agreed to meet for lunch at the café near the El Alamein Fountain in seedy Kings Cross, where he lived, and maybe it was her lack of defences, maybe it was the need to finally get it off her chest, but she had spilled the beans about Sam and his proposal.

"So he proposed a baby before marriage?" Oliver said, biting into a greasy burger and talking as he chewed. "Isn't that a bit wonky?"

"Sam says the true commitment is a child. Anyone can walk out on a marriage and never see each other again, but if you have a kid, you're bound for life."

"Oh that's real romantic. He wants to bind you, does he?"

"I'm not saying that. It's just, well, a baby is a lot more bonding than a marriage, and if we can do that, we can do anything."

"What a load of bollocks! Have a chat to all the single mothers out there, including my own. If things go south, you're the one left holding the baby; he can do a runner any damn time he likes."

"My God, you sound like my mother! This isn't the 1950s, Olie. Men have responsibilities now too, you know. Besides, he doesn't just want a baby, he wants one with me."

"He's smart, I'll give him that," he said, shovelling some chips in now. "He knows your history and figures it's the best way to keep you close—barefoot and pregnant in the countryside."

Roxy grimaced. She hadn't even taken to the barefoot thing yet—*de rigueur* where she lived—how was she going to handle pregnancy?

Oliver's eyes were squinting. "You've never showed any interest in kids before."

"Yes and I was also a selfish, single chick. I'm now pushing forty, and the clock is ticking."

"You're in your midthirties and *clock, schmock*. You have a kid because you want a kid, not because of some inaudible ticking sound or because some hunky bloke begs you for one. You obviously don't want one."

"Why would you even say that?"

"Because you're talking about it with me, your agent of all people. You want me to talk some sense into you."

"No I don't."

"Yes you do."

"Then let's just drop it!" she snapped back.

"Fine by me." He picked at some food between his teeth, then launched into a story about a new client, and Roxy tried to erase the frown from her face and focus on what Oliver was saying. But she was still smarting from the comments and still felt like jumping across the table and throttling him.

How dare he assume she didn't want kids! She wasn't Gilda Maltin. She wasn't married to her career. Barely had a career if truth be told… She felt her frown return. Was that why she was entertaining the idea? Because she had no work lined up? Because she was *bored?*

She shook the thought away and said, "Sorry, I missed that, what did you say?"

"I said, is there any reason you're avoiding that madwoman Maria? She's left a stack of messages, and Shazza's ready to snap." He studied her for a moment. "I thought you were desperate for more freelance."

"I am. I'm just cranky with her."

"You can't afford to be cranky, Rox. Just give us a break and give her a call, hey?"

She groaned. "I already have. I'm going in to see her after this."

Roxy felt like she'd waved the white flag too quickly, had been so keen to teach Maria a lesson, but Oliver was right. Beggars couldn't be choosers.

"Now, back to the book," he said as he patted down his pockets, looking for something. "I tracked down the owners of Phoebe's old Coogee place, and it turns out you were right. The current lot have gone away, but they'll be back late Wednesday. Can meet with you Thursday morning."

Roxy did the maths. "That's when I was leaving."

"How important is this house to your story?"

"Extremely! It's where the whole story began. Phoebe's given me some colour, but I'm not sure how much she really remembers. Be good to get in there, see if I can colour in between the lines."

"Okay, so stay a few extra days. What are you running back for? Sam monitoring your ovulation schedule, is he?"

She glared at Oliver but let that drop as she gave it some thought. It wasn't a bad idea. Her mother had already requested a meeting with Sam. She knew he was returning from his work trip on Wednesday. Maybe she could convince him to fly to Sydney the following day and they could drive home together after that.

She smiled, remembering her first journey in his rattly old Jeep, how Lunar had been watching from the back as the fireworks exploded between them.

Maybe that's what they both needed, she thought. *Another lovely road trip.*

"Earth to Roxy!" Oliver said, shaking the memory away. "So, their names are Mr and Mrs Woo, that's all I've got. Oh, and a mobile number." He had finally located the slip of paper it was jotted on, and he handed it over. "That's Mrs Woo's digits. Text her and set something up."

"Did she sound okay about it?"

"More than okay, she sounded thrilled to have you there. Even gave you permission to take photos if you like." He smirked. "I know a good photographer you could hire, just back from Berlin. And I bet he won't ask for a baby in return."

Roxy rolled her eyes as she got to her feet. *No,* she thought, *he'll ask for my heart, and that's much, much harder to give.*

~~~

Roxy was dashing through the automatic glass doors of Maria's publishing house, head down, mind in the clouds, when she slammed straight into a familiar figure. James Van Beurden was on his way out, dark sunglasses on and a leather satchel under one arm.

"Oh, my goodness, sorry!" Roxy said as the satchel went flying.

"Never mind!" he called back, scrambling to pick it up.

When he returned to his feet, she smiled and said, "What are you doing here in the heart of gossip central?"

He stared at her, confused for a moment, his head tilted to one side, his eyebrows scrunched high above the glasses. Then he gasped.

"Oh, Roxy Parker! Hello! Sorry I didn't recognise you there. How are you going? How's the book coming along?"

"Slowly but surely," she said. "Phoebe's been a bit busy with clients lately."

"Has she? Oh well, I'm sure she'll give you all the time you need." He made a show of checking his watch. "Speaking of which, I'd better dash. I'm running late. But, um…" He reached out and gave her arm a squeeze. "Good to see you again, Roxy, and thank you… for everything you're doing for my wife."

"Not at all, James. And good to see you too."

Roxy watched him scurry away and wondered again why he was there—especially on a Saturday—and if he'd deliberately avoided answering her question or was just caught up in the moment.

In any case, she was also running late and didn't
~~~

have time to give it more thought. She went straight to the lone security guard behind the front desk to check in, then watched as various staffers wandered in and out, all in casual gear, takeaway cups in hand, most looking grumpy that they had to work weekends.

"Well, well, well, didn't you take your sweet freakin' time?" Maria boomed and Roxy swept around. "Come here, gorgeous," Maria said, crushing her to her chest.

The way Maria acted you would think they were best friends or, at the very least, old mates. In fact, they were more like polite adversaries these days. As the past editor of *Glossy* magazine—and now managing editor of a stream of women's, gossip, and lifestyle titles—Maria once provided Roxy with enough freelance articles to help prop up her mortgage, but this had recently waned.

It wasn't Roxy's only issue with Maria. She had always been a little too brash for her liking, a little too *gung-ho*. She'd sell her grandmother for a good story. Hell, she'd sell her for a couple of lines of gossip and chuck her granddad in for good measure. The truth was, Roxy didn't really trust Maria, but she needed her from time to time, and this was one of those times. She just didn't like having to admit as much.

"I'm surprised to find you here on a Saturday," Roxy said as Maria winked at the guard, then led the way to the lifts.

"I have no life, you must know that by now."

The editor placed her security badge against the elevator shaft, which immediately opened, then whisked them up. They passed *Glossy*'s floor and continued skyward, towards the executive level.

"You're up with head honchos these days, I see."

Maria sniggered. "I *am* the head honcho these days, Roxanne. Keep up." She stepped out of the lift. "Why else do you think I'm here?"

"I thought the heads played golf and the staffers did all the hard yakka."

"Yeah, well, those days are gone. We're all clinging on by our oily fingertips, and we're down to skeleton staff. I sacked twenty people last month. That was a freakin' delight."

"Yikes. So I shouldn't take it personally that I've had no work all year?"

"Christ no!" She belly laughed. "There's nothing personal about this industry, love. It's all about the moolah." She rubbed bejewelled fingers together as if rubbing cash, then waved a hand outwards as they exited the lift. "The fab offices haven't changed though."

And she was right. Located in the heart of the city, not far from Phoebe's apartment, the publishing headquarters were stylish and well equipped, but it was the city view that really impressed—the Sydney Harbour Bridge and Opera House gleaming through floor-to-ceiling windows beyond.

Maria continued marching across the open-plan space until they got to a large inner office, glassed in on all sides. She waved Roxy inside to a replica Eames leather chair in front of her desk and then dropped into her own Eames, no doubt the genuine item.

"Can't offer you anything. My assistant's above working weekends for nothing, and I'm above fetching coffee. So let's get straight to it." She waited a beat and then said, "Forgotten Phoebe."

Roxy frowned. "What about her?"

"Wants to be remembered now, I hear."

Roxy rolled her eyes. *Of course.* That's why Maria had called her in. It had nothing to do with freelance work. "Who told you?"

"Jesus, woman, I'm not the head of a dozen magazines for nothing! I have my sources. And you're one of them, so spill."

"Spill what? I'm ghosting her autobiography, end of story."

"I want the exclusive. Extracts, the lot."

"I can't help you there, Maria. Talk to the publisher. Or, better yet, talk directly to Phoebe. She runs MakeAMark, but I'm sure you already know that. And I'm sure you've already approached her. Am I right?"

Her smile deflated. "She's playing coy. Pretty bloody rich for a PR slut. She's not doing any interviews, would you believe? No extracts, nothing."

"I can't help you, Maria. I'm just the hired gun."

"Then give me some goss. We'll pretend we never met."

Roxy laughed. "You're incorrigible! You know very well I've signed a confidentiality agreement. I can't share a word."

"Then let me share something with you."

Maria leaned back in her leather seat and squinted at Roxy. Her mind was ticking over, she was trying to work out her next move, and Roxy could sense that things were about to turn strange. Her headache started hammering again.

"I have a source," Maria said eventually, slowly. "He has some information about your client. I'm happy to hand that over to you in exchange for a deal."

"What kind of information? What exactly are you

talking about?"

"He knows where the parents are."

Roxy stared at her, gobsmacked, and Maria cackled with delight.

"I *knew* that'd get you hooked."

"Are you being serious?" Roxy leaned forward again. "He *knows* where Karen and Shane Fisher are now? Really?"

Maria nudged her eyebrows high. "Really."

"Oh my God, this is huge!" Roxy's eyes were saucer wide. "So where are they then? What's the story?"

Maria waggled her finger in the air. "Not so fast, my pretty. I'm going to need something in return."

Roxy's eyes narrowed. *What a surprise.* With Maria Constantinople there was always a catch. "I told you before. I can't hand over extracts even if I wanted to; that's up to the publisher. And they probably need Phoebe's permission."

"I don't care about any of that. I'm telling you, I have something better. I have a lead that will leave your original story reading like a lawn mower catalogue."

She mock snored as Roxy's eyes squinted.

"So, what? I have to pay you for this lead? I'm confused."

"No, silly girl. I figure you can use my information in your original book, make it ten times better, in which case we need to renegotiate the royalties so my source and I get a cut—"

"Hang on, what?"

She held up a spidery finger. "Hear me out. Alternatively, and this is my personal favourite, you forget that little book you're writing for Phoebe and sign up with me instead."

"You want me to write a book for you?"

"God no! Who reads books these days?" She mock snored again. "I want *us* to do a series of articles—gripping, revealing, extraordinary articles and really string it out." She winked. "And believe me, you will want to string this one out. It's a whopper!"

Roxy sat back and digested all of this as Maria rattled on.

"Then, after that, sure, you can chuck a book out. Why not? But, again, I'd need a cut, so would my source. Best of all, no matter what, we wouldn't need to get permission from Ms Van Beurden. We can do what we like, so it's a win-win for everyone! Well, except her of course, and Horowitz, but let's leave him out of it for now."

Roxy's eyes were practically slits in her face. It all sounded very dodgy, and she smelled a rat. A big fat one. "Why don't you just take your *information* and get your source to write his own story, run it whenever you damn well like, permission or not? Why bring it to me?"

"Because I'm giving you a break, Roxy."

"Why bring it to me?" she repeated, and now Maria shifted in her seat, trying to feign nonchalance.

"Because you already have half the story, you might as well get the full enchilada."

Roxy sighed. "One last time, Maria. *Why me?*"

"Goodness, aren't you Ms Paranoia!"

Roxy groaned and went to stand up; that's when Maria held a palm out.

"Okay, don't get all snippy! The truth is we don't quite have all the facts. It will need a little, shall we say, *investigating.*"

"Again, why don't *you* do all of that? Or did you sack all your investigative reporters last month?"

"Because I know you have a hard-on for mystery, Roxanne Parker, and can't walk past one without sticking your big schnoz in. It's what you do. You're very good at it. You solve this one, it's a boon for all of us. Besides, you have just the right contacts."

"Phoebe's not interested in—"

"I'm not talking about Phoebe."

Roxy chewed on her lower lip, unsure what was happening or what she should do about it. "You're going to need to give me something, Maria. I can't just promise you a cut. How do I know you're not bluffing?"

"I guess you won't know unless you agree to my deal, but I promise you, this information will crack the story wide open."

Roxy felt like cracking her head wide open. This was so typical of Maria. *It was all too clandestine for her liking, too underhanded.*

"Goodness, Roxanne, no need to look so worried. I'm throwing you a bone here. Hell, I'm chucking the whole skeleton at ya!"

"More like a bomb," she muttered back.

"Trust me, sweetie, what I'm offering you—this information I have—is amazing. You will thank me later. I know it."

Roxy rubbed her head, which was still pounding like a jackhammer. She wasn't strong enough for this conversation. Not right now. She sighed and scooped up her handbag.

Maria frowned. "I thought things were grim up north."

"They're grim everywhere, you said it yourself, but not grim enough to sell out my client, or my agent for that matter." She got to her feet. "Thanks for the coffee. Oh, hang on, you didn't get me a coffee."

"Well, if you change your mind, you know where to find me."

"I won't be changing my mind, Maria. My only client is Phoebe Fisher, and she only wants to show how well things have turned out. She's not even remotely interested in finding her folks, and neither am I. So you'll have to take your little bomb and detonate it elsewhere."

Maria was smirking again as she watched Roxy walk out. She knew the ghostwriter well, and she figured she'd be back. Roxy hadn't just caught the bomb Maria had lobbed at her, she had a hunch it was now exploding through her brain.

CHAPTER 24

"What do you think she *means*?" Roxy asked Gilda just half an hour later after she had fled Maria's office and headed straight for her friend's apartment.

She found Gilda nursing her own hangover, still in baggy pyjamas, a stack of copied pages on the coffee table in front of her sofa, a half-eaten block of chocolate in her hands.

"She's winding you up," Gilda said, holding out the packet. "Need a sugar hit?"

Roxy shook her head. "But what if somebody out there does know where the parents are now? And does have vital information?"

"What information? Who is this mysterious information-wielding person, and why haven't they come forward sooner? Why go to a gossip tart like Maria? Why not the police?"

"I gather he wants to make money out of it."

"Then why not take it to a publisher? She's just playing you, Roxy; it's what she does."

Roxy ignored that for the moment. "How could he possibly know where the Fishers are and not say something after all these years?"

"Your question relies on a faulty premise: that Maria

is telling the truth. We all know she's full of crap, especially when it comes to you. She's a manipulative schemer."

Roxy sat down and thought about that. "I don't know. She's slippery, sure, but she's also smart and she wouldn't waste her own time unless it had some merit. She left me a stack of messages, even called Oliver to track me down, and she hates Oliver. I think this is serious, or at least she thinks it is."

"Why doesn't she just hire one of her staffers to look into it?"

"Says I have the right contacts or something."

Gilda held her palms out like she finally understood. "And by that she means you have *me*!" She shook her head. "Please tell me you didn't mention any of this to Phoebe."

"Of course not!"

"Good. Then keep it that way. All it would do is get her hopes up, and it really is sleazy. Some nutter obviously gave Maria a salacious tip-off that's so vague that even she can't be bothered investigating and certainly doesn't want to spend her time and money on it, so she's handed it to the only person she knows who jumps at a mystery at the drop of a hat. She's right about one thing. You are physically incapable of walking past one. You just can't help yourself."

"I'll take that as a compliment, shall I?"

"Hey, I'm equally as guilty and she knows that too. She knows she can drop her little grenade and you'll come straight to me—" She gave her a pointed look because that's exactly what Roxy had done. "And we'll both look into it, whether we're paid to or not. She's wasting your time and mine. Then, if we do uncover something interesting, she gets a cut. It's a total scam."

"I don't know…"

"Just focus on the person who *is* paying your mortgage. Phoebe. Forget about this mysterious stranger and just write the book you're being paid to write." She took another bite of her chocolate, and said, "How is the book coming along?"

"Fine."

"Good, then get that done and get back to your lovely man."

"I didn't think you liked him."

"I like him well enough! At least I know he likes you, and that's more than I can say for Wiles."

Roxy squinted. "Sorry, I did mean to ask. Have you spoken yet?"

"He dropped by late last night. Hammered on the door when I wouldn't let him in."

"That's good."

"Not for neighbourly relations it's not." But she smiled. "We made up."

"Okay, that's even better, right?"

"Again, not for the neighbours. It got a bit noisy."

They both laughed at that.

"So… all is forgiven?" Roxy was talking about Gilda forgiving Wiles, but her friend misunderstood.

"No, he's still furious I went over his head, off on my own tangent. He brought it up again this morning. Told me I was to leave it alone. Said that was an order."

"Ouch. And what did you say?"

"What could I say? As he likes to remind me, he's my boss."

Roxy stared at her and then down at the printouts on the table. "So what's all this then?" She scooped up several of the pages. "Paisley Smith's mobile phone records? Someone's not very good at following orders."

"A little light reading can't hurt," Gilda said, before blowing a puff of air through her lips. "I really wish I could let this go, but there's something strange going on, I can smell it."

"And *I'm* the one who likes chasing mysteries?"

"This is my actual profession, Roxy."

"Tell that to Wiles."

Gilda lobbed a cushion at her head. "I'm serious about this! And if Wiles sanctions me, then so be it. I think your first instincts were right. I don't think it was misadventure or suicide. I think there's more to it. If it wasn't murder, then I think Paisley Smith was driven to kill herself."

"By a violent son?"

"Maybe? I don't know. Yet. But like Bev the boss said, there were secrets in that family, and I intend to uncover them, starting with her phone records."

Roxy glanced at the pages again. "Found anything interesting?"

"Hmmm… There are a few numbers in there that I haven't been able to identify, and Presley Smith is refusing to return my calls, so he's no help. But check out the one at the bottom."

Roxy scanned down as Gilda explained. "It's from a pay phone at the domestic airport. That's the final call Paisley received, just before she upped sticks and took off for Sydney. We know she texted hubby soon after, but *who called her*, that's what I want to know?"

"Has to be somebody old or foreign, who else uses pay phones at airports?"

She groaned. "Now I have to go in and trawl through all their CCTV footage, see if anyone using the phones looks vaguely familiar. Imagine how thrilled Wiles will be when I tell him that."

Roxy winced and dropped the pages back. "Then I'll leave you to it."

As she walked out, she stopped and went to turn around, then stopped again.

"You okay?" Gilda asked, watching her from the sofa.

"Yes, sorry, I'm seeing things." There was something familiar about the phone numbers on Gilda's printouts… "Good luck with your search!" she said and left it at that.

As Gilda continued scanning the phone records, Roxy returned to Lane Cove to roll up her sleeves. Mystery or no mystery, she had a book to write—a genuine, *paid* assignment—and it wasn't going to write itself.

For the rest of the weekend, she planted herself in her stepdad's study and began compiling her first draft. She only had half the story at that stage, but it was a start. She was secretly relieved that Phoebe had begged off the weekend in the end—something about "more problems to sort out"—because it gave Roxy a chance to put her thoughts in order… and her life while she was at it. Between mad bursts of typing, she made a few important calls.

The first was to Sam. "I have a proposition for you."

He jumped at the idea of joining her in Sydney, meeting her mother, and then accompanying her home again.

"I thought you'd never ask. I do have the following fortnight off if you want to stay longer."

"Oh I think a few days will do it." Roxy shuddered at the thought of her mother interrogating Sam for too long. "I'm so sorry. I should have thought to invite you here. I just thought after all your work trips, you'd want to stay put."

"And I do. But I also want to meet your folks. Your mum and *stepdad*, that is." He knew what was what. "I'll get my flight organised, and I'll text you with the details." He paused. "So I gather you told them about the baby idea. Were they shocked?"

"Oh, um, not really," she stammered. "They were fine."

Then she told him she loved him and quickly hung up, wondering as she did so, why she was now lying to both her mother and her boyfriend. And wondering which lie was worse.

~~~

Max got the text and frowned. Typical Roxy. It read, *Busy weekend but I might have some work for you next Thursday if you're free.*

He read the message again, the subtext not lost on him. She was warning him off getting in touch, telling him they could only see each other next Thursday and only as colleagues.

Nothing had changed. Nothing ever would. He reached for his phone and placed the call.

Within seconds a woman picked up. "Hey, Max! I wondered if you'd buzz."

"Can we… can we meet up? I need to see you."

"Sure, honey." There was a slight hesitation. "You really want to do this?"

"I have to."

"Okay, come on over. Just don't forget you need to pay the doorman on the way through."
~~~

~~~

Maria Constantinople had grown impatient, so when the phone finally rang, she scooped it up and barked hello.

"Sorry," the man said. "I have been busy."

"Like you're the only VIP in the village," she retorted. "So I planted the bomb."

"And?"

"And I think you'll find she's very responsive."

The man said nothing for a moment. Then, "Okay, good. And you didn't mention me?"

"Stop panicking. I told you I wouldn't."

Another sigh of relief. "I meant what I said, Maria. My name cannot be associated with this, at least not until… until after. Then I better get what I'm due."

"Oh settle down, you'll get plenty after that. And then some. It will all be worth it in the end."

"Good. Just don't forget why I'm doing this. Don't forget our deal."

"I won't. Now take a chill pill and relax!"

"Relax? Are you serious?" He laughed but it was an ugly sound. "You have no idea who you're dealing with. I just hope you never find out. I just hope to God it's worth it."

He hung up while Maria sniggered at her reflection in the glossy office window.

Oh it's already worth it, she thought, clicking her nails together. *No matter what happens with Roxy, I've got the story of the decade! Two decades, in fact!*
~~~

CHAPTER 25

The sun was just sneaking through the blinds very early Sunday morning when Gilda got the call. She answered it half-asleep but was wide-awake within moments.

"A body? Where?" She listened for a little more, dropping her head into her chin as the man on the other end spoke.

Oh damn it, she thought. *Damn it, damn it, damn it.*

She looked up, her head aching from another late night, then glanced at the radio clock and said, "Pick me up on your way. I'll be ready in ten."

Fifteen minutes later Gilda was directing Wiles back to the highway from her house, and the fastest route down to Gerroa, keeping the conversation neutral the whole way lest she scream out the words, "I told you so!"

Two hours after that she was balancing precariously on a jagged, oyster-covered rock, looming over the body, one gloved hand on her hip, the other holding out a soggy driver's license.

She didn't need the ID, however, to know whose body it was. Despite the broken bones and smashed, blood-splattered face, it was very clear that this was Presley Smith, the grieving husband, now gone to meet his wife. At least that was Flannery's assessment.

Gilda turned and stared up the craggy cliff towards the houses at the top, narrowing in on a nondescript weatherboard structure sitting in the premier spot.

It made for quite an impressive diving board.

"Surfer found the body about three hours ago," Wiles said. "Local lads suspected suicide even before Flannery had ID'd him. Devastated over his wife's death, they think. A specialist medic's coming down from Wollongong now, so we'll know more soon enough." He noticed her stony expression and added, "Of course we won't *jump* to any conclusions."

He was trying to lighten the mood, but Gilda was not laughing. Presley Smith might very well still be alive if Wiles had let her investigate properly, and she had to use every bit of willpower she had to keep that to herself. There was no point starting another argument, and even she had to concede that all the signs pointed to suicide.

"You said it yourself, Gilda, how close the couple were," Wiles said, reading her mind. "How they lived for each other. You heard that from both the son and her boss. He was obviously distraught. He might have been suicidal."

She nodded but all she could think was *How very convenient for Bob.*

The embittered son was finally free to sell his house to the highest bidder. The real estate agents were probably hammering the FOR SALE signs in now.

"Where is Bob Smith?" she asked, and now Wiles was staring upwards.

"Flannery's with him. He'll have to identify his dad,

but after that I want to get the body back to Sydney. I want Vonnie to take a look."

"Tell her to check for handprints on his back."

When the two detectives arrived, Bob was slouched in a white resin chair out on the overgrown lawn at the back of his house, Flannery in a matching chair beside him. Several more were stacked nearby, and a few items of clothing flapped about on a bedraggled clothesline. Elsewhere Gilda spotted buckets of dying seedlings and empty pots that hinted of a gardener who'd given up. Or perhaps it was their life they'd given up on, she thought, as she took the chair Wiles was offering her from the stack.

He helped himself to another, and they sat in a circle for a while, Bob just glaring at the ground as if he hoped it would swallow him up. There was no view of the cliff or the beach from this side, and Gilda guessed he had chosen the spot deliberately, and she wondered if guilt was the motive.

When he finally looked up through his smudged brown curls, Bob's eyes were red and puffy.

"Shall I fetch some teas?" Flannery offered and Wiles nodded.

"Make Mr Smith's strong with extra sugar." He turned back to Bob. "How're you holding up?"

"Oh, I'm terrific." His tone was droll. "Nothing like both your parents killing themselves to make you feel real good about yourself."

"I'm sorry, Mr Smith, I know this is hard. If you'd like, we can come back later."

Gilda shot Wiles a glance but was relieved to see Bob shaking his head.

She leaned forward, eager to get on with it.

"When did you last see your dad, Robert?"

He frowned at her. "Just call me Bob. I couldn't pull off Robert if I tried."

She nodded, agreeing with him. "Bob it is then. So, can you tell us when you last saw him?"

He produced a soggy tissue and wiped his eyes. "Um, yesterday arvo. About six, before I went for some beers at the bowlo."

"Bowlo?"

"Bowling Club, down in Gerringong."

"And your dad didn't go with you?" He shook his head. "Were you with anyone? At the bowlo?" He shook his head again. "And what time did you get back?"

She was establishing his alibi, but he didn't seem to notice or care.

"I dunno. About tenish. Went straight to bed. Didn't even realise he was missing until…" He nudged his head towards the house, towards Flannery, she assumed.

"How was your dad, Bob?" Wiles asked now. "When you left him. How did he seem?"

"All right." His foot began tapping and he was staring at the ground again.

The detectives shared a look, and Gilda said, "Did you have a fight?"

His eyes swung back. "What? No!" A pause, and then, "Look, we had words, that's all. Anyway, it was all your fault!"

She glowered back. "How so?"

"You shouldn't've come! Dad was furious you'd gone through Mum's stuff. Said you had no right! Spitting chips at me."

Gilda tried very hard not to squirm as Wiles now

stared across at her.

Bob sniffed loudly. "I told him to get stuffed, he told me I was an ungrateful shit but it's nothing I haven't heard before, and I left. End of story."

An ungrateful shit? That sounded familiar to Gilda. Wasn't that what Beverly said Paisley had called him just a month before she died?

Constable Flannery appeared with a mug of tea and glanced between the detectives. Wiles waved him on, so he stepped forward and handed it to Bob before stepping back. Bob took a few tentative sips, then looked up sharply.

"Is that when he did it, do you think? When he threw himself over? Straight after our fight?"

Wiles cleared his throat. "The forensic team are at the scene now, and there'll be an autopsy, we'll talk to witnesses, but…" He lowered his voice. "I suspect it happened late last night, mate, or very early this morning, otherwise someone might have found him sooner."

"I just can't believe he did it." A sob caught in the back of his throat. "I mean, I know Mum's death broke him, but I didn't think it'd…" His voice cracked. "I didn't think it'd *kill* him."

"He loved your mother very much," Wiles said. It was not a question, and Gilda wondered if the comment was directed at her.

"It was only ever Mum," Bob replied, his tone now bitter again. "She's all he cared about. Isn't that the whole reason he's lying down there now? Because he certainly didn't care about me! If he did, he might have the courtesy to hang around, make sure I'm okay. You've got to believe me. He didn't give a shit about me."

Gilda nodded, thinking, *I do believe you, and that's what's got me worried.* She suspected it was easier to shove an unloving father from a cliff than a devoted one.

"Any idea what you'll do now?" she asked. "Will you stay? Sell up?"

She was trying to trap him, of course, steer the interview away from suicide and back to murder, but he was shaking his head.

"Told you before, I won't be selling this house. I guess I just stay in this shitty little town for the term of my natural life."

He tipped his untouched tea on the grass and stood up. "Sorry, I… I can't do this now."

Then he walked inside, leaving Gilda feeling very perplexed.

"Why wouldn't he sell, do you think?" Gilda asked Wiles as they drove back to Sydney that afternoon.

They had spent the bulk of the day questioning the locals, traipsing the beach and the cliff top for clues, asking if anyone had seen anything, but there was not so much as a clue worth jotting in their notepads.

Judging from the position of the body, they suspected he had fallen (been pushed?) from a small lookout, imaginatively called Lookout Point, about one hundred metres from the Smith house. It was bordered on one side by a national park and on the other by what looked like a freshly built Greek palace with a thick fence of shrubbery separating it from the public space.

Pity the place doesn't have security cameras, Gilda thought as they knocked on the door in vain. And pity the owners were nowhere to be seen.

The medic had already checked the body and

concluded that death had occurred sometime between 11:00 p.m. and 5:00 a.m., and the tide tables seemed to confirm it. Any earlier or later and his body would have been spotted or washed away.

That left Bob's alibi wide open.

"So why wouldn't he sell?" Gilda asked again, and Wiles glanced across at her, deep in his own thoughts.

"Um, I don't know, Gilda, I guess it's his family home, the only home he's ever known. Didn't you say he was born there? Maybe he wants to die there too?"

"He doesn't seem very attached to the place to me, and I don't get the impression he was very close to his parents either. He seems more angry with them than anything else, and I understand why. If it is suicide—"

"If?"

"Then he'd want to get the hell out of there as far enough away from the parents who deserted him as he can. And I'm paraphrasing Bob there, by the way."

"Everybody grieves in their own way."

"Sure, but tears don't pay the mortgage. He doesn't have a job, lived off his folks. Neither of them are here anymore, so what's he going to do for cash?" She shook her head. "Nah. I think he's either bullshitting us, trying to throw us off his scent and is probably on the phone to realtors as we speak, or he comes into some money now they're both dead."

"You really think the son did this? Somehow drove both his parents to suicide or killed them or something so he could access the will or sell their house?"

She held up a finger. "Multimillion-dollar house, don't forget. And we've seen people do worse for less." She shifted in her seat and stared glumly out the window.

Wiles released a hand from the steering wheel and

reached across to squeeze hers.

"I'm not trying to dismiss your ideas, Gilda, but we need to think logically here." He released her hand to continue steering. "Remember, this is a house he was going to inherit eventually anyway. He had no reason to kill them. He was living there rent-free. Was given spending money, didn't even have to do chores, didn't you say?"

"Yes, but I think the gravy train was coming to a grinding halt. I have both parents on record now saying he was—and I quote—'an ungrateful shit.' Maybe they were calling time on his freeloading and..."

"And what? He forced his mum to sit in a hot car and die? He pushed his dad over a lookout just metres from his house?"

"They did have a fight; he's already admitted that. It makes you wonder."

Wiles scoffed. "No, it makes *you* wonder. It makes me think your friend Roxy is rubbing off on you again. How long's she been in town? A week and you're already grasping at straws."

"Hey, Roxy can't take credit for that. I've always been a straw-grasper."

She offered him a smile, but it was more than that. It was a truce of sorts. And it did the trick.

Wiles said, "I guess it can't hurt to look into it."

She turned to stare at him. "Really?"

"I'm just talking about the will, okay? See if there's a family lawyer and see what he—or she—has to say. Maybe you're right. Maybe there was an inheritance worth shoving your dad off a cliff for."

CHAPTER 26

Monday morning came way too fast for Roxy's liking, and she slapped at her mobile alarm as it woke her up. She hadn't made huge progress on the first half of Phoebe's book and only had a few working days left to complete the interview. She wasn't sure it would be enough. There were still so many questions to ask, so many facts to check, yet it didn't stop her from making another detour on her way to the York Street apartment.

Micky DeSanto arrived at the downtown bank just as she did, and he looked at her with a wary grin.

"You're diligent," he said, and she hoped she could say the same about him.

Despite trying to focus on the book all weekend, trying to ignore what Maria had said, it occurred to Roxy that Gilda Maltin wasn't her only contact.

Micky was a copper once. Maybe he knew more than he was letting on. And if he didn't, maybe his ex-colleague did. Or, here's a thought, maybe one of them was Maria's mysterious source?

"I'm sorry to take your time again," she said, "but I have to ask you this." She crossed her fingers internally and said, "You haven't been speaking to

Maria Constantinople, have you?"

He looked at her blankly. "Maria who?"

She stared back, unsure if he was lying. "Managing editor of a bunch of national magazines." He seemed genuinely bemused, so she said, "Never mind. What about Gary Pollard."

"What about him?"

"You said he moved to New Zealand. Can you narrow it down a bit? I'm keen to chat to him too."

He shook his head. "Maybe Wellington? I'm not sure, sorry. Why?"

"It's something you said, how he had an even crazier theory about the Fisher case than you, but you didn't elaborate. What was that theory?"

He shrugged, his eyes sliding away. "He never told me what it was."

"I'm having trouble believing that, Micky."

His eyes snapped back. "Believe what you want, that's what I do. Helps me sleep better at night."

"What are you talking about?"

He was scanning the streets around them, like someone could possibly still be watching after all these years. "I think Pollard uncovered something. Something big."

"Did you question him on it?"

"A few times, sure, but the truth is I didn't really push it, and he wasn't exactly encouraging me to."

"What do you think he uncovered?"

"I don't know, and frankly I didn't want to know." He glanced around again. "But something, er, *strange* happened in that house, something I still haven't got my head around."

She waited, leaning in.

"Look, Pollard wouldn't say any more than that.

Told me it wasn't worth it and I should just stay out of it."

"Out of what?"

He shrugged. "That's when he got nervous. Real nervous. I began to wonder whether somebody had got to him, some gangster involved in the family's disappearance, maybe? When he vanished soon after, I hoped to God he'd got away because…"

She waited but he'd clamped his lips shut.

"Because the alternative was much worse?" she suggested, and he nodded.

"Maybe Pollard found out too much. Maybe he went the way of the Fisher family. I honestly don't know. But like I said, I didn't want to know. I figured whatever Pollard knew wasn't going to do the Fishers any good anymore, and it sure as hell wasn't going to help me."

"What about Phoebe? Weren't you supposed to be helping *her*? Didn't she have a right to know?"

He waved at someone inside, then turned back again. "Look, I'm real sorry about Phoebe, really I am. Whatever happened to her family, it's tragic, but it's over now. It's done. Nothing is going to bring those people back. All this muckraking, all it's going to do is bring more harm and heartbreak. It's best to just try to forget. To leave it alone."

Roxy frowned. "Is that a suggestion or a threat?"

Micky smiled sadly as he pulled the bank door open. "It's just the words Pollard used before he vanished."

As Roxy made her way to Phoebe's apartment, her brain on overload, her nerves jittery lest she spill any of this to her client, Gilda was heading back to Gerroa but this time with Wiles's blessing. Not that it would have stopped her, she decided moodily, as she continued past the Wollongong exit.

She was going to talk to a solicitor about a will. The Smith's Last Will and Testament to be precise. The problem was she didn't have a clue who the family solicitor was or if a will even existed. There was no central will registry in the state, and Gilda could find no evidence that the Smiths had lodged one with any of the private services online or the practicing solicitors in the local area. And as Bob wasn't returning her calls, she had little option but to drive south again and ask him in person.

Which brought a fresh new problem. The Smith house looked deserted when she arrived.

Gilda hammered on the door and called out Bob's name, even tried dialling his mobile number, but there was no ringing sound coming from inside, so at least he wasn't skulking in a closet. Perhaps he'd gone for a surf, she thought, then dismissed it just as quickly. He seemed too slack for that, far too apathetic.

Then she had a thought. It cheered her up enormously.

Gilda didn't need Bob. She knew someone else who didn't like to gossip but did it anyway.

Beverly Wendt was just finishing with a customer when Gilda walked into the post office, and she quickly waved her to the side, her face drawn.

"We just heard about poor Presley," she said. "It's just dreadful! We all wish we could have done more!"

"That's why I'm here, actually. Can we have a quick chat?"

She nodded. "Just let me get Dean to take over."

Once Dean was ensconced in her place, Beverly buzzed Gilda through to the back of the premises to a poky meeting room. They each took a seat, and then Gilda produced her notepad.

"I'm having trouble contacting Bob Smith and—"

"Oh my! You don't think he's also…" She couldn't finish that sentence, and Gilda quickly shook her head.

"I'm sure he's fine." Actually, she had no idea if that was true, but she needed Beverly to stay focused. "I just need to ask him a question, about their family solicitor, if there is one. We're trying to track down her final will. You don't happen to know…?"

She trailed off as Beverly was shaking her head.

"Sorry, we weren't that close, Paisley and me. If there was one, she never mentioned it."

Damn it, Gilda thought for the second time that morning.

"But she did use the bank on the corner, the building society across from the fried chicken place, same as me," Beverly continued, and Gilda looked at her puzzled. She added, "It's just, well, they might know more. Maybe she kept the will in a safety deposit box there?"

Gilda smiled. "Of course!" *Why hadn't she thought of that?*

She thanked Beverly and then handed her a card as she was escorted out. "If you do happen to see Bob or hear from him, could you give me a call?"

"Yes! I do hope he's okay."

"I'm sure he's fine," Gilda repeated, thinking, *But if I'm right about all this, that won't last long.*

Five minutes later, Gilda was introducing herself to a

teller at the front of the Wollongong Building Society, a 'small bank with a big heart.' Ten minutes after that she was being offered a seat in a plush meeting room. It was a lot plusher than the one at *Australia Post*.

"The manager, John Fazelle, won't be long," the woman told her and left her to it.

Five minutes after that a young man strode in, taking Gilda by surprise. He was the antithesis of your stereotypical bank manager, with sandy coloured, windswept hair, a suntanned face, and hefty biceps straining beneath his regulation bank shirt. He looked to Gilda like he might be more comfortable managing the surf.

"I wondered when you lot would be in," he said, pulling out a chair across from her and slapping a file on the desk.

"Oh?"

"Yeah, we heard the shocking news about the Smiths, and I've gotta confess even I took a quick review of the lease"—he glanced down at the folder—"just to make sure it was still in order."

"Oh yes…," said Gilda, not quite sure what he was talking about but playing along anyway. "And it is?"

"Yeah, yeah, all good, nothing changes, nothing at all. We're not about to boot Bob out, so he can rest easy. The home lease is for the term of his natural life, not just his folks."

Term of his natural life? Where had she heard that phrase before?

"It's all part of the original agreement set up by my predecessor," the young man was saying. "I mean, I get why Mr Smith would like to sell." He whistled. "Bloody top spot he's got there. Best surf on the coast if you ask me, and he'd make a killing. My dad reckons you couldn't give the place away twenty years ago, but it's real estate gold now so…" He opened the file and glanced down at the contract inside. "Anyway, as you know, it's not his to sell."

"That's right," she said, thinking, *How would I know this? What am I missing here?*

The manager was closing the file again as if the conversation was done, so she took a punt and said, "Just to clarify, if you will. Why exactly can't Bob sell?"

The bank manager bat his blond eyelashes a few times. "Because you own it, of course."

"I do?" Now Gilda was the one blinking rapidly.

He chuckled. "Not *you* obviously, but New South Wales Police." Registering her surprise, his smile began to evaporate. He looked down and back. "You… you did know that, right?" He wasn't smiling anymore.

"Are you saying the police department actually owns the Smith house in Gerroa?"

Fazelle's tan had evaporated, and he was rubbing two hands across his face. He looked like he might pass out. "Please tell me I didn't just let the cat out of the bag?"

Gilda leaned forward and smiled. Oh yeah, the cat was well and truly running free. She just didn't know what kind of cat it was or why it was in the bag in the first place.

She brought out her notepad and said, "So, *John*, you've been most helpful. What else can you tell me?"

CHAPTER 27

Wiles couldn't quite mask his annoyance as he walked into his office to find Gilda sitting at his desk, staring at something on his computer screen.

"You can't be there, Gilda." He indicated the seat and she jumped up.

"Sorry, I was checking a few things while I was waiting for you."

He frowned as he closed the door behind him and circled around the desk. "I've told you before, we need to keep things professional at work. You can't just—"

"Hey, I was in your chair, not your lap." She couldn't remember the last time she'd been *there*. She shook the thought away and said, "Listen, I have extraordinary news."

No sooner was the information out, Wiles was shrugging like he didn't think it was extraordinary at all. He took his seat and placed his fingers, steeple-like at his mouth.

"So, let me get this straight. The Smith's bank manager told you that the police force *owns* their house? Outright?"

She nodded gleefully. "And they lease it back to the Smiths—just Bob now of course—for the term of his natural life. Extraordinary, right?"

"What were you doing talking to the Smith's bank manager?"

Gilda's smile deflated. "I think you're missing the extraordinary bit—the Smith house is owned—"

"By us, yes, I did get that. What I want to know is why you were even talking to the Smith's bank manager when I specifically asked you to interview the family lawyer." He held his fingers out. "Don't answer that. On second thoughts, I don't think I want to know."

"I couldn't find the lawyer, couldn't find Bob either, for that matter. So I spoke to the bank manager, hoping he might have their details, but he didn't. Or he wouldn't say. After letting slip about the lease, he went all quiet on me. There's something seriously strange going on though. I suspected it from the start. This proves it."

"All this proves is that the Smiths don't own their own house and you can't follow orders. Although I already knew that."

"But why would *we* own the house?"

He paused. "There are reasons."

"Such as?" She already had a hunch, but she wanted to hear him say it.

"The Force does have residential assets, Gilda, nothing surprising there. It's clearly part of the portfolio. Maybe it's been flagged as a potential future police station..."

"A quiet street in a small village with a killer outlook? Give me a break. And it still doesn't explain why the Smiths have been given the right to live there."

"Maybe it was obtained under the proceeds of a crime act and they're just renting it out to the Smiths."

Okay, that made a tiny bit of sense. "But why would

they get to live there for the 'term of their natural lives'?"

"They could be victims of crime. Maybe they sued the force for some reason and it's part of their compensation."

"What crime? What lawsuit? I've spent the past hour processing their names through the database, I even Googled their names and guess what? Nothing. I mean, there are a million Smiths, of course, and don't get me started on Bob Smith, but there's virtually nothing on a Paisley or a Presley Smith of Gerroa. I did find a couple of similarly named Canadians, but no one of the right age living down the southeast coast of Australia. It's like they don't exist, at least not online, which in this digital age has to be a miracle in itself. Which brings me to the next reason the NSW Police Force might own their house. The *obvious* reason."

Wiles held his hand up like a stop sign, his eyes darting back to the door. "Don't even say it, Gilda. Do not utter the words."

"But—"

"I'm serious." He leaned forward and dropped his voice. "I don't know what you've stumbled into, Gilda, but I'll take it from here, thanks. That means do nothing. Don't drive down south, don't keep poking your nose in—"

"Poking my nose in? Are you serious, Wiles? Isn't that my job? *Our* job? To poke?"

He cocked his head to one side, looking at her like an impatient parent. "Just leave it with me. Please."

She glared at him and crossed her arms as he rifled through his desk, producing a memo and handing it across.

"I know things have been very quiet. I know

you're bored—"

"Bored? You think I'm doing this because I'm *bored?*"

Her voice had risen, and he glanced towards the closed door again, his own tone much softer. "Just use this time to boost your skill set." He thrust the page in her hands. "This is a three-day IT training course. Fully paid for. Bit of fun, and you get your IT skills up. Might help next time you do a Google search."

She stared at the page and back at him. *Really? He was shoving her off to school?*

"What's going on, Wiles?" He looked at her, expressionless. "Why do you want me off this case?" She sat forward. "You've been trying to douse me down since about day two. What do you know that you're not telling me?"

He rolled his pretty blue eyes. "Just call the number at the bottom. Trinie Baker. Great girl. She told me there's still some free spots. You can start tomorrow."

Gilda stood up, huffed, and went to storm out, then turned back. "I cannot believe you, Wiles. I've just brought you something amazing, and instead of thanking me, you're pulling me off this case? Why?"

Wiles leaned back in his chair and closed his eyes briefly. When he opened them again, he looked weary.

"What do you want me to say, Gilda?"

"I want you to stop treating me like a junior subordinate and be honest with me! I want you to tell me why you're pulling rank, when you've never done that to me before. Never."

He stared at her but said nothing.

She shook her head. "I want to hear you say it, Wiles. I want you to confirm what I already know, what blind Freddy could see. It's the reason you've suddenly gone cold."

Now he was crossing his arms, barely meeting her eyes.

She shook her head, then lowered her own tone as she said, "The Smiths were in witness protection, weren't they?"

CHAPTER 28

Lorraine's face lit up like a sparkler when she opened the door to Gilda, and the younger woman wondered whether Roxy's mum was finally warming to her or if she was getting better at faking it.

"Good to see you again, Mrs Jones. Is Roxy in?"

Lorraine leaned in and offered a soft cheek to kiss. "Good to see you too, Gilda. Yes, she's just back from her interview. You'll find her up in the guest bedroom, pretending to work."

"Thanks. I'll find my way up."

Gilda discovered Roxy lying on her childhood bed, her head in a Swedish crime novel.

"Hard at it, I see," Gilda said as Roxy scrambled to hide the book, thinking it was her mother.

"Pretending to be," she said, laughing. "I'm just trying to unwind. Mum thinks I'm working."

Gilda smiled. "Pretty sure she doesn't." She stepped across to the window seat and dropped into it. Then jumped up again, too excited by her news to sit still.

"You okay?" Roxy asked.

"I've uncovered a secret about the Smiths that you simply won't believe."

"Don't tell me! They're double agents, working for the Russians!"

Gilda stared at her. "What? No! This is serious, Roxy." She took a breath, waited a beat. "They were in a witness protection program!"

"What?" Roxy hadn't been expecting that.

Gilda's face clouded over. "At least I'm pretty sure they were. Wiles won't confirm it—infuriating! I think he's the one who's been lying to me, not Bob. I can't believe I blamed Bob for the death of his parents, but now… wow, this changes everything…"

Roxy pushed the book aside. "Sit back down, Gilda, and let's see if we can get some sense out of you."

Gilda did as she was asked, telling Roxy about her trip down south and exactly what the bank manager had told her, followed up by her strained conversation with Wiles.

"He's been acting strange since the start. I wonder if he found out early in the piece and has been trying to get me off the case. Now I know why Bob says he won't be selling the house. Turns out it wasn't his to sell. Not strictly speaking anyway. The police own it and obviously moved the Smiths into it."

"But why?"

"Who knows? They might have been police informants, or they might simply be innocent bystanders who witnessed a crime and have been in hiding ever since."

"What kind of crime?"

"Don't know, but they might not even have been witnesses, yeah? They might just be closely related to the witness and have been moved for their own safety. Especially if the case was never resolved."

Roxy chewed her lower lip as a tiny bell began to

tingle in the back of her head. "So they're probably not from Gerroa?"

"Doubt it, no. They would have first been taken to a hotel somewhere or a safe house, some secure location, and then placed in the house in Gerroa, which might have been purchased for them or already part of the department's portfolio. It makes sense now I think of it—safe houses usually are in out-of-the-way places, sleepy villages. They wouldn't have been able to tell a soul. They would have been given new identities, a full backstory."

"Smith's a nice common name."

"Exactly! They probably got to choose their first names, and I've seen her house. She adores paisley print; no wonder she chose that name. And him? Maybe he was an Elvis Presley fan, I don't know, but it certainly explains why Paisley—or whatever her real name is—babied her son. She was obviously just protective, as you would be, hiding out from danger."

Roxy felt the bell tingle again. "How long do you think they've been there?"

"At least twenty-three years. Bob was born there, remember?"

The bell quietened as Gilda added, "Protected witnesses usually live in multiple locations, get moved around a lot, so I can only assume that Bob's birth changed that."

"But why would they still be in hiding after all this time? Surely the case has come and gone through the courts?"

"Maybe the criminals got off, but the Smiths' lives are still at risk. Even murderers can get out eventually and wreak revenge. The irony is—and I've seen this plenty of times before—the criminal gets his freedom while the poor witnesses stay locked away in their hidden world forever. Makes you wonder who's really being punished."

Roxy cocked one eyebrow. "I saw that view. I walked their beach. Doesn't look too punishing to me."

"Maybe that's why they insisted on staying there? Look, it's all guesswork on my part. That's the thing. It's a very closed, secretive world."

"And Wiles won't tell you anything?"

"Don't think he could even if he wanted to. But it doesn't excuse his secrecy! I am supposed to be his partner, in both senses of the word. Why couldn't he be honest with me?"

"You really think he's known from the start?"

"All I know is, the only reason I found out is because the bank manager's a spring chicken with a big mouth. But we know their mortgage was taken care of, and they were probably put on welfare until things settled, then their jobs might even have been found for them."

"The postal jobs, that makes sense. But what doesn't make sense to me is, if they were whisked away in the dead of night and relocated, and it's all top secret, why didn't someone say something? Surely their friends and any other family would have been wondering where the couple went? There would have been missing persons reports with the local police."

"Maybe there was. Or maybe that was kept under wraps."

"Okay, but the media would have been onto it. There would have been stories, Gilda. I mean, this is around the time Phoebe's family vanished, after all. Someone might have linked the two." She stopped, eyes wide. "I wonder if they had a dog?"

"Didn't see one."

"But you wouldn't. It'd be long dead by now…"

Gilda looked confused, but Roxy's inner bell was clanging loudly now. She cocked her head to one side and said, "I can't believe you haven't worked it out, Gilda! Around the same time that Phoebe's two parents and baby brother go missing, the so-called Smiths suddenly show up in Gerroa—two parents and a baby boy. Maybe even a dog called Bouncer?"

"What are you saying?"

Roxy's eyes were bulging now. "I'm saying, I think you just found Phoebe's missing family."

CHAPTER 29

As Gilda struggled to get her head around that, Roxy's brain was buzzing with excitement. She loved nothing more than a good mystery and believed she had just solved one of Australia's greatest.

"Think about it!" she said, her eyes darting across her friend's face. "The Fishers must have gone into witness protection! It makes perfect sense! It explains how they could have vanished so quickly, so easily, so *completely*, without a single trace. They would have had a lot of help packing, moving, changing their identity. How else do you just vanish overnight?"

Gilda listened to that carefully, her brain working overtime, but it didn't take long to push the pause button. "It's a great theory, Roxy, but it doesn't add up."

"Spoilsport!" Roxy spat back. "Why?"

"Hey, don't get me wrong, I *wish* it was true. It would be amazing if it was, but let's look at the facts." She produced a finger and held it up. "For starters, Bob was born in Gerroa, remember? Didn't you say Phoebe's brother was five when they went missing?"

"Nobody remembers their birth. Bob's parents

could easily have lied to him about that or he could be lying to you. You should check the birth records with the local hospital."

"There wouldn't be any. Bob said it was a home birth."

"Well, how convenient is that?"

Gilda held up a second finger. "There's also the minor matter of Bob's age. He's twenty-three. That makes him *two years* younger than the Fisher kid."

"Or so he thinks! Maybe his parents lied to him about his age too. Again, it wouldn't be hard to fake a young kid's age, especially a boy. They're usually immature for their age."

"Okay, then I have a third point, and you're not going to like it." She gave Roxy a moment to brace herself. "There is no witness protection program I know of that would take three out of four family members—and their dog no less—and leave a vulnerable child behind. One the criminals could kidnap for leverage to get the other three back. Who would do such a thing? It just wouldn't happen."

"Could it have been a mistake? The family were whisked away for whatever reason, maybe Micky D was right and they had some info on some underworld figures back then and poor Phoebe really was forgotten. By the time they worked it out, it was too late."

Gilda looked at her, almost with pity. "They would just squirrel her away to join her parents the minute they realised their mistake. They were just two hours down the coast! It's nonsense!"

"Still," Roxy said, the idea exploding. She loved this idea and wanted to cling to it for as long as she could, but slowly, annoyingly, she began to realise that Gilda was right. Phoebe was the sticking point. There was no way they would leave a ten-year-old behind. It made no sense. She had no other family to take her in. Although…

Roxy clicked her fingers in the air. "It could explain why Margie took the kid under her wing! She knew they'd botched up and felt sorry for her or was protecting her or something."

Gilda snorted. "So now *SuperMeans* is in on this botched operation? Ridiculous, Roxy. Margie's not a babysitter. She was the nation's top detective at the time! And again, remember, this was twenty years ago. Surely at some point they would have reunited the child with her family? Nope, the parents are either long dead or horrendous human beings who abandoned their daughter. There is no other explanation."

Roxy scowled. "I like my explanation better."

Gilda smiled. "I know you do, Roxy, and it would make a terrific ending for your book, but this is real life. Even if it were true, there'd be no happy reunion for poor Phoebe anyway. If they really are her parents, they're now both dead, remember?"

"Knowing how Phoebe feels, she'd probably dance on their graves. But you know, it might explain why they both killed themselves. Could be guilt."

"What, after twenty years, guilt finally catches up with them? That's a bit of a—" She stopped, held a hand to her lips.

"What?"

"I can't believe I've been so stupid!" She jumped up. "I've been so excited by the witness protection theory I haven't thought this through."

"What?"

"I don't know if the Smiths are really the Fishers, let's just leave that aside for now, but if the Smiths really were in witness protection then you have to wonder, *who* were they hiding from? And has that person finally found them?"

"You think Paisley and Presley were murdered by some third party?"

Gilda wasn't listening now; she was rifling through her oversized handbag looking for her phone.

"Who are you calling?" Roxy asked when she pulled it out.

"Bob." Gilda scrolled through her contacts. "If the Smiths were in witness protection, that means Bob's life is also in danger."

Ten minutes later, Gilda was glaring at her phone. "Ring, you blasted thing!" She'd left multiple messages for Bob, trying to sound calm, and her concern was growing with every second.

"You really think he's next on the hit list?" Roxy asked.

Gilda shrugged one shoulder. "He was nowhere to be seen when I dropped in there this morning, and he hasn't answered his mobile all day. I mean, he's a millennial; he's supposed to be glued to that thing!"

She began pacing Roxy's room. "They were *obviously* in witness protection; there's no other explanation for why the police would own their house or none that I can think of. And now two of the three are dead. And the other one's missing."

"Maybe he's been moved to a new location?"

"I hope you're right. I really do." She stopped and put a hand to her mouth. "I wonder if my investigation has put his life at risk? He did blame me for his dad's death. Maybe he's right."

"Who else did you tell this to?"

"No one, apart from you and Wiles."

"Did Wiles make enquiries?" Gilda didn't know. "Or maybe the bank manager alerted the witness protection people about his gaffe and that's what triggered it."

"Again, I can only hope," Gilda said, heading for Roxy's door.

"Where are you going?"

"Back to Gerroa. I need to find Bob."

"Now?"

"Not now," Gilda scoffed. "I'll go in the morning."

"What about Wiles?"

"What about him?"

"Won't he be furious?"

"So? Bob could be in danger, I think Wiles's fury pales in comparison."

As Gilda took off, her mind galloping ahead, Roxy reached for her book but could no longer focus. She dropped it back down, jumped up and took over from Gilda's pacing, her mind returning to her witness protection theory and whether the Fishers really could be the Smiths and vice versa.

If you could get past the niggling issue of Forgotten Phoebe, it sort of, kind of, *almost* made sense.

It certainly explained why Micky's partner Gary Pollard suddenly clamped up and then vanished. Micky said Gary had a secret he refused to reveal. Perhaps he had also stumbled on the truth and was ordered to stay quiet? Or worse, put into witness protection in New Zealand for his own safety?

Roxy thought of Maria then and wondered whether that was the bombshell she was about to drop. Was that why she wanted Roxy to investigate? Because she knew of Roxy's friendship with Detective Inspector Gilda Maltin and knew that the only one who could probe deeper was someone on the inside? A cop?

She scowled and threw herself on the bed. Gilda wasn't going to be much use. She had already dismissed Roxy's theory and was a little preoccupied right now. What's more, if Gilda couldn't get Wiles to 'fess up, how on earth was Roxy meant to uncover the truth? Witness protection meant secrecy at an extreme level, a super secret if you will.

She jumped up. SuperMeans! Of course! If anyone knew the truth or had the contacts to uncover it, it was ex-Detective Chief Superintendent Margaret Means. She just had to work out a way to broach it without having her head bitten off…

CHAPTER 30

It was the penultimate interview with Phoebe, and while Roxy was keen to tick off all her remaining questions, she simply couldn't get Gilda's revelation out of her head. Yet the detective was right. It wouldn't be fair to mention anything to Phoebe until she had triple-checked all the facts. That's where SuperMeans came in.

Roxy had texted her client overnight, begging her to invite her adoptive mum to join them for the interview.

"I just want to get an idea of how great you are together."

It was a lie, of course. What she really wanted was the complete opposite—to separate the pair and get Margie all to herself. And she knew just how to do it.

No sooner had Phoebe welcomed her in and whisked her out to join Margie on the balcony when Roxy asked for a beverage.

"Of course," Phoebe said. "I'll grab you a coffee, two sugars, right?"

"Actually, I'd love a smoothie if you've got one."

"Smoothie?" Phoebe's left eyebrow twitched.

"Yeah, I haven't had time for breakfast."

"Oh, right. I think I could pull something together. I have some bananas and some strawberries—"

"Perfect! And maybe some toast if you have it?"

Margie went to get up. "I can do that for you, Phoebe, if you want to get started—"

"Actually I need to double-check some spelling and stuff with you, Margie"—Roxy interrupted her—"if you don't mind?"

Margie's lips drooped downwards, and she returned to her seat.

As soon as Phoebe had closed the separating screen doors, Margie said, "So, what's the big secret?"

"Sorry?"

She exhaled impatiently. "I wasn't a top detective for nothing, Roxy. Smoothie, indeed. You're trying to distract her. What is it you need to ask?"

Roxy smiled. Gilda was right. Nothing got past *SuperMeans*.

She took the closest seat to her and said, "I know I'm not being paid to solve the mystery but…" She hesitated, trying to decide how to play it. "Well, I heard an interesting theory about Phoebe's parents, and I wanted to pass it by you."

Margie's eyebrows rose ever so slightly. "A theory? From whom?"

She shook her head. "You might have been a good detective, but I'm a good journalist and we never reveal our sources."

The woman drooped her lips again and said nothing.

"I was told there might be a chance that Phoebe's parents went into witness protection." She waited a beat, but Margie was just staring across at her, as if waiting for the punch line, so she said, "If it is true, I don't expect you're going to confirm it to me. I know how these things work, but I do think Phoebe has a right to know, don't you?"

Margie surprised Roxy by nodding. "Of course. If it was true." She blinked at Roxy. "You can't possibly think that's true?"

"It does make a weird kind of sense."

"I don't see how." Margie sat forward. "Shall I explain to you how witness protection works?"

She shook her head. *Gilda had already done that.* "I know—they never leave a child behind."

"Actually, sometimes they do have to separate families."

"Really?"

"Sure, but in those rare cases, the best interests of the child are always paramount—that's enshrined in the Family Law Act—which usually favours some ongoing contact with the parents. And I can tell you this, Miss Parker, Phoebe has never had so much as a postcard, let alone a phone call." Roxy frowned as she added, "Besides, most families transition back to the real world eventually—assimilation is paramount to the success of the program—but, well, I haven't heard from Karen and Shane, have you?"

The older woman scoffed at Roxy's burgeoning scowl. "Don't beat yourself up," she said. "That's one of many theories that did the rounds in the early days, and it's not the silliest one I've ever heard. It would explain how they managed to vanish so easily, but even if it was a major clerical error of some kind, there is one other problem with it."

"Oh?"

"Me, of course! Even if the Force had stuffed up and abandoned the poor child, I would have found out about it. I would have been told, and I would have corrected everything. I mean, I was no fan of Shane and Karen, I've told you that, but..." Her frown returned suddenly. "You haven't mentioned this theory of yours to Phee?"

Roxy shook her head no.

"Please don't. It might get her hopes up, and I won't see her disappointed again. I won't."

"Duly noted," Roxy said, feeling a deep despair. It really was such a neat solution. If only it all clicked into place. "Can I ask you this then, since we're being so candid with each other? Why *did* you take Phoebe in? Really? Why did you give up your career for a child you barely knew?"

For just a split second Margie looked annoyed, but then the mood shifted again and she sighed. "You're not the only one who thought I was crazy."

"I don't think—"

"I did it because it was the right thing to do, Miss Parker. Because what was the point of being in the Force if I didn't do what was right?" Margie's voice was louder and a little shaky, a rare show of emotion, and she checked herself, dropping her voice again. "Listen, I can see you need some convincing, so I'm going to try to explain. Off the record, yes?"

She glanced inside, then back at Roxy, who was nodding.

"After it happened, when no family or friends stepped up, I watched that little girl get shipped off to foster care. The Department had no option but to put her in the system, and it worried the hell out of me, to be frank. It was as though she would be doubly punished for her useless parents." She sighed. "You have to remember, foster care was a very different beast back then. We didn't have the best checks and balances. There were a lot of creeps knocking about, people fostering for all the wrong reasons. I heard rumours about the foster family she'd been sent to, and frankly, I was worried—"

"Who was it?"

"I'm not naming names!" She sounded outraged. "But I can tell you this. A year later that family was struck off the carers' list, and six months after that the father was indicted on child pornography charges. I shudder just thinking about how close Phoebe came to… Well, anyway, I took her in. I had to rescue her from that."

Now Roxy was sitting back in awe. "Okay, wow." Now it made more sense.

"Phoebe clung to me that day her parents vanished," Margie continued, her eyes fixed somewhere on the horizon. "She would not let me out of her sight. She was in deep distress, and it ripped my heart out to see her taken away. I had to help her. Or what was the point of my career? Of everything I had worked for? I had to step up."

"Here we go!" came a singsong voice from the doorway, and Margie snapped her eyes to Phoebe, who was holding a frosty glass and a plate of toast, and continued talking as if she'd been shooting the breeze.

"So it's been a wonderful twenty years, Roxy, and Phoebe's been a delight from the start."

Phoebe cocked her head and laughed. "Liar! I was a little brat, but you wrestled me into shape."

They all laughed at that and, as Roxy consumed her second breakfast for the day, Margie and Phoebe swapped stories about each other until Margie finally held a hand up and said, "It's time to leave you young things to it. Don't get up ladies, I'll see myself out."

As she got to her feet, she turned to Roxy and gave her a warm smile, her tone light, her voice steady.

"Just don't forget, Miss Parker, I get to see the *entire* manuscript before it goes to print."

It was a threat, of sorts, and they both knew it.

~~~

Gilda was starting to get weary of the road to Gerroa, as scenic as it was, and she suspected Wiles would have a conniption if he knew where she was headed—in the opposite direction to the training course she'd promised to attend—but what choice did she have?

If she really had stumbled on the truth—if the family really were in witness protection—that put the Smiths' supposed suicides in a whole new light. Every single thing needed to be reexamined. Starting with Bob.

Gilda didn't know if the son had been moved to a new location, but she had to find out. Maybe her queries had been the catalyst for Presley's death, or maybe it was irrelevant, but either way she had to look out for Bob. And for all she knew, he could still be in that house on the cliff, avoiding her calls, oblivious to the danger.

She glanced at the car's dashboard clock. It was close to 9:30 a.m. now. Her training course would be kicking off. They would be clicking on their name tags and beginning the introductions—"Say your name, where you're from, and tell us something interesting about yourself!"

Hello, everybody. I'm Gilda Maltin. I'm from the Homicide Division, and I'm incapable of following orders.

She hoped Trinie, the trainer, wasn't a Goody Two-shoes who'd chase her up with her boss.
~~~

And she hoped her boss would forgive her in time, although, if truth be told, it didn't bother her as much as it should. She was far more concerned about Bob.

As she took the Gerroa exit, Gilda gave fresh thought to Roxy's suggestion, to the very notion that the Smiths could be the Fishers, but she couldn't make it stick. There were just too many inconsistencies, although… She bit into her lower lip.

Wasn't that what witness protection was all about? Hiding people through half truths and lies?

She gave her shoulders a little shake and told herself it was nonsense. Surely there was no lie large enough to explain why you'd leave a child behind.

By the time Gilda got to the Smith house, she was convinced of two things—the Fishers were not the Smiths, and Bob Smith was in mortal danger. She kept returning to the words his father used at the mortuary that day. How he told her that life had not been rosy and how his wife would never go to Sydney, and certainly not alone.

"You bastards are lying to me! Why are you lying?" he had bellowed.

Gilda assumed it was the grief talking, but now she had to wonder. Did Presley have a good reason to distrust the police? Is that why he called it a "setup" the next time they met, why he said there was something fishy going on?

"Paisley wasn't leaving me, and she was not suicidal!" he'd said. *"She was murdered, that's all there is to it!"*

And then he'd gone oddly quiet, like he'd said too much, and Gilda had sensed a secret, just as Beverly Wendt had. Was *this* the secret? Was this family in hiding from some Sydney-based criminal who had finally tracked them down? A shiver ran through Gilda's body as she recalled Presley's final words, words she was now determined to disprove.

"You will never find the truth, young lady. Don't waste your time."

As she hammered loudly on Bob's door, not so much as a creaky floorboard answering back. Gilda felt her stomach drop.

Come on, Bob, she thought. *Please be in there. Just open the door!*

"You right, love?" came a crackly voice from the other direction, and Gilda swept around to see an elderly lady standing in the front garden of the house next door, a wilted rose in one gloved hand, a bedraggled straw hat in the other.

Gilda turned and made her way over, producing her badge and introducing herself as she went.

"You live here?" she asked, indicating the brick house behind her.

"Well, I'm not pruning the roses for nothing."

Gilda smiled. *Was everyone in this country a smart arse?* "Do you mind me asking, how long you've lived here?"

"Five years, give or take."

Gilda's heart flagged. Not long enough to know when the Smiths really moved to the area or whether Paisley really did have a home birth.

"I'm looking for Bob Smith. The son. Have you seen him in the past twenty-four hours?"

The woman shook her head. "I heard about his folks though. One of your lot came by a few days back. Poor lad. He'd be off licking his wounds, I'd say."

"Any idea where he might be doing that?"

"Not a clue. Like I told your young lad, they kept to

themselves that mob. Never very interested in socialising and whatnot. I like a neighbourly neighbour, myself. It's why we moved up from Melbourne. That and the weather, of course. We thought it'd be a lot friendlier round these parts. Ana's all right, I s'pose; that's the Greek lady on the other side. Stops in for a chat from time to time; helps me with the washing. But they're not here much, sadly. But this mob…" She nodded towards the Smith house. "Well, they were never rude, not that, and I wouldn't want to speak ill of the dead and all. But they might have been happier if they'd just reached out. Just made a bit of effort. It doesn't hurt to say hello to each other occasionally, does it? You come off as a right snob if you don't bother."

Perhaps they weren't being snobs so much as protecting themselves and everyone around them. But Gilda couldn't say that of course, so she went to thank her when she remembered Roxy's request.

She almost winced as she asked, "Can you recall if the Smith family ever owned a dog? A white Labrador?"

The woman was shaking her head. "I don't think so, my dear. They might have kept to themselves, but I would've noticed a dog. I'm a bit of a dog person. Had a King Charles spaniel myself. Little Bessie. She was a lovely thing. That's what kept us in Melbourne for so long. Didn't want to move her in the end."

"Okay then," Gilda said quickly, keen to move on. "Thanks for your help, Mrs…?"

"Pat O'Connell, dear. Just call me Pat."

"Thanks, Pat." Gilda produced a card and handed it to her. "If Bob does show up, do you mind letting me know? I'm a little worried about him."

"You don't think he might top himself too, do you, love?"

"I just want to make sure he's okay."

The woman looked at her like she didn't believe her. "Right you are."

She turned back to her roses while Gilda returned to the Smith house and then made her way down along the side fence. She had better check the place out properly.

The backyard was empty when she reached it, the washing still flapping about in the breeze, the plastic chairs still in the circle where they'd had left them. It all felt a little desolate and deserted, but then it hadn't exactly radiated life last time she was here.

She strode to the back windows and peered through but could see nothing except the Smiths' sparse furnishings and that ever-present paisley print. She knocked firmly on the back door several times, then waited a beat before moving away, disappointment coursing through her.

Gilda knew there wasn't a police station in Gerroa, but perhaps she'd better go and see Oscar Flannery in the neighbouring town and get him to look in on Bob later. Maybe he'd come home eventually, maybe he'd been moved elsewhere. Maybe he was already dead. Either way, she couldn't keep lying to Wiles and driving all this way to check.

Perhaps it was time to hand this one over. Perhaps it was time to bow out.

As she reached the corner of the house, Gilda took a final glance back, when something caught her eye. She stopped and squinted.

What was that in the far corner of the garden, just poking out through a crop of weeds behind the dilapidated wooden bench?

Gilda made her way across the lawn and past the forgotten pots, then stepped around the bench. She squatted in the long grass and reached for the fireweed, brushing it aside to reveal two crudely cut pieces of wood, tied together with rotting string. It was a bespoke wooden cross with one word scratched into the front, almost faded with age but clear enough to send shivers through Gilda again.

The word looked eerily like "Bouncer."

CHAPTER 31

"What the hell is this?"

Wiles slapped a file onto the desk in front of Gilda, his lips set in a grim line.

She took a deep breath and said, "Hi, boss."

It was her way of conceding who was in charge, but he didn't seem to notice.

"What is that?" he repeated.

She didn't look down. "It's my report. On the Smiths' deaths. My theory."

"I'll get to your so-called theory in a moment. What do you think you're doing? I told you to stay out of it. I told you *not* to go down to Gerroa again. Do you remember that?" She nodded, trying not to frown. "I told you I would investigate further. You… you've written down the words…" He hesitated as though scared of even saying them aloud and whispered, "Witness protection. Do you know what you're playing at? How dangerous that can be?"

"Two of the Smiths are already dead, Wiles, it doesn't get much more dangerous."

"It does if you're Bob Smith."

"I'm worried about him."

"As you should be! But you've just made it official,

revealed some intelligence that until now was classified."

She sat forward. "So they really were in witness protection?"

He ignored this. "And why, for the love of God, are you linking this to the Fisher case? What were you thinking?"

"It's just a theory."

"It's fantasy! Absolute fantasy! Where's your proof?" He nodded at the file. "A dead dog called Bouncer? That's it?"

She shook her head. "Actually it's more than that. The timing is suspiciously similar, the makeup of the family. I'm just saying, we need to investigate further."

"Investigate? A family in witness protection?"

"A *dead* family now, or at least two out of three of them are, and if we're not careful, it'll be the trifecta."

"And this!" He slammed a fist on the file. "This is being careful?"

Gilda recoiled. They'd been bickering a lot lately, but his aggression surprised her. She had never seen him so angry, and she was used to cranky bosses. Gilda had always been a rule breaker, and Wiles had once found that amusing. She guessed those days were over.

"You may very well have jeopardised that young man's life. If Bob Smith turns up in a body bag, you can pat yourself on the back."

"Wiles!" she said, aghast as he drew in several deep breaths.

He rubbed a hand across his goatee, then yanked out the seat in front of her desk and dropped into it.

"Why can't you just follow orders, Gilda? Why is that so freakin' difficult for you?"

She offered him an apologetic smile but knew better

than to say anything. He needed time to calm down, to remember she wasn't the enemy, despite her reckless behaviour. Because he was right, she had been reckless. Bob's life may very well be in danger, and her inquiries would not have helped.

Eventually he said, "About the Fishers." She nodded, still staying mute. "Even if I agreed with you, and I'm not saying I do, your theory is absurd. There is no way the Fishers are the Smiths. Witness protection would never—"

"Leave a child behind?" she offered. "I know, that's what I kept coming back to." She sat forward and lowered her voice. "But maybe, just maybe, for whatever reason, they *did*."

"There is no reason, Gilda. The few times when children are separated from parents—and it's a last resort—they keep in touch, the matter is swiftly resolved, everything goes back to normal. There's nothing normal about the Fisher case. I've got kids. I know how things are. There is no way the parents wouldn't reach out to her eventually. It doesn't make any sense."

"Maybe Mrs Fisher did and that's why she's dead." She held a hand up as he began to speak. "No, listen; hear me out. Phoebe could be the reason that Paisley was in Sydney that day. It's where she lives. Maybe Paisley looked in on her daughter secretly quite often, or maybe it was a one-off, I don't know, but whoever she was hiding from might have seen her and that's how she ended up dead."

"Gilda, need I remind you that when it comes to Paisley Smith, there is no evidence of homicide. No signs of coercion or violence. She sent her husband what appears to be a suicide note for God's sake!"

"Or was it a confession? Think about the note, what did it say? *'I'm sorry. I have to do this. I hope you will understand.'* Maybe she was telling Presley that it was time to approach Phoebe, to tell Phoebe everything."

"Why now? After twenty years, why suddenly catch a dose of the guilts?"

Gilda smiled. "I think the book brought her out from the cold."

"The book?"

"Roxy's book." He groaned loudly but she held a hand up again. "Phoebe's autobiography has had a bit of press; the story's back in the news. Maybe that's what started all this, what triggered everything after all these years."

Wiles had stopped groaning. Encouraged, she rattled on. "Maybe Paisley went to see Phoebe, to finally confess, and was spotted by the very person she'd been hiding from. Maybe they kidnapped her and somehow fabricated the suicide. I'm not sure about that part of it."

"That's a truckload of maybes, Gilda. You haven't even got to Presley's death yet."

"His is the easy one! Whoever killed Paisley must have checked her ID, learned where she lived and confronted Presley at the lookout that night. Pushed him over. Which is exactly why we have to keep this case open. I don't know anything about witness protection, but I do know homicide and both deaths could be homicide. I think we have to look closer."

"No, Gilda, we don't." He sighed heavily now and leaned forward in his chair, shaking his head. "I told you before, this is beyond us. I don't have the authority to look into it, let alone get the answers you want. And you certainly don't."

"Why not? Why can't you look into it?"

"Ahh! You are so infuriating!"

"I am?" She bat her eyelashes, pretending to flirt, but he wasn't taking the bait.

"I knew this would happen. I knew this would be a problem."

"What?"

He rubbed his goatee, shaking his head. "If you were any other officer, I'd have your badge by now. Our job was to look into Paisley Smith's death. The coroner has confirmed it's 'suicide or misadventure.' I've just spoken to Vonnie, and she's going to make the same finding for Presley. Whatever their motivation, whether they really are hidden away in witness protection, suicide is not a stretch. The social impact on program participants is well documented. Who wouldn't be depressed, living in hiding? Even if you are right about the book, that's even more reason to take your own life. The story was coming out again; how much more could they bear?"

Gilda sat forward. "So you do agree the Fishers are the Smiths?"

His hand was back up, like a stop sign. "I didn't say that, and it's out of our hands. You need to stop meddling."

"*Meddling?* Is that what you call investigating these days?"

"Gilda…"

"You're like a scared old man," she said, her voice rising despite her best efforts. "What happened to the curious guy I used to admire? I had a crush on you for years. You were such an extraordinary detective. Now…" She frowned. "What happened to you?"

"I got promoted! I'm head of Homicide, Gilda."

"So?"

"So, I don't answer to you, I answer to the Director of Crime Operations and…"

He didn't finish that sentence, but she took it as an admission of sorts. "You've been told to shut this down, haven't you? I knew it. You're deliberately derailing this investigation."

"Don't be ridiculous."

"And now you're lying to me."

"Gilda, I just want to come in, do my job, get paid, and go home again."

She looked at him with horror. "Well, I don't! I still have some spirit and some bloody gumption. And I want to find out what happened."

"You want to rock the boat."

"Yes, if it means uncovering the truth, and I don't care whose toes I step on to do it. And I'm disappointed that you don't." She exhaled. "Look, I don't know what's going on with us or even whether I care anymore. But I can't do this without you, and so I'm asking as a colleague, as a fellow detective, not as your"—she pointed from him to her and back again—"whatever it is we are these days. *You* can find the answers. You have the contacts. You could find the truth if you wanted to."

"Well, I don't!"

He stood up and strode across the room, then turned abruptly and strode back, leaning down and across the desk towards her.

"This is really easy for you, Gilda. You still think it's all a lark. But I've got two mortgages to pay now and two kids to finance. Have you seen the size of the house my ex-wife just bought? Maybe when you grow up and get some responsibilities, you'll understand."

Gilda's jaw dropped; she didn't know how to answer that.

He straightened up. "You're going to leave this case alone, that is an order. You will not be rocking the boat, and neither will I."

Gilda blinked up at him, incredulously. He didn't seem threatening now, just pathetic.

She shook her head sadly. "Then don't rock the boat, Wiles. Whatever you do, protect your lovely salary and keep paying your lovely mortgage, because it's about all you'll have to keep you warm at night."

CHAPTER 32

The moment Gilda walked into Peepers café, Roxy knew she had struck gold. There was a glint in the detective's eyes, and she could barely constrain her smile as she made a beeline for Roxy's table. But she also looked weary, and Roxy was tired too; she'd done an all-nighter on Phoebe's book but was keen to hear Gilda's news so agreed to this early catch-up.

Sometime in the past twelve months Roxy had morphed into a morning person, and sunrises didn't freak her out quite as much as they used to.

"Bob had a dog, didn't he?" Roxy said, one step ahead as Gilda closed in.

"Better than that," Gilda replied, pulling out a seat and dropping into it. "The dog's name was Bouncer."

Roxy squealed, catching the eye of the patrons around her and causing Gilda to place a finger at her lips.

"It's classified. I'm *this* close to being fired." She indicated an inch with two fingers. "In fact, if I hadn't been sleeping with my boss, I'd be gone already." The glint had vanished. "We had another fight."

"Oh honey. I'm sorry. Are you okay?" She shrugged.

"It must be hard going out with your boss."

"Especially when he's so damn straight." She paused so they could order breakfast from the passing waitress, then said, "He didn't used to be like that. But…" She was lowering her voice again. "I think he knows the truth and has been silenced."

"By whom?"

"Federal Police, probably. They oversee the program. Think about it. If the Smiths really are the Fishers, then what an almighty stuff-up, leaving a ten-year-old to fend for herself! No wonder he's scrambling to shut it down."

"And no wonder Maria looks so proud of herself."

"Hang on, Maria Constantinople? What's she got to do with any of this?"

"Don't you remember? She told me she has some secret information about the Fisher family and where they are now. Said it would blow the story wide open. What if her source—whoever that is—knows something about all this? That could be what she's hiding."

Gilda looked queasy. "If Maria knows, the whole world will know."

Roxy was shaking her head. "I don't think so. I mean, Maria might have some inkling, but she doesn't have the whole story, certainly not enough to run a giant exposé. If she did, it'd already be front-page news. She's obviously got a few pieces of the puzzle but not quite enough, which is why she came to us."

"Still, I'd better alert Wiles. Whatever the truth is, they will have to contain it."

"You really think Wiles is hiding the truth from you?"

"Maybe. Probably. I don't know." She grimaced.

"I just wish he'd be honest with me. He's my partner!" She deflated into her seat. "Oh who am I kidding? We're not partners, never were."

"Come on, Gilda. You guys make a great couple."

"No, not really." She paused as two frothy lattes were placed in front of them. "We've been going out a year, Roxy, a full twelve months, but we're still sneaking about like school kids. I'm keen to bring it out in the open, but he keeps shutting the door—in every sense! He doesn't want to tell his kids, he doesn't want work to know. Why are we even bothering?"

Roxy reached out and squeezed one of her hands. "I'm sorry, honey. I didn't realise. But it could be worse. You could be going out a year and your partner already wants to chain you to the kitchen sink."

"Sorry?"

Roxy shook herself out. "No, I'm sorry. You've got bigger fish to fry."

"No! Tell me! *Please!* I need to think about something else or my head will explode."

"Well, I'm not sure this is going to help but…" She sighed again. "Sam wants to have a baby."

Gilda nearly choked on her coffee just as their matching poached eggs arrived.

Roxy smiled. "Don't worry. I haven't agreed to anything, but I'm not getting any younger, and I don't know, it might be nice."

"*Nice?* Roxy, having a kid is not *nice*. It's full on! It's farewell sleep-ins and bye-bye catch-ups with your BFF."

"I don't get those now anyway! We're up early every morning feeding the animals, walking Lunar. I've become a morning person, and I barely recognise myself! And it's not like I ever see you."

"Whose fault is that?"

"It's no one's *fault*, Gilda. It just is." She forked some egg in her mouth and chewed glumly for a while. "It just makes me realise that life has moved on and maybe it's time for us all to move on with it."

"What does Max say?"

"I don't need Max's permission to have a baby, Gilda. He doesn't get a vote in this."

"We all know which way he'd vote if he did." Gilda stared at her food gloomily, her appetite lost as she thought about Max and their recent rendezvous. "You've got two gorgeous men fighting over you, and I can't even get one to hold my hand in public."

Roxy shook her head just as a text came through from Phoebe. "Sorry," she said after reading it. "We still have so much to tick off. Says she's free now if I am."

"Then go! Finish that damn book."

"I haven't even finished my breaky." She pushed her half-eaten eggs aside, then pulled some cash from her purse and stood up. "Are you going to be okay?"

"Of course! I'm a survivor, you know me."

Roxy leaned in and gave her a hug. "So what do I do about Maria? She's left me a thousand messages."

"Nothing! Do not speak to her. Leave her to me."

"Okay, and what about Phoebe? What do I say to her about the Smiths?"

"Again, nothing! Wiles is right about that at least, a few dog bones don't make a case. Besides, if it is true, it needs to be presented to her carefully, with all the facts in place. You can't say a word, Roxy. Promise me!"

"All right, settle down. I agree with you. The poor woman's had enough shocks for one lifetime." She grimaced. "Speaking of shocks, Sam's flying in to meet my mother tomorrow, God help us. So Caroline's trying to get the girls together for a final drink at Pico's tonight. About sixish. You up?"

Gilda lifted one shoulder half enthusiastically. "It's not like I'll have a hot date or anything."

Roxy smiled. "I'll remember to bring my violin along."

Roxy had never been a great keeper of secrets, and as she worked her way through the final questions with Phoebe, she struggled to stop herself from bursting out with the words: "I think I found your parents!"

The fact that they were now dead was one reason to shut right up. The realisation that she might have it all utterly wrong was another good one. So she kept it to herself, but Phoebe clearly sensed something.

During their lunch break, as they sat eating takeaway sushi, Phoebe said, "Are you okay, Roxy? You don't seem quite yourself today. A little preoccupied."

"Oh, I'm fine," she lied. "I just want to make sure I get everything I need, that's all. This is our last official interview, after all."

"Mmm, but there is this amazing invention they call a telephone, even better ones called email, WhatsApp, Skype…"

Roxy feigned surprise. "Oh, they sound helpful!" She laughed. "I try not to hassle my clients after the interviews are done, otherwise it can drag on forever."

"I'd rather you hassled me, Roxy, then get something wrong. Now, shall we get back to it? I will need to end right on the dot tonight." Phoebe was checking her watch as she pushed her sushi plate aside.

"Another crisis?" Roxy asked.

"No, my darling James is taking me out to dinner."

"Lovely. Where will you go?"

She shrugged and her face clouded over. Now it was Roxy's turn to ask, "Are *you* okay?"

"Yes! Well… I don't know." She gave Roxy the once-over. "You don't have children, do you?"

Roxy was surprised by the subject change and said, "No. Why?"

"Oh, it's just… Look, I probably shouldn't be saying this, and please don't put this in the book, but James wants to have a baby."

Roxy feigned surprise. "I thought you said that wasn't happening."

"I did. He agreed. But now he's had a change of heart." Her left eyebrow crinkled again. "I don't know what's happened to make him change his mind, but I'm still not sure. Why haven't you had kids? If you don't mind my asking?"

Roxy almost blushed at that. "Oh, just haven't got round to it, I guess. My partner wants them, I'm just not sure yet. I mean, you really have to be into kids, right?"

"Exactly! That's what I said and… after my childhood, I just don't know…"

"What are you worried about?"

Now she was blushing. "It's silly really. I just… Well, I wonder whether I'll be as bad as *them*." She blushed deeper. "What if it's hereditary? What if there's more of those people in me than I realise?" Phoebe had shrunk back into the couch and was chewing her nails, her usual confidence now evaporated. She looked less like a PR princess and more like a frightened child. "What if…," she began, "what if I have an evil streak in me too? What if I do something terrible to my own child?"

Roxy gasped and reached across the couch to grab her hand. "You'd make a terrific mum!" she told her, but even she had to wonder.

What had Phoebe's parents done to vanish so completely? What murky world had they belonged to? Even if her theory was correct and the Fishers had become the Smiths, she still didn't know why they were in hiding. What had happened to make them flee in the dead of night, and why did they leave young Phoebe behind?

Something extraordinary must have gone down. Something so extraordinary they could never come back.

As she placated the usually unflappable Phoebe and pulled the interview back on course, it occurred to Roxy that there were still so many questions about that *fateful day*, and neither of them was likely to get the answers they wanted, the answers that would help Phoebe sleep better at night.

CHAPTER 33

It was close to drinks time, and Gilda was trying to determine whether her new strappy dress was a little too strappy for Pico's dingy wine bar, when the doorbell rang. After peering through the peephole, she slapped a frown to her face and swung it wide.

Wiles was standing outside, a bottle of champagne in his hand.

"That better be bloody French," she said, turning to leave him standing there.

Wiles smiled and followed her inside, then through to the bedroom where she continued getting ready.

"I'm meeting the girls," she said. "I haven't got long."

"This won't take long." He placed the bottle on the bedside table and sat down on the edge of her bed. "I'm sorry about yesterday. You were right about one thing. I was being overly cautious. I wasn't doing my job."

Gilda was now standing in front of the vanity, applying makeup. She stopped and stared at his reflection in the mirror. That was quite a confession, but she wasn't ready to fall into his arms just yet.

"But you weren't right about everything," he added,

bringing back her frown. "I wasn't playing you, Gilda, or lying to you. I knew nothing about witness protection before you mentioned it, and nobody had asked me to shut it down."

"So why then?"

"Because I know how these things work. *Witness protection*, Gilda! Do you have any idea what a can of worms that can be? It's way above our pay grade and a really dangerous part of policing. People don't go into protection because they witnessed a misdemeanour, you know."

"So, what? You were protecting me?"

He looked abashed. "I know you don't need protecting, and I know it was stupid of me, but I just wanted a chance to look into it discreetly, and sorry, but you're about as discreet as a foghorn."

She smirked now, but he had a point. "And?" she said, reapplying some mascara.

"It's murky, Gilda. Very, very murky. And it's not strictly witness protection."

She turned to face him, mascara brush in hand. "It's not?"

"Well, it is and it isn't. The commissioner who oversees the program on behalf of the NSW Police Force is being very evasive, and I'm not sure if that's protocol or if he's genuinely clueless. The inside word, however, is that they are witness protection, but there's nothing official. No paper trail."

"Isn't that how witness protection works though?"

"Yes and no. I mean, there's always some trail, some link, certainly back to the commissioner, but the only name I can find—and don't even ask me how I got it—is a Nowra detective called Bob Ingram."

"Nowra? That's down near Gerroa!"

He smiled. "Don't get excited. Ingram's now dead. And don't let that excite you either, he was a chronic smoker; lung cancer took him about twelve years back. I'm struggling to unravel any more than that. Apart from one very shady source, I can't get confirmation that he was even on the Smith case."

Gilda smacked her freshly glossed lips together and turned to face him again. "Maybe that's where they got their name for their boy?" she said. "Bob?"

"It's a pretty common name, Gilda."

"Okay, so what about the Fishers then? Can we link them to the Smiths?"

"If there is a link, I can't find one and nobody's saying, not even Mr Shady. But then they wouldn't, right? It's witness protection. The truth may never be revealed."

"And what about Maria Constantinople? Did you investigate her source? She might know more."

Gilda had called Wiles earlier that day, alerting him to what Roxy had said, but he was now shaking his head.

"Doreen went to see her this arvo," he said. "Thinks the woman's bluffing. Says she's just trying to get an angle but doesn't have anything conclusive."

Gilda's eyes narrowed. She didn't trust Maria at all and wondered who was bluffing whom. If she had to put money on it, she'd be betting on Maria.

"So what happens now?" she said, sitting down beside him. "And don't tell me to leave it alone. I have to find the answers, Wiles. We must be able to link the two, and not just to prove a point. I can't help thinking if the Fishers really are the Smiths, it's not so much about what they witnessed or who they were hiding from, the real question—the *real crime*—is why did they leave Phoebe behind and never get back in touch? At the very least, that question needs to be answered. Somebody allowed that to happen, and they may just be the biggest criminal in all of this."

"I agree."

"You do?"

"Yes, I've had a quiet word to internal affairs. If—and it's still a big if—the Fishers are the Smiths, then what happened to make them desert the kid? How did that even come about? How was that allowed, and if it was an accident, how was it not rectified? Somebody must know."

"What if that somebody is now buried with sooty lungs?"

"Then we keep digging."

Gilda stared at him. "Whoah. The boat's really rocking now! Aren't you scared you'll lose your fancy promotion?"

"Okay, I deserved that." He smiled sheepishly again and took her hands in his. "I miss you Gilda, I want us to work."

"I do too, but not like this. Not the way it's been." She pulled herself free and stood up. "I know I'm fabulous, darling"—she followed that up with a grin—"but I'm not getting any younger and I'm sick of all the subterfuge. I want a man who'll stand up for me. Who'll stand beside me. Who'll take me to Pico's and introduce me to his kids and brag about me to his colleagues. I know that can't be you, I know that."

"I can try, Gilda."

"I don't want you to *try*. I want what Roxy's got."

"What's Roxy got?"

"She's got a man who desperately wants her baby."

"You want a *baby* now?" He looked stunned.

"No! I couldn't think of anything worse. The point is I want a man who *would* have a baby with me, if I wanted one. Which I don't."

"Thank God," he said, then realised how it sounded and added, "I'm sorry, Gilda."

"Yeah, I'm sorry too. But I'm grateful you're looking into this case. I know you're going out on a limb for me, and I appreciate it."

"But it's not quite a baby, right?"

She reached down and kissed him lightly on the lips. "Let me know how you go."

Then she plucked the unopened champagne from the table and handed it back.

"You gave up a bottle of Veuve Clicquot? Are you *insane*?" said Caroline as they sat sipping glasses of Australian sparkling wine at the bar soon after.

It was a good drop, but it wasn't top shelf.

"You're missing the point, Caro," Gilda snapped back. "I thought Wiles was Mr Right, but who was I kidding? He was barely Mr Okay. Why am I so bloody hopeless at this relationship thing?"

"Oh darling," Caroline said. "I can get you a new man in minutes."

Both Gilda and Roxy snorted.

"What?" Caroline said.

"I don't think she wants a new man, Caro. She wants the *right* man. And, no offence, but you're not exactly an expert at that."

Caroline humphed. "And *you* are? Miss 'I love you, Max! I hate you, Max! I love you, Sam! I don't know if I want your baby!'"

Roxy's jaw dropped, and she glared at Gilda, who

looked suddenly contrite.

"You were late. We got chatting."

"Gossiping more like."

"Well, I think it's charming," Caroline said, now taking both women by surprise.

"You do?" said Roxy.

"Yes! I think this will finally give Max the signal he needs." She took a sip from her glass. "I'm sorry, Roxy, you know I love you, darling, would *adore* you as my sister-in-law, but I love Max more. You've been avoiding him since he got back, and his heart has been smashed enough. It's time to draw a line in the sand."

"She can do that without falling pregnant to another bloke!" Gilda retorted but then added, "She's right though, Rox. Max is seriously screwed up, and I'm not sure how much more of him I can take."

Roxy frowned. "What are you talking about?"

"He's been dropping in to see me late at night, boring me senseless with endless chatter about you—should he keep trying? Should he leave you alone? Poor bugger's been paying me for my time with the finest Swiss chocolate and single malt, but it doesn't make it any more palatable." She rolled her eyes. "Honestly, it's like I've got *Bold and the Beautiful* on a loop. I think it's time to cut him loose."

Roxy scrunched her eyes and sighed. "You're right. I know you're right. I *have* been avoiding him, but what else can I do? I was perfectly fine when Max was in Berlin. I met Sam, I was happy, we were discussing babies and a future. Then Max returns, and suddenly I'm full of doubts." She opened her eyes and held her glass out for a refill. "I don't want to be full of doubt! I want to be happy again. I'll just have to keep my distance."

"Aren't you meeting him tomorrow for the shoot?" Caroline said and Roxy flinched.

"Yes, but that's purely professional. I just hope Max realises that."

So did Gilda. She needed an early night and wasn't up for another boozy episode of her favourite soap.

CHAPTER 34

Max Farrell didn't look at all dramatic or depressed when Roxy pulled up in front of Phoebe's childhood house the following day. In fact, he looked both happy and professional. He already had his tripod set up, a camera attached, and was gesticulating with one hand as he conversed with a short, plump woman standing beside him. She had long black hair and bright red glasses on.

"Mrs Woo?" Roxy said as she walked up.

The woman turned around. "Oh hello! You must be the author? Roxy Parker? Your photographer here has been explaining shutter speed to me. I'm afraid it's beyond my 'leetle grey cells'."

Max laughed, offering Roxy a smile. "How were your drinks last night?" he said, no trace of irony or hurt or the fact that he'd been crying into Gilda's lap.

"Good, yep, great," she replied, turning back to Mrs Woo. "Thank you so much for letting us do this."

"Not at all! I was most excited to get the call. It's not every day your house gets to be in print."

"It's not exactly *Architectural Digest*, Mrs Woo."

She giggled. "Still, it's very exciting to me. I love a good mystery. I'm a big fan of Agatha Christie!"

"You don't say? So you never had a problem with the history of the house?"

Mrs Woo was giggling again, oblivious to the pain that at least one person had felt there. "I think it gives it an edge! I love it! So, what pictures do you need to take?"

Roxy turned her attention to the house, which Max was now quietly photographing, adjusting the lens from time to time, zooming in, then getting a long shot. He looked up at the question, awaiting Roxy's response.

She said, "I guess that depends how much has changed. We're really only interested in the house from a historical point of view. I know the exterior looks fairly similar, but I'm keen to see how much of the interior still reflects the day Phoebe's family vanished."

"Oh no, then you will be disappointed," Mrs Woo said, her tone now mollified. "We are doing renovations, but it has been renovated before. As you can see, the old garage has been turned into another bedroom and… well, come in, I'll show you."

Roxy glanced at Max, who turned and gave her another smooth smile. "Go ahead. I just want to get a few more out here, then I'll grab the lights and see you inside."

"You need a hand?"

He shook his head and returned to his camera, so she followed Mrs Woo, who was now waiting at the open front door.

As she stepped inside, Roxy kicked herself for not bringing Phoebe along. She knew it would be unpleasant for her client, but she still wished she'd thought to ask. Who better to know what had changed and what had remained the same?

Roxy had a basic idea of the home layout, but the

place looked very different to what she'd imagined, and as they walked between rooms, Mrs Woo confirmed this.

"The last owners moved the kitchen from the front of the house to the back, added that extra bedroom and then knocked out a few walls in the living room. We want to put at least one back, make it a little cosier."

Roxy nodded, taking notes. When they got to the dining area, she stopped and stared. The back wall had been stripped and sanded, but she caught a busy pattern underneath layers of paint.

Mrs Woo giggled. "Along the way, somebody had wild taste!" She pointed to what looked like the remains of stripped and fading wallpaper. "Who would want to paper a dining room in paisley?"

Roxy's eyes were bulging now. She knew of at least one woman, and it made the hair on her arms stand on end.

"Are you okay, Parker?" asked Max, appearing beside her. "You look like you've seen a ghost."

She wrapped her arms around herself and nodded. "That's exactly what I've seen." She turned to him. "Can you take a photo of that for me?"

"Sure." He went to set the tripod up in the doorway, but she pointed at the far corner.

"I need a close-up of that peeling paint and the paisley wallpaper underneath. It's not for me, it's for Gilda."

He looked bemused but knew better than to ask questions and did as instructed while Roxy followed Mrs Woo, who was continuing her tour of the house, oblivious to what she'd just unveiled.

Annoyingly for Roxy, there were no other signs that

the Smiths might once have lived here, but Roxy now felt exhilarated, eager to finish the job and talk to Gilda.

"And here is my backyard," Mrs Woo was saying as she opened the laundry door that led out.

"I don't think we need to go out there," Roxy said.

She had already scoped the back, and there wasn't much to see—just a boring rectangular space and a few droopy palms.

"It is dull," Mrs Woo agreed, "but we're going to fix all that. Turn it back to what they had originally. I can't believe they took it out!"

Roxy went to enquire further when she heard Max call from inside. She excused herself and headed back.

"I've taken a quick snap of each room. Do you want me to focus on anything else?"

She shook her head. "I think that will do it, but thank you. Oh, and can you do me a favour and get that close-up to Gilda? You've got her mobile number, right?"

His eyes narrowed, wondering if she knew about his secret rendezvous with her bestie, but she just bat her eyelashes innocently so he nodded and said, "Want to grab a bite to eat after this? Promise I won't jump on you this time."

Roxy's heart dropped. "Sorry, Max, I can't."

She had to collect Sam from the airport soon, but she didn't want to tell him that. She wasn't sure if it would make him feel better or worse. And she wasn't exactly sure how she felt about it either. He shrugged like it didn't matter anyway and began packing up his camera as Mrs Woo approached.

"Any chance I can get some prints of the photos?" she asked Roxy. "I'm making a scrapbook of the house, a record of before and after."

Roxy nodded, then thanked her for her time and stepped outside to put a call through to Gilda.

"I'm at the Baker Street house now," she said. "Phoebe's old place. And I've spotted something on the dining room wall that you are going to want to see."

"Should I come over?"

"No need. Max will text the image to you soon. Show Wiles. I think it's going to blow you both out of the water."

"What is it, Roxy? Tell me!"

She laughed. "Just you wait, it'll be worth it, I promise." She noticed the time and frowned. "I've got to go. I've got to stop at Olie's and drop the last of the tapes in for transcription, then I'm picking Max up from the airport, and I'm running late."

"Max or Sam?" Gilda said and Roxy smacked her forehead.

"Sam, I meant, *Sam*. I'm picking Sam up. Shit!"

Gilda laughed. "You better get Max out of your head, honey, before the plane lands."

~~~

Max was the furthest thing from Roxy's mind as she pulled her car through the turnstile at Sydney's domestic airport that afternoon. Sam didn't get much of a look-in either. Now that she was there, all she could think about was poor Paisley Smith and her hot, tortuous death.

She'd made good time, and there was still ten minutes before Sam's flight landed. Instead of parking on a shady lower level, Roxy kept circling up and to the top of the car park. She wanted a good look at the place where Paisley had perished.
~~~

Was this also the place of Karen Fisher's demise?

It was now early afternoon, and as she drove slowly across the top level, her windows down, she could still feel the intensity of the heat shimmering up from all that bright cement. Roxy shuddered.

What a way to die.

Looking around, she could see no trace of the horror that had unfolded just last week, no fluttery remains of police tape, so she circled back and then downwards, parking undercover and noticing as the temperature dropped ever so slightly inside the car. She parked, locked her vehicle and bolted for the arrivals lounge.

Sam was just striding through the doors when she got there, and he spotted her first, waving then rushing up.

"God, I missed you," he said, dropping his carryall and pulling her into a hug.

Roxy melted into Sam's chest and reminded herself his name was not Max.

"How was the trip?" she asked, pulling away eventually.

"Boring, actually." He brushed a hand across his stubble. "But I think I finally nailed Sudoku."

"Good, you can show me. I'm useless at that stuff. Come on, let's get out of here quickly, or we'll have to remortgage the cottage to pay for the parking."

He laughed, grabbed his bag and followed her out.

By the time they got across the Sydney Harbour Bridge and into the lower north shore, Roxy had caught up on Sam's news and given him a brief précis of Phoebe's book. She omitted all mention of the Smiths and witness protection. Gilda had sworn her to secrecy, and it would only complicate the conversation. Besides, she needed the extra time to prep Sam for her mother.

She needn't have bothered.

As soon as they parked in the driveway, Lorraine came flying out to greet them, Charlie close behind, and she almost pulled Sam out of his seat to swamp him with a hug.

"I'm so delighted to finally meet you," she said when they were settled in the living room with cold drinks. "I'm glad you could find the time. I know you're very busy with your fly-in-and-fly-out work."

Roxy pulled Charlie aside and whispered, "Who is this person and what has she done with my mother?"

He laughed. "She's just happy you've found yourself a lovely man." Roxy rolled her eyes. "You can't blame her, Roxanne. She wants to see you settled, then she can stop worrying about you."

"She doesn't really worry about me that much, does she?"

"Of course she does! She's your mother, she worries you'll be on your own for the rest of your life, and I guess we won't always be here for you to turn to."

"Why? Where are you going?" He gave her a look that said *Be serious*, and she smiled. "She worries about your lack of commitment, Roxy. It's become a bad habit, one I'm hoping Sam can break."

Roxy nodded but was not sure to whom he was referring—Lorraine or herself.

By the time dinner was done and the couple were left to themselves, sipping the last of their wine in the backyard under a hazy moon, Lunar firmly parked at Roxy's feet now, Sam turned to her and said,

"You never told me your mother was so lovely."

"She's not! I have no idea who that woman is, but I do hope she hangs around for a while." She smiled. "I think she's just excited by the idea that you might actually make an honest woman of me."

"Yeah, about that… I didn't think you *wanted* to get married. I was a bit confused why she kept asking about the date and the venue. I nearly told her I'd check your ovulation schedule and that a home birth would be nice."

Roxy stared at him, openmouthed. A home birth? *Really?* She decided to let that one go for now and said, "Sorry, Mum misunderstood the situation, and I didn't have the heart to correct her. She's an old-fashioned creature, and I'm not sure she'd cope with the idea that we'd be having a baby out of wedlock."

Let alone in a remote cottage, she thought, shuddering to herself.

"So we are then? Having a baby?"

Roxy tried for a smile, but she honestly didn't know.

He frowned and dragged her closer. "Look, Roxy, I thought we were on the same page with this, but obviously we're not. Every time I mention it, you go all quiet. I don't want to foist this on you. I'm older than you, so I'm ready, but you have to be ready too. You have to be one hundred percent into it. This is a big deal."

"I know, and I… I'm just not sure."

He stood up. "Then we don't do it. Not until you are." He reached down and kissed her on the lips. "I might take Lunar for a quick walk before bed. Looks like we need some bonding time, and I could do with the fresh air."

"In Sydney? Good luck finding any!"

She smiled as she watched them depart, but her heart was feeling heavy again. She'd never seen her mother so happy, and she knew Sam was the perfect partner. Would make a perfect dad. But he was right. She had to be fully committed to the idea, or it just wouldn't work—for him, for her, for any future child.

She thought then of Phoebe and wondered about last night's dinner with James. Had he convinced her to have a baby too? Or was he now as disappointed as Sam? At least Phoebe had a legitimate reason to use the handbrake—she'd had a traumatic childhood—but what excuse did Roxy have?

Chewing on her lower lip, Roxy frowned and wondered why she thought she even needed one.

CHAPTER 35

Gilda stood before the large whiteboard, chewing on the end of a blue marker pen.

"Impressive," came a voice behind her, and she turned to see Wiles standing at the doorway to the conference room.

She glanced back at the names and arrows she'd scribbled and said, "It's a tangled web, but I think I can make it work."

He closed the door, then stood beside her. "Okay, talk me through it."

Grabbing a plastic ruler from the table, Gilda pointed at the words "Family #1."

"So," she said, "twenty years ago next month, Phoebe Fisher wakes up to find her parents, Shane and Karen, and her five-year-old brother, Daniel, missing."

"And the dog, don't forget the dog," he said, smirking just a little.

"Oh I haven't forgotten; he's right there in the centre." She tapped the ruler at the name "Bouncer" jotted on the board. "So, maybe they went into witness protection, maybe they didn't. We don't yet know. Cut to the Smiths."

She moved the ruler to the words "Family #2."

"Around the same time, give or take a few years, a similarly aged couple turn up in a sleepy village called Gerroa. They have a young son and a dog called—wait for it—Bouncer." She tapped the name again. "Now this family, we can both agree, *were* in witness protection, although no one's prepared to admit that and the only person who knows is six feet under."

The ruler came to rest on the name Detective Senior Sergeant Bob Ingram/Nowra.

Wiles nodded and took the ruler from her, pointing it back to the word "Bouncer."

"So when it comes to actual evidence, all we've got is a dead mutt, is that correct?"

"Not exactly."

Gilda turned and produced a printed photograph, which she stuck to the board with a magnet. "I also have this."

It was a photo of the paisley wallpaper from the Fisher house that Max had texted across.

She said, "We all know you change names when you go into witness protection. That's standard procedure. Smith's a pretty common name, a classic choice if you want to hide out. So is Bob. But Paisley? That's an odd one. Why would you choose that?" She pointed to the print. "I think Karen Fisher was a big paisley fan and that's where it came from. This picture shows the old wallpaper in the Baker Street house. That print is everywhere in the Smith house in Gerroa. I think it's another link. And I think if we dig deeper, we'll find more."

Wiles made a clicking sound with his tongue and studied the picture closely.

"I don't know, Gilda. I'm still not sure it's evidence of anything other than two families with similar tastes."

Before she could interject, he added, "But what about Bob? If you can link *him* back to the Fishers, you've got your case. Get his DNA, compare it with Phoebe's, and you'll have your answer."

"It's not that simple," Gilda said. "He's still AWOL. But I do have other options, sir."

"Sir?" He laughed. "You haven't called me that in a while." His smile deflated. "Does this mean we've officially broken up?"

Gilda dropped her head to one side. "I'm not sure there was much to break up, do you?" She turned back to the board. She didn't want to get sidetracked. "I'd like to return to Gerroa. Go back and canvass the other neighbours. I only talked to one woman on one side. Maybe somebody has been there longer? Might know exactly when the family first showed up and whether they had a boy and a dog in tow. I don't believe that home birth story for one second, and somebody has to know the truth, even if they don't realise they know it."

"All right then, off you go," he said, and she stared at him surprised. His blue eyes twinkled. "It's not like I'm going to be able to stop you, is it?"

She smiled. "Finally you're working me out. I do think it'd be worth my time. I'd also like to talk to the bank manager again, if I can. At the very least he must know the date they were given the house. It has to be in the lease agreement. Bob says they've been there at least twenty-three years, but if it turns out it was just twenty, well, it makes a lie of that home birth story and it's another solid link."

"Good idea, but Gilda?"

"Yes?"

"I hate to rain on your parade, really I do, but even

if you did prove it conclusively—that the Fishers are the Smiths and vice versa—what are you going to do with that news?"

"What do you mean?"

"People in witness protection have the right to absolute anonymity. It's vital to protect themselves and their loved ones. The commissioner who oversees it has extensive powers to protect them from everyone, including curious detectives and their nosy mates. Even if you did officially connect the two families, you can't say anything to Roxy, let alone Phoebe Fisher."

"Even if it involves murder?"

"Especially then. It's illegal for anyone to reveal the whereabouts of someone in the program, and that includes you."

"You don't think people have a right to know? After twenty years of wondering? You don't think Phoebe has a right to know why her family went?"

"Rights and the law don't always match up, Gilda."

"Tell that to Phoebe and Bob."

The Smith's bank manager did not look quite so relaxed when he sat down to meet with Gilda the second time around, and with good reason.

"Seems I overstepped last time, breaching client confidentiality," John Fazelle said. "I won't be making the same mistake, Detective Maltin, so you're wasting your time. Unless of course you have some kind of warrant?"

She shook her head. "I don't want to put you in an awkward position, John, but I am most concerned about Bob Smith's safety. Both his parents have died under, frankly, suspicious circumstances. He's gone missing from the house, and I really need to find him. I just have one question for you, and then I'll be on my way."

The manager's eyes narrowed, like he was trying to decide if she was tricking him again. "I may not be able to answer it."

"Let's give it a whirl, shall we?" Gilda crossed her legs and took a deep breath. "I know you can't say anything more about the Smith's, er, *unique* housing situation." She didn't dare use the words "witness protection," and maybe he didn't know the full story himself. "But I would like to know *when* they first acquired the house in Gerroa. I just want the year, that's all I ask."

He frowned. "Can't you look that up at your end?"

"I could but there's a lot of red tape to wade through. It could take months, and Bob may not have that much time."

"Hey, I'm sorry if Bob's in any danger, but I can't tell you that, Detective. It's confidential and you know it. I couldn't even tell Bob when he asked. I know it broke his heart, and I can only hope it didn't cause friction with his folks. To be honest, I was shocked they hadn't told him themselves. I figured he had a right to know; he was so keen to sell the house. But it is sealed information and I told him he'd have to bring it up with them. Was out of my hands."

Gilda had a finger up. "Hang on, sorry, can we back up a bit here. Bob Smith came in and spoke to you about the lease?"

Fazelle frowned again. "I already told you that. He dropped by and asked some questions. I explained that they didn't officially own the house but that he could remain there for the term of his natural life."

"Yes, you said he was surprised." *Hang on.* "When was this?"

"About five, six weeks ago."

"So let me get this straight. Are you saying that Bob found out about his, er, *unique housing arrangement,* a month before his mother died?"

Fazelle was gawking now, unsure what to say or perhaps terrified he'd put his foot in it again. He folded his arms over his chest and refused to answer any more questions, but it was all making a terrible kind of sense to Gilda suddenly. She couldn't believe she'd missed it!

The bank manager hadn't just spilled the beans to her, he'd spilled them to young Bob. Had Mr Fazelle used the actual words "witness protection"? Or had Bob worked it out as she had? And if so, how angry would that have made him, knowing his parents had lied to him his whole life?

Mad enough to kill?

Gilda thanked the scowling banker for his time and stood up, her mind racing backwards again.

Perhaps she'd been looking in the right place all along. Perhaps it wasn't some master criminal from two decades ago who had caught up with Paisley and Presley Smith. Perhaps it was the lie they had fed their son.

~~~

Maria jumped on the phone when at last he called.

"I think she's onto you," she said. "I think Roxy Parker already knows."

A long pause. "Are you freakin' kidding me?"

"Sorry, mate. I told you she was a bright spark."

"You're the one who'll be sorry, lady. You must
~~~

have said too much."

"Don't threaten me, my sweet. The cops have already done that."

"*Cops?* Are you serious?"

"Settle down. It's no big deal. Roxy must have told her cronies, and one of them paid me a little visit yesterday, just sniffing around, trying to shake me. It didn't work."

"What did you tell them?"

"Nothing! I played my part beautifully. I batted my eyelashes and acted very coy. But we can't be coy for long. I'm telling you, Roxy knows something and that's why we need to come out with it now. While we're still in a bargaining position. There's no more time to waste."

"Whoah! Hang on now. It's more complicated than you think."

More dangerous too.

"Listen, I really don't care. You want this story told, you want your money, you need to get in here and give me your side of it, *pronto.* Otherwise we'll miss the opportunity."

Otherwise I'll miss my exclusive.

A deep sigh, a slight hesitation, then, "I can't get there until tomorrow at the earliest."

"That'll do," Maria said. "In the meantime, what should I tell Roxy if she calls?"

"If she really does know the truth, tell her to watch her back."

~~~

Gilda stood outside the bank, wondering about her next move, how to flush Bob out, when her phone
~~~

rang. It was Wiles and he sounded pumped.

"I just got a call from Flannery."

"In Gerringong? Did he find Bob?"

"No, but he found a witness to Presley's suspected murder."

"You agree it's murder now?"

"I did use the word 'suspected,' Gilda. According to Flannery, last weekend a woman heard two people arguing at the cliff top, the one Presley Smith fell from. Apparently there were two voices, a heated argument, and then a scream."

"Okay," Gilda said, reaching for her car keys and beeping her vehicle to life. "Why are we only just hearing this now? It's been a week! I'm close to Gerroa. I'll head straight down."

"No point, not today. The witness is from Melbourne. She owns a holiday house on the other side of the Smiths, just near the lookout. She heard the argument late last Saturday night and drove back to Melbourne early Sunday morning, didn't think anything more of it. It was only when she was lining up the cleaning lady in Gerroa today that she heard the news about Mr Smith. She's only just put the two together."

"Okay, so how soon can we interview her?"

"She'll be back in Gerroa midmorning tomorrow. It'll have to wait until then. But here's what I can tell you, what she did tell Flannery over the phone. Apparently she didn't just hear an argument, she heard someone yell 'You ruined my life, now it's your turn' or something to that effect."

Gilda gasped. "That has to be Bob, surely?"

"Bob? I thought he was off the suspect list now."

"He was, but then I spoke to Loose Lips Fazelle, the bank manager, again. Turns out Bob never knew about his family being in witness protection, and he found out a month before his mother died. I think the timing is very suspicious. He must have been fuming, especially if he confronted his mum and learned he had a sister too. That he'd been ripped away from her at an early age and been lied to his entire life. I mean, that'd make me see red."

As an only child, Gilda's lifelong dream had been to have a sibling. It was partly why she and Roxy connected so well—they were like surrogate sisters.

"Okay, well let's wait and see what this witness has to say tomorrow. Hopefully she'll identify Bob as the one arguing with his dad on the cliff top and we'll be able to wrap it up. In the meantime, I'll get Flannery to keep looking for Bob."

"Don't worry," Gilda said. "I think I know how to lure him in."

CHAPTER 36

It took just one word to bring Bob out of hiding, a name he had long forgotten. His own.

"Your real name is Danny," Gilda had texted him soon after talking to Wiles. *"Want to know more, meet me at my office."*

She then attached the address for command headquarters. And here he was just a few hours later, sitting in Interview Room Two, his right foot tapping away maniacally, a three-day growth lending him an older, edgier, slightly sinister look.

Gilda hadn't expected to lure him quite so quickly—would have preferred to have spoken to the witness first, but she wasn't about to look a gift horse in the mouth. And besides, she had something else in her hot little hands. Something she would have found a lot earlier if only Wiles had half her gumption.

She shook the thought away and turned to Doreen, who was standing beside her, watching Bob through the one-way mirror. Wiles wasn't able to make it, but she didn't need him, she was feeling confident.

"You ready?"

Doreen nodded.

As the two detectives sat down at the table in front of Bob, he stared at them with a mixture of curiosity and concern. Gilda placed a folder in front of him and then leaned across the table to press Record on a built-in voice recorder.

He glanced at it warily, then back at her. "I thought you were going to give me some information?"

"I will, but first you need to give me some."

She paused to tell the recorder who was present in the room, then added the time and date while he kept darting wary glances between Gilda and the recorder and back again. Then she formally cautioned him and asked if he'd like a lawyer.

He looked like she'd flipped and said, "I can't see why."

"Let's get on with it then," she replied, swallowing her relief. "So, Mr Smith, where were you on the night your father fell from Lookout Point?"

His foot stopped tapping. He looked confused by the question. He said, "I told you before. I was at the Gerringong bowling club."

"You were there until closing, around 10:00 p.m., that's correct." Thanks to Flannery, they already had a witness statement; the flirty barmaid remembered him. "Where were you after that?"

"Home, like I said. Asleep in bed. Why?"

"So you didn't follow your father to the lookout that night?"

"What? No."

"You didn't get into an argument and push him over?"

"What?" Bob sat forward, eyes wide. "Never! Why would I do that?"

"Because you had found out about your past."

He sat back. Said nothing.

"I spoke to your bank manager, Bob. Or would you like me to call you Danny?"

He looked stung then, but remained quiet.

"You discovered that the house you thought your parents owned was actually owned by the police. That probably had you puzzled for a while, but then you somehow put it together. You confronted your folks about it, didn't you? You accused them of lying. You were angry, and who could blame you? Did you get into a tussle with your dad over it? Is that what happened?"

"I told you, I didn't see him that night."

"You followed him to the cliff. You argued, he fell."

He shook his head vehemently. "No, I wish there was a camera on that stupid hill. I'd prove to you I wasn't there."

She smiled and reached for the folder, her trump card. "There mightn't be a camera at Lookout Point, but there are cameras all through Sydney airport."

He looked confused by the subject change, then began tapping his foot rapidly.

She opened the folder to reveal a series of A4-sized images. They were a little grainy, clearly taken from an overhead camera, and they revealed a busy space, people walking in all directions, some wheeling luggage behind them, others hand in hand with loved ones.

"Lucky for me, these just came through." She tapped a nail at a figure at the far side of the image. "That's you, Bob."

He didn't bother to look down, but it was clearly Bob, a bag flung over one shoulder. She pulled another image out, tapped again. "And here you are at the phone booth." She looked up. "What happened? Forget

to pack your mobile? Oh, and here's my favourite…"
Another image, another tap, this one showing Bob
walking through automatic glass doors. "That's the
terminal's exit to the car park. The top level of the car
park. The day your mother died."

She waited for that to sink in, which it did, rapidly.
He was now sitting back, his arms folded across his
chest.

"So? I met up with Mum. It's not a crime."

"You didn't just meet up with your mother, Bob.
I think you confronted her in the car park that day.
Things got out of hand, and you killed her."

"No way! Nuh-uh, that's not what happened."

"Talk me through it then."

Bob pushed the dark curls from his eyes and
collected his thoughts.

"Look, okay, you're right. I spoke to that dude from
the bank. Johnny something or other. I wanted a proper
valuation on the house. The real estate agents are
always beating it up, but I wanted to know just how
much we could make." He scowled. "Mum and Dad
were always whinging about having no money, always
broke. I couldn't understand why they didn't just sell
the bloody house, move into something smaller and
enjoy life a bit more, you know? Maybe take an
overseas trip."

"And?"

"And it was valued at over two million bucks,
did you know that? So I asked him what was left on the
mortgage, to get an idea of what kind of profit we could
make. I… I just wanted to get the facts lined up and
convince them it was worth selling."

"Except it wasn't theirs to sell, was it?"

He scowled. "I couldn't believe it! When the bank

guy told me it belonged to the police force, I was shocked. Why would you guys own our house? So yeah, I eventually put two and two together. More like two hundred and two hundred. The more I thought about it, the more it all made sense."

He leaned forward now, his foot tapping away again. "I always knew something was off. We have no rellies, barely any friends and, apart from occasional drives, we never went anywhere. I can't believe I didn't see it sooner." He shook his head. "They lied to me about my age, did you know that?"

Gilda said nothing.

"I was always so much bigger than the other kids in my class, so much more mature. I asked for my birth certificate once, and Mum said I didn't have one. Something about how you don't get an official certificate with a home birth, and that sounded weird to me, but what would I know? I thought maybe I was adopted. I let it go. But when I heard about the house, that's when I thought… Well, I didn't know what to think."

"So you confronted them?"

"I waited until Dad went to work, and then I asked Mum. I knew if I spoke to them together they'd close ranks. They always closed ranks, that's how they got away with their lies."

"Divided we fall?"

"Something like that."

He sniffed and she realised that he was close to tears now. Doreen noticed, too, and produced some tissues.

He blew his nose noisily, then said, "Mum refused to admit it, of course. Said I was delusional. Had always been away with the fairies, with my crazy nightmares about monsters and my invisible friend Fifi. But I could tell I had unsettled her. I knew something was up. So I did a bit of digging on my own. I spoke to the guy who used to live next door."

"Guy?" Gilda hadn't met any guy.

"Yeah, bloke called Thomas. He sold his house to Pat O'Connell about five years back. Moved into the old folks home. I looked him up, asked him questions, did my sums. It was all a fucking lie!"

Bob's voice was firing up, but it was catching too. He was verging on tears again, just holding himself together. "Thomas remembered the first day I arrived—and it wasn't by natural birth in the dining room I can tell you that. He laughed when I said that. Remembers me helping my folks carry boxes in. Said I wasn't much use but I had a crack."

He smiled at the memory, one of the few real memories he'd ever been told. He seemed lost in his thoughts now, so she tapped the image again.

"So you confronted your mother again?"

He shook his head. "I'd had enough of the lies. I packed some stuff and took off. Got the first train to the airport."

"Where were you going?" Doreen asked now.

He scowled at her. "What did it matter? I just needed to get away from them and their lies."

"So what happened?" Gilda asked.

Bob's jaw tightened, and he looked down at the photos. "I was just walking around, trying to decide where to go with the little money I had." He glowered now. "But I couldn't do it. I couldn't just vanish like *they* had done. It wasn't right."

Gilda found the picture of Bob at the public phone. "So you called your mum."

"My phone had no charge, but I did have some

coins, so I called her mobile. I told Mum what I was doing, and she begged me to stay where I was. Promised to finally tell me the truth. Said she needed to talk to Dad, then she'd drive straight up. Could I please wait. Just give her until one o'clock. Said she'd meet me at the terminal, in the car park at the top."

"Why the top?"

He shrugged. "I guess she figured that'd be emptier, easier for me to find her? I don't know."

"Okay, we're getting somewhere. So, your mother drove to the terminal to meet you. Then what?"

"I went out at one, like I'd promised. I found her car, I got in and we started to talk. But she was full of shit! She didn't want to tell me the truth. She started some new fairy tale about how the police rent houses to poorly paid postal workers and it's all federal government run. It was just more lies, so I got out and she screamed and begged me to get back in. She begged me to come back home with her. I told her I wasn't going anywhere until she told me the truth. For once, I just wanted the truth. You don't think I was owed that?"

Gilda said nothing but she did think he was owed that, and so much more. "So what happened next?"

He sniffed again. "So we sat there for bloody ages, just brooding. I could barely look at her. She disgusted me. I just needed her to stop bloody lying!" He sniffed louder and took another tissue. "Finally, finally she did! I went to get out for the second time and she said, 'Okay, it's true! We used to live in Sydney, we were put into witness protection. You weren't born in Gerroa.'" He looked at Gilda with wrenching eyes now. "Why did she have to say she nearly died giving birth to me in the house? I mean, why make up shit like that?"

Gilda was more interested in why they went into hiding, but he swore he didn't know.

"She wouldn't tell me that. Said it was safer if I didn't know. To be honest, I didn't want to know. It was bad enough knowing my whole life was a lie, I didn't really need to hear all about their sordid past. I mean, what kind of crap did they get mixed up in that made them have to run and hide like cockroaches? I wasn't sure I could ever look either of them in the eye again after that."

"What else did your mother tell you?"

He looked at her sharply. "Wasn't that enough?"

"She didn't mention where exactly you were from, any other… family, perhaps?"

Gilda wasn't sure how much to share about Phoebe Fisher, but he was shaking his head firmly. He didn't seem to know anything about his sister or the house in Coogee. Paisley must have taken that information to her grave.

"The only thing Mum told me was that they tried to make my life as happy as they could, as comfortable as possible. Even named me after my favourite TV character at the time." He snorted. "Bob the Builder! Can you believe that? I was named after a cartoon character, a bloody TV tradesman!"

No wonder he wanted to change his name to Robert, she thought. "Okay." It was time to keep the interrogation rolling. "So what happened after your mother finally confessed?"

"Nothing." She stared at him. "Seriously, nothing happened. I just got out of the car and went back to the terminal. I was furious, sure, but I didn't kill her if that's what you're driving at. I got out and I walked away. And she was alive when I did it, I promise you that!"

Gilda didn't believe him, but she let it go for now. "Then what happened?"

"Sweet F-all. I just sat at Mackers for another hour, sipping a coke and pretending I had somewhere else to go." He glanced at the folder. "Surprised you didn't get happy snaps of that. Then I got real and caught the next train back to Gerringong, hitched my way home from there. I wasn't going anywhere. I have no family, no money—they made sure of that. Always discouraged me from working. It was like they were keeping me tied to them. Tied to their miserable lies."

In many ways Gilda felt bad for Bob. He *had* been lied to his whole life, but as she rounded up the photos and placed them back in the folder, she kept thinking his folks were also right. Whatever their reason for running, it wasn't such a bad life. They'd given him a beautiful home in a cosy and safe part of the world. Surely that was something. And surely he could have left Gerroa at any time and got himself a job, got himself a life.

She cleared her throat. "So what time did you get home that day?"

"Don't know, about sixish, give or take."

"And what did you think when your mum didn't return home that night?"

"I just assumed she was working late at the post office, making up the hours she'd wasted driving to Sydney." His eyes welled with tears. "I nearly died of shock when Dad got the call, when he told me... when he said her body had been found. That she was still at the airport..." He choked and swiped another tissue.

"What about your father?" she said.

"What about him?"

"You must have confronted him too."

"You'd think so, wouldn't you? But, no, I was a coward. Dad was so distressed about Mum and couldn't understand why she'd gone to Sydney. We used to go on drives all the time, but always together, the three of us. I… I didn't have the heart to tell him it was all my fault. That she'd gone to see me." He gulped. "That the last thing I said to her was 'Go to hell.'" He blinked back a tear, swallowed down a lump.

"But he must have known," Doreen said now. "He eventually saw the text from your mother, right?"

"If he knew, he never said a word to me."

Gilda wasn't buying it. "You already told us you fought with your father the night he died."

"To be honest, that was just about money, that's all that was. I asked for a tenner, he told me to get stuffed. Then I took off for the pub, and he… he just vanished."

"He didn't vanish, Bob, he fell from the cliff above your house, right after he had a fight with someone. I think that someone was you. I think you *did* confront him just as you had confronted your mother."

"What? No!"

"I think you loaded up at the bowlo, then went home and demanded the truth from your dad. Maybe he stormed off to the lookout, you followed, and things got out of control. Maybe you didn't mean to push him—"

"No! It's not true. I didn't hurt my dad! You have to believe me!"

Gilda pulled her chair back and stood up. "I don't have to believe anything you say anymore, Bob. I already have you at one crime scene, and I have a witness who's about to place you at the other."

CHAPTER 37

It was midmorning on Saturday, and Sam had taken the Jeep to meet his Newtown tenants, so Roxy took the opportunity to finish packing. They were due to head off at first light the next day, and her bedroom looked like it had exploded.

Lorraine and Charlie were hosting a farewell barbecue at Lane Cove that evening, so she wanted to have it all packed in the car before her friends arrived. She winced at the thought of the evening ahead. This would be the first time most of them had met Sam, including Max. She bit into her lower lip, wondering whether she should have left him off the invitation list, when her mobile rang.

Deep in thought, Roxy answered it without realising it was Maria.

"Got a minute?" the brassy editor boomed, then before she had a chance to reply, she said, "We need to talk. You need to come to my office, now."

Roxy hesitated. "I'm not allowed to speak to you, Maria."

"I don't think you have much choice, my love," she said before hanging up.

An hour later, Roxy was crossing the empty foyer of the publishing house behind Maria, who was clickity-clacking her way to the elevator shaft, her tight skirt squeezing her ample buttocks in all directions. She wondered idly why the woman didn't just wear a tracksuit and trainers. It was Saturday after all; the place was virtually empty. Who was she trying to impress?

The question was answered when they stepped into Maria's plush office.

"Meet Gary Pollard," she said, sweeping a hand towards a beefy fifty-something covered in tattoos who was sitting in front of her desk.

The man stood up and stepped across to Roxy, one hand extended.

Roxy tried to hide her elation as she introduced herself. "I'm Roxy Parker."

"I know who you are," he said, his deep voice almost deadpan. "You're the one writing what amounts to fiction."

She frowned but let that drop. "And I know who you are. You're the missing detective from the Fisher case. You've finally come out of hiding?"

"I wasn't in hiding. I was just keeping my distance."

She took the seat beside him and said, "From what? Or should I say, from *whom*?"

Maria held a spindly finger high. "Not so fast, people, we have the small matter of a contract to sort out."

Roxy turned her frown upon Maria. "I'm not signing any contract, Maria. I've told you before, I'm not selling out my client."

"Even though her whole story's a lie?" This was Gary, and his voice was now dark and growly.

"If it is a lie," Roxy said, "you're welcome to give me

the truth and I can present all that to Phoebe, or better yet, why don't I take it straight to the police?"

"You have no idea who you're dealing with, do you?" he said.

"And neither do you," she spat back. "I'm not Maria Constantinople. I don't sell people out for royalties."

"Now, now, kittens, let's all just take a nice deep breath," Maria chimed in, clearly not taking offence. "Mr Pollard here has some vital information on the Fishers, Roxy, and you would be an utter fool to ignore it." Roxy went to interrupt, but she held her finger up again. "You might not sell out your clients, love, but do you really want them looking foolish or, worse, like liars? Do you really want the truth to come out *after* your book is published? Because it will come out, Roxy, it will all come out in the end, and not only will Phoebe look ridiculous, so will you. Worse, you'll look like the worst fact-checker in publishing history. You'd be lucky to get another ghostwriting gig after that."

Roxy scowled and sat back. "What do you want, Maria? What is all this?"

"We just want a cut, Gary and I."

"Why? You have plenty of money!"

"Well, I don't." That was Gary again, his eyes cloaked. "That Fisher case destroyed my life. I had to leave the Force, move countries, lost my entire family because of it. Can barely scratch a living together. I don't just want the truth out there, I want someone to pay for it."

"So that's me? I have to pay for it?"

Maria laughed. "Not *you*, sweetie! The Fishers, the publisher, Steven Spielberg if he buys the film rights. It's a win-win! What Gary has to say will blow your little 'where is she now?' book out of the water.

You won't regret it, I promise you that. Now…"

Maria produced a large A4 envelope. "I've taken the liberty of drawing up a contract. I know how these things usually work. You're getting a very lovely sum for the book you're ghostwriting and some royalties, and we just want a tiny cut. That's all we ask, just a teeny, weeny percentage. If we give you this information, it will make your story ten times better and you'll make ten times as much, so it's only fair. And think of the future! You'll have more work than you ever dreamed of."

She flung the envelope across to Roxy, who did not pick it up.

"Mr Pollard would like two percent of all proceeds—just two percent, nothing major—and so would I."

Roxy gasped. "Are you serious?"

"Very much so. Which is why I've left Oliver out of this. He's a fool and he'd talk you out of it, but I know you, Roxy. I know you want the answers, the real truth about your client. And Mr Pollard here can provide the lot. You just have to sign on the dotted line."

Roxy considered all that, her eyes squinting. Maria was right. She didn't care about the money; she cared about the truth, the whole truth, and about getting the story right. But didn't she already know the truth? Or at least some of it?

Perhaps it was time to up the ante.

"I don't need to sign a deal with you, Maria, and I don't need your information, Mr Pollard. I already know exactly what happened."

Maria's smile wavered slightly. "Really?"

Roxy's smile grew firmer. It was time to take a risk and reveal her hand. She just hoped Gilda would forgive her. "I know the Fishers didn't just vanish," she said. "I know they went into witness protection."

She watched as Maria swapped a worried look with Gary, and, emboldened, she added, "And I know there was a major botch-up and poor Phoebe was accidentally left behind."

That's when the cards began to fall around her feet. Maria flashed Gary another look, this one much more relaxed, while he leaned back in his chair with a smirk.

"You don't know anything, you foolish woman," he said. "You're in way over your head. You have no idea."

Now feeling nonplussed, Roxy jumped to her feet. He was right; she *was* in way over her head. They obviously knew more than she knew, and she didn't like being the one in the dark. It was too disorienting.

"I need to get out of here," she said, stepping towards the door. "I'm sorry, Maria, but I can't do this."

"Did she tell you what happened in the house?" Gary called out, and she stopped in her tracks. "Did Phoebe tell you what really happened long before her parents vanished? I bet she didn't. I bet they kept that little secret under wraps."

Roxy stepped back towards him. "What are you talking about?"

He sniggered. "Something dark happened at 53 Baker Street, Coogee, something sinister that set it all off. I bet she didn't share that little anecdote with you during all your lovely interviews."

Roxy had no idea what he was talking about, and her curiosity was piqued, but her instincts were screaming again and she knew she had to get out. She had to speak to Gilda and Oliver and even her client, so she feigned disinterest and turned her eyes upon the editor.

"I don't have time for this, Maria. I'm leaving for Byron tomorrow, and I've got a book to write." And to Gary, she said, "If you want to write your own version of events—whatever those events are—you go right ahead. I can only write what I know, and if I've got it wrong, then so be it. It's no skin off my nose."

That's when the man's smug look morphed into something darker.

"I'm no book writer," he told Roxy, "but I do know the facts and I can promise you this: until the story comes out—the *real* story, not the bullshit you've been fed—none of us are safe." Then he gave her a pitiful look as he added, "It's not your nose I'm worried about, lady. It's your life."

~~~

Gilda glanced at Roxy's incoming call and let it go to message bank for the third time that hour. She was driving back to Gerroa, Wiles in the passenger seat this time, and she felt buoyed for the first time since they'd discovered Paisley's body slumped in a hot car just two weeks earlier.

Gilda didn't have time for chitchat. Lorraine had already invited her to Roxy's shindig, and she didn't want to discuss the merits of whether Max should get an invite or whatever else Roxy was calling about. She needed to stay focused, couldn't help but feel pumped. She knew this witness was about to help close her case.

Gilda could not have been more disappointed.
~~~

"So let me get this straight," she said, staring at the large-nosed brunette and trying not to look grumpy. "You believe you heard Presley Smith arguing with a *woman* the night he died? Not a man?"

The witness, Ana Loukanis, blew a plume of smoke from thick ruby lips and nodded. They were seated on the deck outside her cliffside McMansion, and she was dragging on a cigarette like her life depended on it.

"And you're absolutely sure?" said Wiles, also feeling the bitter taste of disappointment.

"Yes!" She glanced between them like they were fools. "I did tell the officer that over the phone yesterday." *Duh!*

Wiles exchanged a similar look with Gilda, feeling more than foolish. Had Flannery neglected to tell them the other voice was a woman's? Or had they neglected to ask? In any case, they had made an assumption, a rookie error, and it altered the case substantially.

For one thing, it put Bob Smith in the clear.

Ana brought the cigarette close to her lips again and said, "I know a chick's voice when I hear one, and it was definitely a chick he was arguing with."

Gilda nodded, trying to get her head around that. "So you heard a man and a woman arguing at the lookout around midnight? And the man was definitely Presley Smith?"

"Yes! I know his voice too. He's a quiet bloke, normally, but he can pull off a roar when he wants to. Calling out to the boy, mostly, checking up on him all the time." She tapped the excess ash from her cigarette into an ashtray on the table in front of her. "I don't know what his problem was, but poor Bob couldn't go five metres without being nagged."

With good reason, Gilda thought now. "So, you heard

Presley talking, but you didn't actually *see* him?"

She shook her head firmly. "I was sitting right here, doing just this." She waved her cigarette in their face. "It was dark and there's plenty of shrubbery as you can see. Kostas—that's the hubby—he planted it out so we'd have some privacy. But plenty of people drop by with champers to look at the view. You often hear chatter, gossip, the odd fight."

"And it was definitely a fight?" Wiles said, and she nodded again.

"I didn't hear many words, just a few here and there that didn't make a lot of sense, but at first I thought it was Presley and Paisley having a tiff, then I remembered that Paisley… well, I knew she'd carked it. My cleaner told me that last time we were up. So I guess that's why I stuck around to eavesdrop. I don't normally—"

"Yes, yes," Gilda said, waving her on. She wasn't in the mood for guilty consciences.

"So, as I say, I couldn't make out much, until the woman raised her voice and said something like 'You ruined my life, now it's your turn.' Something like that. I don't know if this chick—whoever she was— pushed him. But she sounded to me like she wasn't about to give him a hug."

Gilda and Wiles exchanged another look. They didn't know a lot about Presley Smith and the "chicks" in his life, but from what they'd been told, there was only one woman and that was his wife.

Or was there?

Gilda sat forward. "Do you think you'd recognise the voice again?"

Ana tapped her cigarette and said, "If she said something nasty, I might."

Gilda paused the interview and pulled Wiles aside.

"We need to get back to Sydney. We need to speak to Roxy."

He tried very hard not to frown. "Why, what are you thinking?"

"I think there's only one woman in the world who could accuse Presley of ruining her life, and no one knows her better right now than her ghostwriter."

CHAPTER 38

"Phoebe Fisher?" Roxy said, glass of bubbly at her lips. "You seriously think Phoebe pushed Presley Smith from a cliff top?"

"Shh!" Gilda said, taking Roxy by the elbow and drawing her away from the group towards Lorraine's well-tended garden.

They were ensconced in the Jones's backyard, in the throes of Roxy's farewell barbecue. Lorraine was holed up in the kitchen, teaching Caroline how to make a decent potato salad—*'I cannot believe you never learned how to make one!'*—while Charlie was holding court at the barbecue, marinated rump steaks and lamb sausages sizzling away in front of him. And standing in a circle around him were all the men from Roxy's life—Max, Oliver, Lockie and Sam. Even Lunar was there, drooling from the smell of all that luscious carnage. The men were nursing matching beers and appeared to be making small talk.

Or at least Roxy hoped that's what they were doing as she watched Max and Sam interact with each other.

She had only just introduced Sam to the group when Gilda appeared and dragged her away, and she was secretly relieved, and not just because of her ex.

"I've got something to tell you," Roxy said, but Gilda held a palm up.

"Me first, this is really important."

Then she'd launched into an account of her visit to Gerroa and what the witness had said.

"It sounds bat crazy, I know," Gilda said, stopping when they reached the lush herb patch by the back fence. "But the witness insists it was a *woman* Presley Smith was arguing with that night he fell, and who better to accuse him of destroying her life than the child he left behind?"

Roxy gave it some thought as she sipped from her glass. "It does make sense. She's certainly capable of it."

Gilda's eyes widened. "I was expecting you to tell me I was nuts!" She glanced around, then back. "Has Phoebe ever given you the impression she knows where her biological parents are now? Might want to do them some harm?"

"Quite the contrary. She acts as if she couldn't care less. But there was something I heard today, something I've been trying to tell you."

Roxy then launched into her own account of the morning, of her conversation with Maria and the ex-detective.

"Gary Pollard was not surprised when I mentioned witness protection, and don't get huffy with me, Gilda, he already knew, that much was obvious. But he knows other stuff too, stuff I have no idea about. He used the words 'dark' and 'sinister,' like something very bad happened in the Fisher house a long time ago, before the parents vanished, and I get the impression it has something to do with Phoebe, but I just don't know what."

"Was he saying *Phoebe* did something dark?" Gilda's

eyes lit up. "Was she like one of those psychotic children who boil bunnies and try to stab their brother or something?"

"The neighbours did say the siblings used to fight a lot, or at least that's what they told Micky D back then. Maybe they weren't abandoning Phoebe so much as escaping from her."

That wiped the glint from Gilda's eyes. "What could she have done to make them want to do that? I mean, when kids are evil, *they* get taken away, not the parents. It's crazy stuff."

Roxy frowned. "I know. It makes no sense."

Lockie approached with a cheese platter and held it out. They both waved him off, and Roxy called out "But thank you!" as he returned to the main group.

Gilda waited until he was well out of earshot, then said, "Okay, let's focus on what Ana Loukanis told me today. If Phoebe was the woman she heard arguing with Presley the night he died, how would she have found him, do you know? And why now? We're only just connecting the dots ourselves."

"Actually, I do have one idea. I think Phoebe's husband might have found out."

Gilda's glint was back and she waved her on.

"Okay," Roxy said, "so I didn't think much of it at the time, but I ran into James Van Beurden in the lobby of Maria's building."

"When was this?"

"Last Saturday. About lunchtime. He was coming out as I was going in, and he didn't really explain what he was doing there, and I didn't press him on it. They do publish a couple of financial magazines, so maybe it had something to do with that. But now I think about it, he was a little jittery; he dropped his satchel. Maybe he'd just been to see Maria. Maybe she was playing both of us, and he took the bait. Paid Gary for the information and handed it to his wife."

Gilda mulled it over as Roxy added, "That might not have been his first visit. For all we know, Maria could have told him ages ago and maybe Phoebe had something to do with her mother's murder too?"

"Except Bob's already admitted to meeting his mum at the airport and leaving her in a hot car."

"Yes, but didn't he say he left her *alive*? Phoebe might have met with Paisley at the airport later, or…" She clicked her fingers. "Maybe Paisley arranged a little reunion between the two siblings and it all went belly up. Maybe Danny's covering for his sister!"

Gilda wrinkled her nose. "I don't think Bob even knows about Phoebe. He seemed genuinely in the dark on that."

"Either way, you should check to see if Phoebe's car went through the airport turnstile that day. You should also check her phone records again."

"Why?"

"Because I think it's *Phoebe's* number I couldn't quite place. I've been trying to work it out since I saw the list of numbers on your table that night."

"You've lost me now, Roxy."

She drained her glass and said, "You had a list of the calls to Paisley Smith's mobile; you were checking them that night I popped in. One of them looked familiar to me, but only just. Like it was new and I couldn't quite place it."

"You think that was Phoebe's number?"

"Possibly. But it wouldn't be hard to check. You could also check to see if Phoebe phoned Presley Smith too. Maybe she'd arranged to meet him on that cliff top at midnight and pushed him over."

"Good idea, but honestly, Roxy, with friends like you…" She exhaled loudly. "I thought you *liked* Phoebe."

"I do! I hate saying all this because she is lovely and she has come so far, she's really pulled herself up by her bootstraps, so resilient and strong, and that's why I'm worried. Quite frankly, I think Phoebe Fisher is capable of anything."

"Even murder?"

"Even murdering her own parents."

"Well, what a surprise, they're talking about murder again."

This was Max, approaching from behind, Sam beside him. Gilda gave Roxy a pointed look as they turned with stiff smiles.

"Have you noticed how every conversation with Roxy turns to murder, Sam?" Max asked, and Sam's smile faded.

"Yeah, but I can't talk. That's how we met. I bullied Roxy into investigating my sister's death."

Max looked mortified. "Oh shit, sorry, mate. I forgot about that."

"Nah, don't worry about it. Roxy did an amazing job, so did Gilda."

There was an awkward lull in the conversation as Max continued silently beating himself up while Roxy and Gilda were suddenly mesmerised by the herb garden.

Sam was used to this reaction whenever he mentioned Sunny, and he was used to pulling people's feet out of their mouths and moving things along, so he simply drained his beer and said, "Anyone up for another?"

"I'll come with you," Gilda said, grabbing Roxy's empty glass. "See if I can find Roxy's favourite drop."

As they walked off, Max winced. "Sorry, that was so stupid of me. I forgot about his poor sister."

He'd heard the story but not firsthand from Roxy, and she shook her head.

"Don't be sorry, you weren't to know. How are you, by the way?"

"I'm good. Listen, I got those prints for you."

"Prints?"

"Remember Mrs Woo asked for some copies of the photos I took? They're in my car now. I'm happy to drop them to her. I heard you're leaving first thing."

"It's fine. I'd better do it. She's been so helpful, but thank you."

He shrugged and glanced away, and she followed his eyes to Sam, who was laughing at something Gilda was saying as she opened a bottle of red. They were standing just near the kitchen doorway where a large table was set up with Lorraine's finest china, silverware and crystal wineglasses. She was surprised her mother was risking it and wondered if it meant she was now officially a grown-up.

"You didn't have to come, you know," Roxy said gently. "I would have understood."

He stared at her with a bruised look. "Of course I was going to come. Wouldn't have missed it for the world."

"It's just..." She didn't say it, but he was staring back at Sam again.

"I can see now why they hate him." He caught her sudden frown and smiled. "He's a good bloke, Roxy, a keeper. But then you already know that."

Her frown dissolved, and she felt the lump in her

throat harden. "I was never worthy of you, Max."

He offered her a lopsided grin. "You got that right."

"I'm so sorry about the other day—"

"No, I'm sorry. I do it every time. I put you on the spot, demand things I have no right to demand, and it's just wrong. Gilda reckons I'm on a loop I can't seem to break out of, but it's not your fault, it's mine. The truth is, I just want the best for you, Parker. That's all there is to it." Then he bumped her shoulder with his and said, "Come on, let's get back before they all start gossiping."

As they made their way across the yard, she stopped and said, "Why are you being so kind to me?"

He smiled sadly. "Because I love you, Parker. And I don't know how to be any other way with you."

CHAPTER 39

The sun had barely made an appearance when Sam and Roxy pulled their Jeep up outside the house on Baker Street where it all started, where the chaos all began. Roxy hardly slept a wink last night, and it had nothing to do with Max's conversation or the fact that her new partner was sharing the same roof as her mother (that would take some getting used to!)

She couldn't help thinking of Phoebe and of the words Gary Pollard had said.

"Something dark happened in that house. Something sinister set it off."

What did he mean, exactly? What could possibly have sent the parents into hiding, leaving their eldest child behind? Gilda had promised to call her the moment she connected the dots, but she was relieved to be leaving town, not sure how she could face her client.

It made Roxy desperately sad to think that Phoebe might be involved in the Smiths' deaths. It was not the ending she wanted; it was not the story she had hoped to write.

And it was not what she felt ten-year-old Phoebe deserved. After everything she'd been through,

Roxy didn't want to see her locked up.

Yet the more she thought about it, the more it made sense. If James had learned the truth from Maria, if he was able to track the Fishers down, it didn't seem such a stretch that he'd tell his wife, that she'd confront them herself, that she'd wreak some kind of revenge. Not only was she capable of it, you couldn't really blame her either. Roxy didn't know what sinister event had triggered their departure, but she did accept that the witness protection program should never leave a child behind. And neither should a mother.

Karen Fisher should have stuck by her daughter, no matter what.

Roxy shook the thought away and stared across to the Woo house, her eyes still bleary from the early hour. She was getting used to sunrises, but she needed a coffee under her belt first.

"Is that her?" Sam said, pointing to the Chinese woman who had appeared on one side.

"Yep." She grabbed the folder of images. "I won't be long."

When she reached Mrs Woo, Roxy handed over the prints and apologised for the hour. "I could have left these in your mailbox on our way out of town. We just wanted to get a good start. It's a long drive."

"No stress! We had to be up early anyway. We have the digger coming today." She smiled gleefully. "We are finally putting the pool back in."

"Okay, well, thanks again," she said as she turned to go, then she stopped and turned back. "Hang on, sorry, what do you mean *back in*?"

"Phoebe didn't mention it? The original house had a lovely swimming pool, but it was filled in years ago, and nobody has bothered to resurrect it."

Roxy recalled the large rectangular lawn at the back of the house and felt her inner bell tingle again. "Why would someone fill it in? Aren't pools a selling point in these parts?"

"That's what we said! We didn't even know it was there until we saw the original plans. I guess after the drowning, nobody's ever wanted to jinx it, but we're not superstitious."

And now the bells were well and truly clanging. *Phoebe had mentioned a drowning in the neighbourhood. She never said it was at her house.*

"What happened, exactly?" she asked, but she knew the answer even before Mrs Woo replied.

"A child drowned here, sadly. A young girl, I believe. One of the neighbour's kids."

"Was it Mrs Dorey, from number 51?" She pointed to the house next door where the old lady used to live, but Mrs Woo's eyes were heading in the opposite direction.

"Oh no, it was number 55. You know, the grumpy lady? The one who used to be a detective."

Roxy raced back to the car, wrenched the door open and reached for her phone.

"Everything okay?" Sam said, and she shook her head.

"Sorry, honey, but we're not going anywhere just yet. Give me a few more minutes." Then she dialled Gilda's mobile.

"I was about to call you," Gilda said as she answered. "I've trawled the phone records, and I can't find Phoebe's number, but I can find a number for—"

"Margie Means?"

There was a pause, a grumpy sigh, and, "How the

hell did you know that?"

"I didn't, I'm just guessing, but I think it all relates to a drowning that happened at the Fishers' house. It just doesn't quite add up…" She chewed her lower lip. "Tell me this, do you have any idea when and how Margie Means lost her child, her biological child? I got the impression from Phoebe it was during childbirth but—"

"Yeah, you said that the other day, but I thought it sounded wrong. Doreen's just pulled up the file on Means, and it turns out her daughter, Melanie, was much older when she died. Like, nine or ten."

Roxy felt her stomach lurch. "Does it say *how* she died?"

"Yeah. Accidental drowning, backyard pool, but it doesn't say where."

Oh I know where, thought Roxy, her eyes back on Mrs Woo's house. She just needed to find out *why*. Mrs Dorey had told Phoebe that the supervising mother had been drinking that day, that it was all her fault, but now she had to wonder whether there was more to the story.

Had a young Phoebe done it? *Was that why her parents cut and run?*

"Does it say how it happened?"

"Not that I can see. It's just a tiny archived article."

"Okay, what about the date?"

Gilda paused. "What are you thinking, Roxy? What's this about?"

"Gilda, please, just answer the question."

"All right!" *Tetchy*. "Um, let me see…" There was a bit of keyboard tapping, and then she said, "January 14, 1993."

Roxy did the maths and exhaled. Phoebe would have

been just three years old at the time. Whatever happened to Margie's daughter it could not have been Phoebe's fault. Not really. It had to come back to the supervising mother.

It all came back to Karen Fisher.

"I was just chatting to one of the old-timers in here," Gilda was saying. "We're trying to work out why Means was in touch with the Smiths, whether she was the one who put them into witness protection or if there's something more sinister going on. Anyway, he tells me Margie was at work when she heard about her daughter's drowning, and was absolutely devastated, *inconsolable*, he says, which you would be, of course. Reckons she went off the rails completely after that, and it destroyed her marriage, but she eventually pulled herself together and poured everything into her career. That's why they were all so surprised when she suddenly gave up work to look after—"

"A ten-year-old?" Roxy said, finishing her sentence. "That's the least surprising part of all of this."

There was another pause. "Come on, Roxy, what's going on? What are you thinking?"

"I don't know yet. It's all such a muddle."

"What is?"

"Margie, her daughter, Melanie, little Phoebe. It's like the chicken and the egg, which one came first? Did she take on Phoebe because she lost Melanie? Or was that the reason it all started?"

"Huh?"

She shook herself. "Sorry. Listen, I'm outside Margie's house on Baker Street right now. Can you come?"

"Of course I can. Are you okay?"

"Sam's with me. I'm perfectly fine, but you need

to come quickly."

"I'll come straight over, but here's what you need to do, Missy. Stay with Sam. Don't do *anything*, don't approach anyone, just chill out. I'll be there in twenty."

Roxy made vague promises as she hung up, but she didn't have the patience to stay put and she had too many questions swirling through her head—like, if Margie's daughter really did drown in the Fisher's pool, why did she never say anything? Was she deliberately hiding it from Phoebe, or was there something else going on?

Was *that* the dark, sinister event that Pollard spoke of, the one that set the whole thing in motion? The catalyst for why the Fishers ran?

And if it was, then a whole new suspect had just been produced—a grieving mother who was *inconsolable*, her marriage in tatters, her career almost derailed. She might have pulled herself together, but did she ever get over it?

Or did she continue to nurse an almighty grudge?

"Hey babe, what's going on?"

Roxy wrenched her eyes from Margie's house to Sam, who was leaning across the front seat, staring up at her, a worried look on his face. Lunar looked concerned, too, his head at a curious angle.

"Sorry," Roxy said, holding another finger up. "I just need to send a quick text."

She madly tapped at her phone and only had to wait three seconds when a response came flying back. She tapped again, then thrust the phone into her pocket and turned to Sam.

"I know you're keen to get going, but do you mind waiting here for a bit longer? I just have to pay someone else a visit."

His eyes squinted. "You're up to something, I can smell it. And it doesn't smell good."

"It's going to be okay," she said, leaning into the car to ruffle Lunar's head. "As long as I know you guys are out here watching my back, I'll be fine."

"*That's* supposed to reassure me?" He grappled for his door handle. "I'm coming with you."

"Sam, please. You might scare her off. After all this time, I just can't risk it."

"Scare who off? Roxy—"

"Sam! Don't turn into Max on me, not now. I can handle myself."

He frowned and sat back in his seat. "I know you can, Roxy. Doesn't mean I can't stand beside you while you're doing it."

She leaned into the car and pulled him to her chest. "I'll be fine," she whispered in his ear. "Gilda's on her way. When she gets here, send her to the house next door to the Woos, number 55."

Then she stood up, closed the car door, and strode towards it.

When Margie opened her front door, she did not look surprised to see Roxy standing there. Nor did she look like she'd just stumbled out of bed. Already dressed in loose trousers and a flowing linen shirt, she peered past Roxy towards Sam, who was now standing beside the car, hands on his hips, deep frown etched in his forehead.

"Back for more happy snaps?" Margie said, mistaking Sam for Max. "Don't know why you bother. It's changed considerably since Phoebe's time."

"So I hear," Roxy replied. "That's what I want to

talk about. Have you got a minute?"

Margie nudged her lips down and turned, leaving Roxy to close the door and follow her through the house. She caught up with Margie in the kitchen, where she was filling up the kettle.

"Tea?" Margie called out.

"Sure," she said, buying herself more time.

As Margie set about making a pot, Roxy took a deep breath and said, "Why didn't you tell me?"

"Tell you what, dear?"

"About your daughter and how she drowned in Phoebe's pool."

Margie's back stiffened for just a moment, then she continued spooning fresh tea leaves into a ceramic teapot and filled it with boiling water. She placed the pot on a tray and added two matching cups, a small jug of milk, a dish of sugar and a teaspoon, then led the way to the table where they had sat the first day they'd met.

As she waited for the tea to steep, Margie finally met Roxy's eyes, and they were shiny, like she was holding back tears or anger or something.

"I don't see what my trauma has to do with your book," she said, her voice low.

"I don't mean to upset you, Margie. I understand it was traumatic—"

"You don't understand anything, Miss Parker." Her eyes were still watery, but her voice was as dry as a desert. "My daughter didn't drown in Phoebe's pool. She drowned in *Karen Fisher's* pool. Phoebe's mother. *She* is the only one to blame for Melanie's death, and I won't have Phoebe bear that guilt. I won't."

"So she really doesn't know?"

"Of course she doesn't know, and you will not tell

her. Do I make myself clear? Not a word."

Roxy frowned. "You don't think she has a right to know? You never thought you should mention it?"

Margie nudged her lips down. "What for? That poor child had enough on her plate with her parents vanishing. The last thing she needed was me adding guilt on top of worry." She reached for her cup, wrapping her hands around it. "Phoebe was so young when I lost my child. She was barely three, and the Fishers filled the pool in very quickly after that. It was the only decent thing those people ever did. Phoebe obviously didn't remember it, and I wasn't about to tell her. She didn't need one more reason to hate her folks. It really has nothing to do with Phoebe, and you must not speak a word of it."

Margie's eyes had lost their gloss and were now as cold and hard as her voice.

"I'm not sure I can lie to my client, Margie."

"I'm not asking you to lie. I'm telling you to leave it out."

"It's the same thing. This is part of her history, part of her story. It has to go in, don't you understand that?"

Margie's lips were now a thin, tight line. "You journalists are all the same. All you care about is headlines and scandal. There are human beings involved in this. It could break Phoebe's heart. Don't underestimate how much this will hurt her."

"You're the only one underestimating Phoebe. I haven't known her long, but I don't think anything can make her hate her parents more than she already does, and I also think she's perfectly capable of handling this."

But that wasn't all Roxy was thinking. She now felt positive she'd uncovered the reason Phoebe's folks had run, leaving their daughter behind. It had nothing to do with bad parenting or gambling debts and everything to do with payback.

It all felt so eerily convenient, more than just coincidental—the family who took Margie's ten-year-old daughter away from her suddenly upped sticks and left their own ten-year-old daughter behind.

Were they leaving her as compensation? Was that it?

Roxy felt her confidence slip. It was a crazy theory, even by her standards. People didn't just hand their own child over when they accidentally took another child's life.

Did they?

Margie was watching Roxy keenly as she grappled with the facts, or what she knew of them. Then she did something remarkable that helped Roxy make her mind up. She stood up and stepped slowly across to Roxy's chair. She held on to both armrests and leaned in very close, giving her a smile that made Roxy's blood turn to ice.

"I'd like to give you a little bit of advice," she said, her voice even, her breath warm against Roxy's face. "You need to get up right now, and you need to leave my house. Get back in your vehicle and get out of Sydney. Go back to wherever the hell it is you come from."

Roxy was imprisoned by the woman's arms and she shrank back.

"When you get there," Margie continued, her voice still eerily calm, "you need to write the little book you were paid to write, and then you need to forget all about Phoebe and Melanie and that doomed, dreadful house."

"But—"

She held a finger up, millimetres from Roxy's nose. "I am not finished," she said, her voice still steady. "You need to take the money my daughter is paying you, and you need to let it go. Just do yourself a favour, dear, and let… it… lie."

Roxy blinked up at her, shocked. "Are you threatening me?" She gulped.

Was this little old lady really doing this?

That's when Margie released her hold and slowly returned to her chair. She picked up her teacup and looked across to Roxy, a bright expression on her face. "Of course not my dear, I'm just telling you how it is." Then she took a sip of her tea and said, "Now, if you don't mind, I'd like you to get the hell out."

That's when the doorbell suddenly rang, echoing through the house. Roxy jumped ten inches as Margie's eyes swept across to it. She squinted and looked back at Roxy.

"Who is that?"

Roxy shrugged but she had an idea, and it filled her with relief. Margie might very well be SuperMeans, but like every superhero, she had her own form of kryptonite, and it was now hammering at her door demanding to be let in.

CHAPTER 40

Phoebe almost fell into Margie's arms when she swung the door wide, then she pushed her back gently and said, "Is everything okay?"

Margie frowned. "Of course, why?"

"Roxy texted and told me to get here ASAP. I figured you'd had a fall or something!"

They both turned to look at Roxy, who was still in her chair, her heart rate still galloping from Margie's earlier words.

"Goodness, Roxy," Phoebe said, swinging the door closed and stepping towards her. "You gave me such a fright." Then her usual crinkle appeared above her left eye. "What are you doing here? I thought you were driving back, first light?"

Before she could answer, Margie said, "She was just leaving. Weren't you, Miss Parker?"

"Actually, no," Roxy said, feeling emboldened now with Phoebe in the house. "The truth is, we were just getting started."

"Started?" said Phoebe.

"Yes, Margie was telling me all about your old house, explaining a bit of history to me, what happened there when you were three."

Phoebe glanced between the two women, eyebrows knotting together now, sensing something was not right. They landed on Margie, whose features were stiff.

"Margie? What's she talking about?" She laughed, but it was a nervous one. "What mysterious event happened when I was three?"

"Oh you didn't hear?" Roxy said, getting to her feet. Her legs were wobbly, but she needed to get her blood pumping. "Remember the drowning that Mrs Dorey told you about? The one where some poor child was left to die in a neighbour's pool? That wasn't some child, that wasn't just any pool."

"What are you doing?" Margie's tone was dark and foreboding. "You really think this is going to make Phoebe happy?"

"I'm not here to make Phoebe happy," Roxy spat back. "I'm here to get the facts. I told you that at the very beginning, and nothing has changed. This woman deserves to know the truth."

She turned to Phoebe again. She took a deep breath and said, "Margie's daughter drowned in your swimming pool when she was ten."

Phoebe smiled at her as if waiting for the punch line. Then she scoffed. "I think you better check your facts again, Roxy. Margie's daughter died at childbirth, sadly, and we didn't even have a pool! You tell her, Margie."

Margie just stared blankly at the floor.

"You did have a pool once, Phoebe, but your folks filled it in," Roxy said. "You were so young you wouldn't remember, but Margie just confirmed this to me. So did Mrs Woo, who now owns your old house. I don't know all the details yet, but what I can only assume is that Margie was at work the day it happened and your mother was babysitting Melanie—"

"Don't you dare say her name!" Margie suddenly thundered, catching both women by surprise. "You have no right to come in here and say her name to me! It's none of your business! How dare you try to profit from my daughter's death!"

"I'm not trying to profit, Margie," Roxy replied, but Margie was now clutching Phoebe's hands and pulling her closer.

"I'm sorry I never told you, but I didn't want to hurt you, Phee. I didn't want you to hate your mother any more than you already did."

Phoebe looked aghast. "Is it true? My… my…" She couldn't bring herself to say it so she said, "*that woman*? She was the one who let that child drown, *your* child? Is that what broke up your marriage? What broke your heart?"

Margie nodded firmly. "That's why I offered to take you, because I know what loss feels like. When your parents just took off, I felt your pain, Phoebe. I wanted to help you through it."

"Bullshit!" Roxy said, and now all three of them looked surprised. "I'm sorry, Phoebe, I don't mean to swear, but that is a blatant lie. Your parents didn't just take off. I think Margie arranged the whole thing. She somehow made it happen. I think she took you as compensation for her child."

"*What?*"

"Look, I'm still putting the pieces together, but I think Margie threatened your parents somehow. I think she organised some secret witness protection program, and they handed you over before they went in."

"Witness protection? Goodness me!" The storm had lifted and Margie now sounded mildly amused. "Have you gone completely insane? I have no idea where the

Fishers are now, and quite frankly I don't care to know."

"Then how do you explain your phone number showing up on Paisley Smith's phone records not long before she died?"

"Who?" Phoebe said.

"Your mother, Karen Fisher. I think that's what she changed her name to," Roxy said. "Your dad called himself Presley and your brother became Bob. They moved to Gerroa, on the south coast. I think Margie arranged everything with the help of a corrupt cop friend or two. I just don't know why." She turned to Margie. "Were they really escaping some master criminal? Or was it you they were fleeing from?"

Phoebe had paled. "Margie?" she said, her eyes dancing across the older woman's face. "What's she talking about? What is all this?"

Margie sighed wearily and drew her away from the front door and into the living area. "I am so sorry, my dear," she said, "but I did warn you that woman was salacious. I knew she would try to make this story bigger than it is."

"But… *witness protection*?" Phoebe couldn't even wrap her head around that, and Margie was rolling her eyes.

"It's a ridiculous idea that's been doing the rounds for years. I already told Roxy it was absurd. I told her days ago, and I begged her to keep it to herself. I knew it would hurt you."

"But…"

"Please, sit down and let me explain."

Margie pulled Phoebe to the couch, and they both fell into it while Roxy stepped closer, squinting now, chomping on her lower lip.

Margie said, "Look, she is right about witness

protection," and Phoebe's eyes widened. "But it's not what you think. I *have* placed families in protection over the years, and there *may* be a couple on the south coast—I can't confirm that." She scowled at Roxy, then turned back to Phoebe. "Even mentioning them could put their lives at risk, but they have nothing to do with you or your parents or any of this. Nothing, I promise!"

Phoebe was scraping the hair from her face and tucking it behind her ears, trying to regain her equanimity, and Margie flashed Roxy another scowl before turning gentle eyes upon Phoebe again.

Phoebe said, "But… but why would she say all of that…?"

"I told you before, she's trying to make this story into something that it's not. Listen, my dear, please, just listen." She took Phoebe's chin in her hands and forced her to look at her. "I wish I could give you your happy ending, really I do. But as far as I know, your parents just vanished, and that's all there is to it."

"That's more lies!" Roxy called out, but Phoebe was on her feet again and she stepped in front of Margie and crossed her arms. The look she gave Roxy was withering.

"I think it might be best if you leave."

Roxy frowned. "I'm not making this up."

"I'm warning you, Roxy."

"It's all true. Margie Means is not the woman you think she is."

"Roxy…"

"Please, Phoebe, you have to hear me out—"

"No! I do not!" Phoebe suddenly spat out, her voice trembling, her hands in the air. "I brought you into my home! I told you things that I have told no other living being. And *this* is how you repay me? You make an enemy of the only good person I have ever known?"

Roxy stared at her and across to Margie, who stared back, a very subtle glint in her eyes. She looked victorious, and that's when Roxy realised that she could very well get away with it.

"Please, Phoebe," she repeated, but the younger woman was now pointing at the door.

"Get out before I start screaming!"

And then the doorbell rang again.

Margie swivelled around and glared at the front door, but she didn't look quite so triumphant now, and she didn't look like she wanted to answer it either, so Roxy took some calming breaths and wobbled across.

When she opened it, she found Gilda standing there, her own version of kryptonite just behind her. Bob Smith was frowning as he peered back towards the Woos. Towards the old Fisher house.

"Why does that place look so familiar?" he said. Then noticing Roxy he added, "Hey, aren't you the chick with the sniffer dog?"

"Roxy Parker," she said, producing a shaky hand. "I'm ghostwriting Phoebe's autobiography." She raised her eyebrows to Gilda, who gave her the nod. "I'm ghostwriting your sister's book."

"My *sister?*" Bob's frown deepened just as a loud gasp came from inside the house.

They all looked in to find Phoebe standing at the edge of the living room, one hand at her mouth, her eyes wide. She looked like she'd just seen a ghost.

"Oh my God," she said, stepping slowly towards Bob, her voice now barely audible, her eyes never leaving his face. "It's not… It can't be…"

She stared at the familiar chocolate-brown curls and

deep, dark freckles and gasped again. He looked just like her father used to look, with a smidge of her baby brother thrown in.

"Hello, Phoebe. I'm Detective Inspector Gilda Maltin," Gilda said, holding out a hand as much to shake as to cling to. "And this is Bob Smith, or should I say, Danny Fisher. Your brother."

It was just as well the hand was there because Phoebe had to grab it to stop from falling, but she quickly steadied herself and kept staring at Bob as though worried he would suddenly vanish again.

Bob looked confused by all of this, but then something must have clicked because his own eyes suddenly widened and he said, "*Fifi?*"

Had his invisible friend really come to life?

The siblings stared at each other for a moment longer before Phoebe pulled him towards her chest, her eyes welling with tears while his darted around the room, still trying to work out what the hell was going on, when they finally landed on the stony-faced woman on the couch.

He jumped back and reached for the doorframe.

"Are you okay?" Gilda asked, glancing from Bob to Margie and back.

"It's… it's…" He could barely get the words out, his face ashen, his eyes still locked on Margie. "It's the *monster!*"

CHAPTER 41

Bob Smith's brown curls were shaking violently, one hand pointing towards Margie, the other still clinging to the doorframe like it was the only thing holding him up.

"What's that man going on about?" Margie said to no one in particular. She was still seated on the couch, ankles crossed, eyes rolling.

"What's going on, Bob?" Gilda asked.

He had turned very pale, and she was worried he would drop, so she pulled a chair towards the door and pushed him into it. Meantime, Phoebe was smiling awkwardly.

"That's Margie, Danny," she told him. "Don't you remember our next-door neighbour? She saved me. She looked after me when you guys… when you left."

Why did you leave? she wanted to scream, but she was feeling overwhelmed and he was still trembling like a leaf.

"No, no, no," he was saying, his voice a hoarse whisper. "That's the monster, the one who tried to kill me."

"Oh for goodness' sake!" Margie snapped, making him recoil.

"Keep her away from me!"

Gilda held her palms out. "She can't hurt you now, Bob, you're perfectly safe."

Phoebe looked horrified at all of this and knelt down beside Bob. "What's going on? Why would you *say* that about Margie?"

"She tried to drown me once. That woman! I remember it clear as day. On the beach at Gerroa. She pushed my head down into the water. I nearly died!"

"Oh for the love of God," Margie said while Phoebe stared at her with bewilderment. "I've never even been to the beach at Gerroa! You have to believe me, dear, this lad is very confused. He must have mental health problems."

Roxy stepped forward now. She had been madly clicking the pieces into place, and she had a pretty good idea what this was about.

"That probably wasn't Gerroa," she told Bob. "That could have been Coogee beach, the one just down the road from here. I think that was *before* your parents left. I bet it was a warning to them, a living, breathing threat."

"*What?*" said Phoebe.

"I'm right, aren't I?" Roxy looked across to Margie, who was still seated, staring at her fingernails, looking annoyingly blasé. "You were showing Karen Fisher just how serious you were, weren't you, Margie? She drowned your child, you could just as easily drown hers."

Margie scoffed loudly now. "I didn't drown anybody. And if you bothered to check the lifeguard's report for the day, you'll find I'm the one who saved the silly boy. He'd be dead if I hadn't stepped in."

Phoebe was still trying to catch up. "Roxy, what are

you saying now? Margie would never hurt anyone!"

"No, but she needed your parents to *think* she would. I think it was a warning. I think it was the final straw." She turned back to Margie. "After your daughter drowned, I think you told the Fishers their apology was not enough, that simply filling in the pool was not going to cut it. I don't know exactly how it happened, but I think you demanded a child for a child, and when they refused, you showed them just how serious you were. Maybe you gave them ten years to make it happen, or maybe that was just how long it took, but I think that's why they left you that night, Phoebe, to save you and your brother."

Margie was brushing invisible dust from her blouse, still acting nonchalant while everyone stared across at her, Bob's eyes still saucer wide.

"I had nightmares about her for years," he said. "I will never forget her face."

"Of course you remember me, you stupid boy. You lived next door for five years!" Margie hissed.

It was the first real sign her composure was slipping, and now Phoebe's eyes were wide.

Margie cleared her throat and took some settling breaths. "I'm sorry, it's just very upsetting. Why on earth would I want to threaten a child? It's all lies, just ludicrous nonsense."

"You lost a child. You demanded one back. It's as simple as that," said Roxy, but now Phoebe was walking back towards Margie, dropping on the sofa beside her. She took her hand and gave it a pat, then swept her eyes to Roxy.

"Margie's right. This doesn't make any sense. It's really crazy stuff, Roxy. Margie would never hurt a child and as for the rest of it? Please! As if my so-called parents would just hand me over. They could just as easily have gone to the police."

"Margie *was* the police, Phoebe," said Roxy, and now Gilda was nodding.

"That's true. It was a different time back then. The great SuperMeans ruled the Force, didn't you, Margie?" Gilda didn't sound so gushing now. "It wouldn't have been too hard for you to arrange everything, you had a contact in witness protection. We've already connected you to Ingram. Maybe he owed you a favour. Maybe you had something over his head. In any case, you were able to organise for the Fishers to be packed up and moved out swiftly, overnight, while Phoebe lay sleeping. No doubt drugged or she would have stirred. Did you drug the old lady on the other side too?"

Margie was scoffing loudly again while Phoebe was staring at her, a deep frown etching her forehead. It was one thing to dismiss Roxy's theories—she was a "salacious" journalist—but this Gilda woman was a detective.

Why would she be saying all this?

"You organised for two young, inexperienced detectives to investigate the family's disappearance," Gilda continued. "That was very clever of you. You knew they wouldn't be up to the task, but even if they were, you interfered right from the start. You organised for a cleaner to come in and wipe away any evidence. Was it Mrs Dorey, or did you have someone else in your pocket?"

"More lies and nonsense." Margie's voice was rising now. She turned her eyes to Phoebe. "This is all conjecture, my dear. All fabrications and fantasy."

Roxy held a hand up; she still had a card to play.

She just hoped she'd put it together correctly. "I think you'll find one of the investigating officers will say otherwise." Margie's eyes darted to her and she smiled. "Ex-Detective Senior Constable Gary Pollard has come out of hiding, and he's keen to tell the truth. He knows you organised the cleaner; I'm pretty sure of that. He must have found out and confronted you. Did you threaten him like you just threatened me?"

Gilda frowned. "She just threatened you?"

Roxy ignored that, eyes still on Margie. "He knew you had ties to the criminal class, had several of them in your pocket. He was so worried he left the Force and scuttled off to another country, and I can see why. You really are very intimidating, Margie. You're very good at it."

"I'm a seventy-year-old lady, for heaven's sake!" She turned to Phoebe and grabbed her chin again. "Look at me, Phee. Look at me!"

The younger woman's eyes were wide, her face pale.

Margie said, "Just think it through logically. You weren't just handed over, you were taken into foster care, remember? You're lucky I got you out!"

"That wouldn't have been hard," Roxy countered. "Just make up a nasty story about the foster family and she was all yours. You probably ruined that foster family too. Was any of it true?"

Phoebe's eyes were now dancing between them all, not knowing who to believe or what to think. She was still struggling to grasp what Gilda and Roxy were saying. Struggling to defend Margie on all the charges. Her eyes reached for Bob but he was still by the front door, hunched over in his seat.

Eventually her gaze settled on her ghostwriter.

"Why, Roxy?" she said, her voice barely a whisper,

her expression anguished. "Why are you saying all of this?"

Why are you ruining everything?

"Because it's true, Phoebe, and I think you know it. Deep down, it all makes sense. And it all started because Margie's child accidentally drowned in your swimming pool."

"It wasn't an *accident*!" Margie bellowed suddenly, causing Phoebe to shrink back. "Karen was blind drunk, like she always was. She was *negligent*! She just sat in her drunken stupor and she let my baby die."

"Your 'baby' was ten years old when she drowned," Gilda called back. "She wasn't a baby at all. Karen probably—foolishly—assumed Melanie knew how to swim by that age, and she *should* have known by then. You have a beach just down the road. It was your job to protect your child, not your neighbour's."

Margie didn't appear to be listening to her. She was reaching out to Phoebe, who had slid away from her and was tucked into the farthest corner of the couch, her arms wrapped around herself.

"Please, Phee," she croaked. "It wasn't just the drowning. Your parents were hopeless! Losers! Drunks!"

"They never touched a drop of alcohol," Bob said, catching them all by surprise.

He was standing at the door of the living room, and the colour had returned to his freckled cheeks. "As long as I can remember," he said, "Mum never touched a drop."

"But that's thanks to me!" Margie told him. "What I did… it must have shocked them out of drinking! I saved them. I saved all of you!"

It was a confession of sorts, and everybody knew it,

including Phoebe, who leapt from the sofa like she'd just been bitten.

"This is *true*?" she said. "You really did all that? You took my family from me?"

"No, Phoebe, please! I… I helped you—"

"You helped yourself to somebody else's child!"

"It wasn't like that…"

"You destroyed me! You blew my family apart! You tore me away from the parents I loved."

"Your parents were irresponsible gamblers," Margie said. "They were drunks and—"

"I don't care what they were! They were *my parents*! Don't you get it?"

Phoebe was screaming and sobbing at the same time, hands on her hips, looming down towards the woman, who suddenly seemed older and greyer and not so super anymore.

"I just wanted my mum and my dad and my little baby brother! I wanted my dog Bouncer, and I wanted everything to go back to the way it was." Giant tears were streaming down her face, and she swiped at them angrily, trying to get her words out. "I cried for them all, every night for years and years. I sobbed and wept and you let me! You held me in your arms and you *let me*!"

"Phee—"

"But it's worse than that!" Phoebe said, blue strands of hair now dancing about her face wildly. "You let me believe they didn't *want* me! You told me they deserted me! You said they did it for nothing! That they just packed their bags and took off for no reason! You said they didn't love me! And you let me believe that. All these years, you let me believe they never looked back!"

"We drove past all the time," Bob told her, one hand reaching out. "Every few months, Mum and Dad would pack me in the car and we would drive up here. Just slowly drive down this street. Sometimes they would stop, sometimes they would take off in a hurry, like they were being chased. I never understood it and they never explained why. Eventually I refused to go;   I just figured they were scoping for real estate or something. But now I know, they were looking in on you, Fifi. They were watching you grow."

Phoebe choked back a sob and turned to face Margie with horror in her eyes.

"My God, Danny's right. You really are a monster."

You might as well have punched Margie in the face. She recoiled, her own eyes now wet and wide. "No... Phoebe, darling... I protected you."

"You just wanted a child, and you were prepared to destroy everyone else to get one!"

"No! It wasn't like that!"

"Then what was it like?"

This was Gilda, trying to wrestle back control of the conversation, but Margie Means was too much of a professional for that. She drew her lips together, turned her body away from them all, and stared down into her lap, but enough had already been said.

Phoebe reached for Bob and they fell into each other's arms again, two lost souls clinging to the only light left in this dark and ugly saga, while Roxy sighed wistfully and Gilda stepped towards her mentor and said the words she never imagined herself saying.

"Margaret Means, you are under arrest—"

"What for?" the woman demanded, finding her voice again. "This is all conjecture. You have no proof of any of this!"

"Perhaps not yet but that's not why I'm arresting you." She took a deep breath and said, "Margaret Means, you are under arrest for the murder of Presley Smith. Or should I say Shane Fisher."

Then she recited the woman's rights while Phoebe and Bob stared at her, horrified.

CHAPTER 42

It had been an extraordinary morning, and Sam watched as Gilda marched Margie Means out of the house and into a patrol car that had been idling next to his. Roxy soon followed, and he ran to her, Lunar on a leash by his side.

"I only caught a bit of that through the doorway," he said. "I didn't want to intrude, but, whoah! That was intense."

"And it's not over yet." She leant down to pat the dog. "We're not going anywhere today, guys, I'm so sorry. This has thrown everything up into the air."

"I figured that. Do you want me to hang around?"

"No, go back to Mum's for now, feed this poor pooch." She squeezed his hand. "I need to talk to Gilda and to Phoebe and Bob. I'll get a lift back with Gilda later."

"Okay." He turned, then turned straight back. "You're bloody amazing, Roxy."

She smiled. "I don't think I'm the amazing one here. I think Phoebe is, and Bob. Or should I say Danny. What those two siblings went through is mind-boggling."

She leaned in and kissed him on the lips, then

watched as he returned to the car, letting Lunar jump into the passenger seat as they slowly drove off. Then she remained outside with Gilda, allowing the two siblings to have a proper reunion in private.

"I wished we'd had a chance to chat before all that started," Gilda said, her tone slightly huffy, and Roxy gave her an apologetic smile.

"I'm so sorry. I just wanted to ask Margie about the drowning, try to understand why she hid that from Phoebe. To be honest, I hadn't properly pieced it together, and I might not have if she hadn't suddenly turned so threatening."

"What did she say?"

"To be honest, not a lot. She didn't need to; she was just… *frightening*. You know, I think she really believes she's some superpower who can shove us all around like her minions."

"It certainly worked in the past. If what you say is true, the Fishers were terrified of her, so too Pollard, and he was a big burly cop."

"Do you think she'll ever admit to it, I mean, properly?"

"She'd be stupid if she did. But we have her phone number linked to Paisley's, we have the voice witness, we might be able to find some CCTV from the highway. We might get lucky."

"Do you think she killed Paisley too?"

Gilda groaned. "Sadly I don't. Come on, I need to speak to Bob, and it's not going to be pretty."

They returned inside where the two siblings were now seated on the sofa, conversing quietly. They looked up as Gilda approached, and then Bob frowned.

"You think that woman pushed Dad over the cliff?"

Gilda held a hand up. "I don't know for sure, Bob, but we have a witness who heard your father arguing with a woman just before he fell. We suspect it was Margie."

Phoebe was gasping. "I can't believe she would do that…"

"Seriously?" Bob looked at her surprised. "After everything you just heard?" He turned back to Gilda. "And she must have killed Mum too."

Gilda shook her head. "I don't think so, Bob. We'll check her alibi, of course, and footage from the airport, but I have a dreadful feeling that you were the last person to see your mother alive."

"What? No! I told you before, she was fine when I left her." He turned to stare at Phoebe. "I didn't kill her, you have to believe me! Like I just told you, I was angry with Mum for all the lies, but I didn't want her dead."

"I don't think you meant to do it," Gilda said, pulling up a seat across from him. "I think it just happened. You left your mother in that hot car. She died of heat exposure."

"No! She was alive when I got out, she was still alive."

"How do you know that? You already said you were so disgusted you could barely look at her. Maybe you didn't see what trouble she was in before you exited the vehicle."

He paled. "She was fine… she had to have been. We'd just been talking. I… I was fine when I got out. The heat didn't kill me."

"You're half her age, Bob. In peak condition. But it's not only that. We clocked your mum driving through the turnstile at noon that day. You didn't meet her until one. So she had already sat in that hot car for an hour by the time you got there. Your mobile wasn't working, so she couldn't call you to meet her earlier and she probably didn't want to leave the vehicle in case you missed each other. So she sat there, in the hot sun, for that extra hour. By the time you got in, she was probably already in heat distress."

"But… but her window was down! I remember that."

"On a very hot day, it doesn't make a huge difference," Gilda told him.

"But why didn't she get out? When we'd finished talking, why didn't she…?"

"Maybe she couldn't. Maybe she was already slipping into a coma by that stage. You never looked back, Bob. You didn't stop and check that she was okay."

He let out an agonising roar, one hand at his mouth. "Oh God, I could have saved her." Then he buckled over and sobbed into his lap.

Phoebe stared at him shocked, then placed a hand on his back and rubbed him gently. What could she say? She had spent most of her life hating that woman; she wasn't sure she even knew how to go about defending her now.

Eventually Phoebe looked at Gilda. "Margie said you had no proof, that it was all conjecture. But surely if they went into witness protection, somebody must know something?"

"We're still investigating, but it looks like it was arranged through a Nowra detective, a man who's now deceased. Maybe he took the truth to his grave."

"She'll never admit it," Phoebe said. "If there's one thing I know about Margie, she's stubborn."

"You do have other avenues," Roxy told Gilda.

"I wonder about Margie's ex-husband. We know their marriage fell apart after Melanie died. Maybe he knew something of her plans and had to get out? He might talk. You could also try tracking down the cleaning woman, if she's still alive? Talk to Gary Pollard. He's keen to get the story out."

Gilda frowned. "I have a feeling Margie's too smart for that. There'll be six degrees of separation everywhere we look. As for Pollard, I got the impression he just wanted to make some easy cash."

Roxy shook her head. "No, I mean, yes, he wants compensation for everything he's lost, but I think it's more than that. He's scared. Real scared. I think he wants the truth, to come out so Margie Means is put away and he can finally stop watching his back."

"Seriously?" said Phoebe. "She had that much power?"

Gilda nodded. "She was working in the organised crime unit, knew lots of nasty informants, a few hit men, no doubt. She probably used that threat a few times to keep people quiet."

Phoebe shuddered like an icy wind had just rippled through her and pulled Danny closer as though needing his warmth. "Oh, so much is making sense now! No wonder she forced me into swimming lessons even though I could swim perfectly fine. She must have been terrified I would drown like her daughter had. But I still don't understand why she would do all of that, why she would go to so much trouble… *for me?* I barely knew the woman back then! I'd never even been in this house!"

"Maybe it was less about you and more about revenge," Roxy said. "Maybe she needed your mother to know how it feels to lose a child. She couldn't blame herself for not teaching Melanie to swim, so she had to blame someone. She blamed your mum, and you all had to pay the price."

"She could get away with this!" Phoebe said now, staring at her brother, her left eyebrow crinkled again. "After everything she did to us, she could get off lightly."

Roxy had thought the same thing herself, but now she was shaking her head. "She's lost you, hasn't she, Phoebe?" The woman nodded fiercely. "Then I think you'll find that will hurt more than anything else could."

It wasn't quite a death sentence, but for Margie Means it might come close.

EPILOGUE

The story Phoebe had hired Roxy to write was not the story that ended up in the book, which was now printed, bound in hardcover, and being clutched to Phoebe's chest. Everything had changed, the characters had switched, their motivations all flipped on their heads. Roxy thought Phoebe would abandon the book completely when the truth came out, but she seemed even more determined to get her story told and gave Roxy another two months to research and write it properly.

The real version this time.

"I have spent the past twenty years hating my parents with such determination and idolising that woman I thought was my saviour, but now I know it was all a lie. That she manipulated everything! I need to set the record straight, if only for Mum and Dad's sake and for little Danny who lost his childhood too."

The fact that Phoebe was even using those names showed just how far she'd shifted back towards the truth.

"I'm so sorry I never got to meet them," she said now. "But I don't blame my brother for Mum's death. He had just learned the most horrendous truth.

He wasn't thinking straight when he stepped out of that car and left her there. I just hope he stops blaming himself."

Roxy's hope was that Gilda would find evidence that Margie had met with Paisley at the airport after Bob, but the woman had an ironclad alibi, and so that was on his shoulders. They did learn that Karen and Margie had been in touch over the years, although what they spoke about would go to Karen's grave. Margie was not talking. She was too smart for that. But Roxy suspected they were not happy family chats but probably more threats to keep the Fishers silent. She also believed, in their final conversation, Karen must have somehow let slip that Bob suspected the truth.

So when Karen showed up dead soon after, Margie must have gone into damage control, confronting the only other witness who could testify against her with any conviction—Shane Fisher. Ana Loukanis had positively identified Margie's voice at the lookout that night, but whether he then jumped or was pushed was still a matter of speculation.

SuperMeans never got to Pollard though, and he was finally talking and not just for his own tell-all book deal with Maria. He would testify that Mrs Dorey was the naïve cleaner hired by Margie that fateful day and that her threats had taken him into hiding. Whether it would be enough to convict her, was up to a jury now.

There were also fresh question marks around Mrs Dorey's sudden heart attack just a month after the Fishers vanished, but the fact that the old lady had been cremated made that a moot point.

Still, it sent shivers down Roxy's back.

Meanwhile, the Federal Police were officially in damage control. Word had got out about the witness protection program and how a top commander had misused it for malicious purposes, and there was much back-pedalling and blame-shifting going on. The house in Gerroa was officially handed to Bob as victim compensation, but it would take more than a killer view to get him over what had happened. Roxy wasn't sure he ever would, although she knew he had it up for sale and suspected it was a good start. And with Phoebe by his side, his chances of a happy ending were looking better.

One question remained for Roxy though. Did Phoebe still harbour any animosity towards her folks? Did she wish they had stood up to Margie twenty years ago?

"You mean am I angry that they didn't fight for me?" she said, and Roxy blushed.

Perhaps that is what Roxy meant. It was a classic *Sophie's Choice*, and it was a gut-wrenching one.

"Maybe a little." Phoebe sighed. "But then, as you know, it wasn't just me they were fighting for, it was Bob. And my mother did have her own case of negligence. She had been the one on duty the day Margie's daughter drowned, she was obviously drunk, we can't sugarcoat that, so who knows how much guilt she carried around? How much penance she was prepared to pay?" She sniffed. "I'm just so sorry that I can't ask her myself. Or Dad for that matter." She gulped. "Do you think Margie pushed him? Or did he jump?"

Roxy wanted to believe the former but remembered what Gilda had said. "They had a great love, your parents. Everyone who knew them as the Smiths will tell you that. Perhaps after what they'd gone through together, he just couldn't survive any more loss. Maybe your mother's death was one departure too many."

Both women choked up at that sentiment, and Phoebe reached for a handkerchief in her pocket. Then, surprisingly, she laughed as she dabbed her tears away.

"I can't *believe* you thought I had anything to do with it! That James had somehow helped me track them down to Gerroa and I could do such a terrible thing."

Roxy blushed and apologised. Again. It turns out, James Van Beurden really did have a legitimate reason to be in Maria's building that Saturday and knew nothing of Gary Pollard, had never even met Maria.

"I told you before, Phoebe, it's only because you're such a strong woman. You have to take that as a compliment!"

They both laughed, and then Roxy remembered something. "I once asked you if any answer was better than none, and you replied that nothing could justify what happened. You obviously no longer feel that way."

Phoebe shook her head. "I was such a fool! So willing to believe all the lies Margie had been feeding me back then—that I was *worth* deserting, that it wasn't so strange that my flesh and blood would walk out on me. Every time I even tried to rationalise what happened, she would steer me back to the negative, totally eroding my sense of self. No wonder I thought I'd make a bad mother! Sure, my mother drank, and yes, a child died on her watch, but she wasn't an evil person, not deep down like Margie is. And neither am I." She offered Roxy one of her lovely, beaming smiles. "We're going to start trying later this year, for a baby, James and I."

Roxy pulled her into an embrace. "That's fantastic.

I'm so happy for you."

"The truth is, Roxy, I think my parents were so incredibly brave. They're the true heroes here. They gave up their life to save me and to save my brother. I'm glad I can spend the next part of my life finally believing that."

She sniffed into her hanky and then scowled. "I'm going to look like a panda out there if we keep this up!"

She wiped her eyes again. Then she licked her lips, straightened down her hair, which was now a more subtle shade of blond, and said, "So, shall we face the music?"

Roxy smiled. "Now's as good a time as ever."

And then they gave the nod to a woman who was standing at the edge of the stage, a microphone in her hand, looking across at them expectantly. She nodded back, then looked out at the enormous crowd and placed the microphone to her lips.

"Ladies and gentleman, thank you for coming, and please give a warm welcome to Phoebe Van Beurden, the author of the new memoir *Forgotten Phoebe, Remembering At Last*."

As the crowd in the large hall erupted with applause, Roxy squeezed Phoebe's hand, then stepped back and watched as she walked across the stage and into the spotlight.

"You okay?" That was Max, standing behind her in the shadows.

"Yes," she said, wiping her own tears away. "But it's been a very emotional ride."

"I mean about the fact that she gets to take the glory when you actually wrote the book. I think you should be out there with her."

Roxy shook her head firmly. "It's all part of being a ghostwriter, you know that. Besides, it's Phoebe's story, not mine. She lived it, she survived it, she can take all the credit she likes. Come on," she said, slipping her arm through his, "let's sneak down the back and see if there's any of the good champagne left."

"I think you'll find Olie's already saved you a bottle, and all the gang are there."

She beamed. She hadn't seen them since she'd returned up north to write the book and then wait for it to be edited and published—almost six months. "Thank you, Max."

"It's just champagne, Roxy."

"No." She stopped and turned to face him, squeezing his hand. "Thank *you* for always being there for me, no matter what the cost."

He smiled and squeezed her hand back. Then they continued making their way, but one of them was already bubbling inside. Max didn't know a hell of a lot about women, but he wasn't stupid and he did know this: a pregnant woman wouldn't be asking for champagne.

It was a glimmer of hope and he held on to it as if to a life raft.

~~~~
~~~~

ACKNOWLEDGEMENTS

I'd like to thank my family and particularly my sister Michelle, who's always been one of Roxy Parker's biggest fans and whose subtle—*and not so subtle*—hints encouraged me to embroil her in another adventure. It's been five years since the last Ghostwriter Mystery, and Michelle's right. It was long overdue! I forgot how much I enjoyed Roxy's company and what fun her friends and family can be.

Thanks, Shell, for reminding me.

I would also like to thank the hubby and kids for giving me the time and space to pen another book, and single out our beloved Bluey Kasper. He's a three-year-old Australian cattle dog who loves nothing more than a good, galloping walk, up and down the hills surrounding our property. Annoyingly for Kaspie, over the past six months he was constantly halted midstride as I stopped, grappled for my smartphone and recorded sudden plot lines, dialogue and snippets for this book.

It's done now, Kas. You can walk more freely.

Finally, I would like to thank my beloved readers, many of whom answered a call in one of my CALarmer newsletters to suggest character names for this story. It can be hard conjuring up original monikers and I was overwhelmed with suggestions, but two really stood out:

• Thank you Alice M., who suggested her granddaughter's name "Preslea" and then kindly permitted me to change it to "Presley" as it better suited my purposes. I was short on original male names and this is certainly the kind of name a bloke might give himself.

• Thank you, also, to Nancy Sasser who heard the name "Paisley" in passing and thought it was "rather unique." You're not wrong, Nancy, and it worked so well with this particular plot and one character's particular fetish!

Thanks again to everyone for signing up for another Roxy adventure. I hope you enjoyed it as much as I did.

ALSO BY C.A. LARMER

Blind Men Don't Dial Zero
(Sleuths of Last Resort 1)

POLICE say the case is open-and-shut: The heir to a massive fortune slaughters his parents, confesses to the crimes, then turns the gun on himself. His grandfather says, "Not so fast." With the case now closed, Sir George assembles his own crack team of detectives—five amateur sleuths with a nose for mystery and a need to prove themselves—then pits them against each other to solve it.

"This is a fantastic read! lots of twists and turns and a real page turner! Quirky, interesting and complex characters fill this interesting adventure! Loved it!"
Charlene @Amazon

"Will have even the most seasoned sleuth baffled as these amateurs tackle a wealthy family, loyal employees, and unsavoury boyfriends Action-filled … unforgettable and hard to put down"
Peggy Jo Wipf for Readers' Favorite

After the Ferry: A Psychological Novel

IT'S the 1990s, pre-mobile phones, and a young traveller must make a terrifying choice: Jump ship with a seductive stranger or stay cocooned on the Greek ferry and miss the love of her life?

"A great read…suspenseful and very well written.   I highly recommend this book."
Heather, Booksprout

LARMER MEDIA

ABOUT THE AUTHOR

C.A. Larmer is a journalist, editor, teacher and author of multiple crime series, stand-alone novels and a non-fiction book about pioneering surveyors in Papua New Guinea. Christina grew up in PNG, was educated in Australia, and spent many years working in Sydney, London, Los Angeles and New York. She now lives with her musician husband, boomerang sons and their very cheeky Bluey on the east coast of Australia.

Sign up for news, views and giveaways:
calarmer.com